THE DEVIL'S MERCENARY

Venetia dei Giorlandi was the spoilt daughter of a wealthy Venetian merchant. Proud and beautiful, she scorned the Spaniard her father appointed as her protector on the dangerous sea voyage. Caught up in a holy war between the Turks and the forces of Christendom, Venetia had to learn patience and humility before she could win her way to happiness with the mysterious Roldán Domingo and learn the terrible secrets of his past...

THE DEVIL'S MERCENARY

The Devil's Mercenary

by

Anne Herries

Magna Large Print Books
Long Preston, North Yorkshire,
BD23 4ND, England.

British Library Cataloguing in Publication Data.

Herries, Anne
    The devil's mercenary.

    A catalogue record of this book is
    available from the British Library

    ISBN   0-7505-2276-3

First published in Great Britain 1988 by Mills & Boon Ltd.

Copyright © Anne Herries 1988

Cover illustration © Len Thurston by arrangement with
P.W.A. International

The moral right of the author has been asserted

Published in Large Print 2005 by arrangement with
Linda Sole

Magna Large Print is an imprint of Library Magna Books Ltd.

Printed and bound in Great Britain by
T.J. (International) Ltd., Cornwall, PL28 8RW

Anne Herries also writes as Linda Sole. As Anne Herries she is the author of twenty-nine published novels and as Linda Sole she has published another fifteen novels, as well as a few under other names. Linda loves to hear from readers and they can contact her through her website at: www.lindasole.co.uk

HISTORICAL NOTE

Many of us, at school, must have thrilled to the rhythms of Chesterton's poem *Lepanto*, the one that begins:

> White founts falling in the courts of the
> sun,
> And the Soldan of Byzantium is smiling as
> they run...

while, perhaps, having little idea what it was all about.

As the sixteenth century advanced, it brought nearer and nearer what we should now call a confrontation between the two great Mediterranean religions, Christianity and Islam. The Ottoman Empire, with its protectorates along the coast of North Africa, had the advantage of unity, while the Christian states were divided. Pope Pius V saw that he must remedy this, but it was not easy. The Venetian Republic wanted trade rather than war with the Turks and would in fact have preferred to strike at its rival, Genoa; Philip II of Spain was a devoted son of the Church, but he had his troubles in the Netherlands.

However, at last a Holy League was formed, and a fleet was assembled under the command of Don John of Austria, Philip's handsome young half-brother. Adventurous men flocked to his standard – even from England and France, whose monarchs officially stood aloof. On 7 October 1571, Cross and Crescent met in the bay of Lepanto, within the Gulf of Patras. The battle lasted only one day, but at its end the Turkish fleet was utterly destroyed. The risk that the Mediterranean might become 'a Turkish lake' was over for ever.

THE BEGINNING

'That a son of mine should allow himself to be whipped like a dog – and over a woman!' Baron William Forsythe Dominion glared at the young man standing silently before him. 'I am shamed by you, Roland.'

The youth's bright blue eyes were unflinchingly steady as they met the older man's angry gaze. There was nothing in his expression to show that he felt the sting of his father's scorn far more than the bruises and cuts to his hands and body. More even than the deep wound to his left cheek where the leather thong had cut through to the bone, leaving an angry red scar that was still swollen and painful some ten days after it had been received.

'Well, have you nothing to say for yourself?' the baron demanded furiously.

'There were six of them, Father. I offered to fight a duel – but the earl laughed in my face.' Now there was a flicker of some emotion in the blue eyes. 'It seems he found it beneath his dignity to cross swords with me.'

'And that surprises you?' His father laughed harshly, taking a few strides about the freezing cold room. 'Are you a fool, sir? You are just seventeen, the younger son of an insignificant baron – and you dared to seduce the Earl of Lodeberry's bride within weeks of her wedding!'

'Marietta was desperately unhappy. Her husband is old enough to be her grandfather, with sons almost twice her age, so can you blame her for needing consolation?'

'I sent you to the earl to make your way in the world, not to console his bride!' the baron growled. 'There's little enough for your brother to inherit. I can do nothing more for you.'

'Was it your wish that I should be a lackey? For that's all I was to Lodeberry.' Roland's jaw jutted stubbornly, his thick, dark brows meeting in a frown that was almost as fierce as his father's. 'I have no intention of living beneath your roof.'

'If you expect me to find you another position…'

'No. I shall make my own way.'

'Not at Elizabeth's Court, sirrah! She has no love for Catholics, I dare swear. Lodeberry is a vindictive man. He'll be your enemy from now on. The first time you show your face at Whitehall, he'll have you hounded out.' The baron frowned as he looked at his son. Roland was tall, as tall as he himself, with a fine, muscled physique. From childhood he had been pushed hard, taught to fight and fend for himself. It was a harsh world for younger sons. There was no room for softness in a boy's education. 'So, what will you do?'

'I shall go to my uncle in Madrid.'

'Your mother's brother...' For a moment the baron's face lost its harshness. His second wife had brought him great happiness besides her small dowry – long spent – and his memories of her were still warm. After her death in childbed when Roland was nine, he had waited a full three years before marrying again; an Englishwoman this time, as his first wife had been, with a sizeable fortune to fill his empty coffers. He had never been able to keep money in his hands, though there was always enough to provide for his expensive tastes – and those of his elder son Harold. 'Do you think your uncle will welcome another mouth to feed?'

'I do not mean to be idle, sir. I believe the life of a mercenary will suit me. He has written asking me to visit him. I believe he has some influence with the king.'

'You would fight for Spain?' The baron's lips curled in a sneer.

'For any army that will pay me.' Roland's eyes glittered with pride and anger. 'What choice have I? At least I shall live like a man, not like a lackey!'

'And die like a dog on foreign soil.'

'Perhaps. But you forget, sir, that for me

13

Spain is as much my birthright as England. My mother's blood runs as deeply in my veins as in yours.'

'Ay, and her faith, I'll be bound, for you imbibed it with her milk. Mayhap it's for the best that you go. With a Protestant queen on the throne of England, there's naught for you here.'

'My plans are made. I shall leave at dawn tomorrow.'

'Then we'll sup together one last time.'

'Forgive me, I have business elsewhere.'

'Business? What business?' The baron stared in sudden suspicion. 'You were near dead when your servant brought you here. You'll not risk another beating for that whore?'

'Marietta is not a whore!' Roland's jaw hardened. 'But my business is not with her. Lodeberry has three sons, and before dawn he will lose one of them. Carlton has a mistress, whom he will visit this evening, and I shall be there to greet him.'

'You plan murder? I'll not have it, Roland! You've shamed our name enough.'

'Not murder – a fair fight. This time I'll have friends there to see justice done. He'll meet me in a duel or I'll take a whip to him.'

There was a dawning respect in his father's eyes. 'Why Carlton?'

'It was he who spied on Marietta. He was mad with lust for her himself and spiteful

14

because she would have none of him. He saw me kiss her and ran hotfoot in his jealousy to the earl. If I don't kill him, he'll make her life unbearable.'

'So you'll risk your life for her sake?' The older man's face twisted with contempt. 'Tell me, was she worth the beating?'

A faint smile quirked Roland's lips. 'That, sir, is something neither you nor any man living shall ever hear from me!'

CHAPTER ONE

'Is he not handsome?' the fair-haired girl asked with a giggle as she gazed down at the man who had just dismounted from his horse in the courtyard. 'Stop pushing, Katrine. I was here first!'

The second girl pulled a wry face. 'There's room for both of us, Isabel. Look, he has a scar on his cheek! I wonder how he came by it?'

'No doubt he earned it along with a purse of ducats.'

The third voice was cold and scornful, causing the other girls to part and move away from the window. Their mistress had a sharp tongue and could administer a stinging reproof on occasion.

'What do you mean?' Katrine, always the bolder of the two, risked a scolding. 'Who is he, and why has he come here?'

'He lives by the sword. He is a mercenary – and a Spaniard!'

Venetia dei Giorlandi's lip curled in disgust. She was not sure whether she despised their visitor more because of his nationality or his profession. Like most Venetians, she instinctively distrusted all Spaniards, and she could

17

not understand why her father had invited this one to sup with them. Nor why he had insisted that she must be present. Normally, Marco dei Giorlandi was inclined to indulge his only child, but this time he had been adamant.

'You will dine with us, Venetia,' he had said. 'And there's an end to it.'

Since she had no choice but to obey, Venetia had dressed for the occasion in a gown of green velvet with an embroidered stomacher and hanging sleeves. Her hair flowed on to her shoulders, caught back from her face by a rolled bandeau of velvet slashed with silver, its rich titian colour a foil for the creamy perfection of her complexion. She was a beautiful girl, though her green eyes held an icy pride as she moved towards the window, glancing down at the courtyard.

If she had hoped to catch a glimpse of the stranger, she was disappointed, for he had already entered the house with her father. She turned away, feeling slightly chagrined, pausing to glance at herself in a mirror with an ornate gilt frame. Her surroundings were comfortable, if not as luxurious as her own apartments in the Giorlandi Palace overlooking the Grand Canal, but they were in Rome now, not Venice, and this villa had been taken only for the duration of their stay. Hopefully, that would soon be at an end!

Her father had come to Rome as part of a Venetian diplomatic mission. There was talk of forming a temporary union with several other nations – the most important of which was Spain! – in an offensive against the Turks. The mission had recently become urgent because the Sultan of Constantinople had demanded the surrender of the Venetian-owned island of Cyprus, to which he had a certain if dubious claim.

The girl did not really understand all this talk of Holy Leagues and the importance of saving Christendom from the Turkish fleet. She knew only that her father was deeply worried by the threat against Cyprus. Much of his personal wealth was tied up in the sugar, cotton, and the wine for which the island was famous. She supposed that this must be why he had been so willing to attend the conference in Rome. It was possibly behind his invitation to Captain Roldán Domingo.

Sighing, Venetia made a sign to her ladies to follow her. She knew that she could delay her entrance no longer. Her father would be growing impatient, and she did not wish to make him angry, because he had enough on his mind already. Besides, she had a certain mild curiosity about their visitor. She had heard stories about him from her nurse Almería, a Morisco woman who had come to the Giorlandi palace soon after Venetia's

19

mother had died, when the girl was but seven years old. Almería had cared for her, giving her a mother's love in return for a home where she could practise her own religion without fear of persecution, something she could no longer do in Spain. It was because of Almería's stories that the girl was ill-disposed towards the stranger. If what she had said was true – and there was no reason for her to lie – he must be cruel and utterly ruthless. A man without principles.

She decided that she would for the moment keep an open mind. There must be some honourable Spaniards, although until recently her father had had nothing good to say of them and Almería had fled from Spain because the Inquisition had begun to take an unhealthy interest in her people. While Charles V ruled the huge Spanish Empire, the Moors had given lip-service to the Catholic faith, practising their own religion within the privacy of their own homes. King Philip was less tolerant. He encouraged the Inquisition to root out the heretics, and at last the Morisco people had risen in revolt – a revolt that was swiftly and ruthlessly crushed. According to Almería, Captain Domingo had been the leader of an assault on Galera, only a few weeks previously.

Naturally enough, Venetia sympathised with the rebels. She was just fifteen, spirited and full of ideals. She saw the Moriscos as a persecuted people who had tried to assert their rights and been cruelly defeated. Almería had sobbed bitterly when she heard of the massacre at Galera, and she wept with her. It was not to be expected, then, that she would greet this stranger with any great feeling of pleasure. Nor did she.

Entering the airy chamber with its high, domed ceiling and tiled floor, Venetia saw the two men standing in conversation by the patio. The room, designed for summer use, opened out on to a paved terrace with white columns, a fountain and flowerbeds. It was early spring as yet, but the evening sun crept beneath the arches, dancing like spray from a fountain on the bright jewel colours of the tiles, and on the glorious deep red-brown tresses of the girl's hair, making it glow like fire so that it seemed for a moment that she was touched by heaven's light.

The stranger's eyes narrowed as he saw her, and he seemed to stare at her intently as she approached, sinking into a deep curtsy before them.

'Venetia, my dear,' Marco dei Giorlandi said with a smile of approval, 'I wish to present Captain Roldán Domingo – a member of the Spanish diplomatic mission.'

'Sir, I am ... happy to welcome you to my father's house.'

Her slight hesitation was noted, and a hint of mockery registered in the stranger's eyes.

21

They were bright blue, with an alert, pene-
trating gleam that made her draw a sharp
breath. He was no fool then, this Spaniard!
She decided that Isabel had been right; he
was handsome, despite the thin scar running
from his left eyebrow to his jaw. She found
herself echoing the question Katrine had
asked aloud. Was the scar the result of some
wound on the battlefield? Somehow it did
not look as if it had been made by a sword,
and it had been there for a long time…

She offered her hand, and he took it,
bending over gallantly to touch it with his
lips. 'The pleasure is all mine, lady.'

Why was it that she thought his words
mocked her? She looked up into his face,
seeing the arrogance and pride she had expected, but also something more. A deeper,
intriguing look that made her wonder.

'Venetia, you and your ladies must keep
Captain Domingo company until we dine. I
have some business I cannot avoid.' Marco
dei Giorlandi nodded to his daughter.
'Perhaps our guest would care to take a turn
in the gardens? It wants an hour or more
until sunset.'

'As you wish, Father.' Venetia turned to
the visitor with a slight toss of her head. She
caught a swiftly-hidden smile on his face,
and her manner became even more haughty.
'It is but a small, uninteresting garden, sir,
but if you would care to stroll for a while?'

Her father frowned at her, for it was an ungracious invitation, but the Spaniard's expression did not waver. He offered her his arm, indicating that they should proceed to the garden, and she was obliged to lay just the tips of her fingers on his sleeve. His doublet was fashioned of black velvet, the sleeves slashed to show the white of his silk shirt. His Venetian-style trunk hose were frilled just below the knee and fastened with gold points, and his ruff was of the finest gold lace. On the index finger of his right hand he wore a huge, square emerald ring, but no other jewellery. Compared to most men of her acquaintance he was modestly dressed, though he carried himself with such arrogance that no one could suppose it was other than a matter of choice. His skills as a mercenary were obviously well rewarded, Venetia thought, her face unconsciously reflecting her scorn.

They strolled along the little paths of the neat, formal gardens, followed at a discreet distance by Venetia's serving-women. Katrine and Isabel were both daughters of impoverished noblemen. Without dowries, they had been faced with a choice between the convent or servitude to a girl who was their equal in birth, but more fortunate. Aside from a sharp temper that was liable to explode without warning, Venetia was an indulgent mistress, often passing on expensive trifles that had ceased to amuse her, and the girls knew that they could fare worse. Therefore they had the good sense not to intrude too closely on their mistress, though both were dying to know what the handsome Spaniard was saying to her.

'Have you enjoyed your stay in Rome? I believe it is your first visit?'

'It is pleasant enough here,' Venetia replied with a sigh, 'but I miss my home. One can never be as easy in another's house. Do you not agree?'

'It is different for a soldier. I am seldom at home.'

'No, I suppose not.' She glanced up at him impulsively. 'How can you reconcile your conscience, sir? I understand that sometimes war is unavoidable – but you fight for money.'

'A labourer is surely worthy of his hire?'

'Indeed, that is true, and a common soldier may have no choice, but...' Her eyes flicked to his ring. 'That pretty trifle was not bought with a soldier's pay! I have heard that there were vast amounts of gold and precious stuffs to be plundered at Galera when it fell?'

'The spoils of victory...' He met the accusation in her gaze. 'A soldier must take what he can from life. It is often all too short. If the plunder is fairly won...'

'Men were slaughtered without mercy,

24

women and children sold into slavery. Do you think that fair, sir?' Her eyes blazed with all the passion she felt within her, and he thought that she looked like the Goddess Minerva from ancient mythology, newly sprung from the head of her father Jupiter complete with sword and shield.

'Slavery is a necessary evil.' His voice was flat, without emotion. 'Without slaves our galleys would be too dependent on the wind, often becalmed for the lack of it.'

'Venetian galleys are manned by volunteers.'

'Are their lives any less wretched because of that? They live in their own filth, exactly as our slaves do.'

'But they are free men.'

There were free men in Spanish galleys, too, but he did not remind her of that. 'A man is not a slave simply because he wears a chain about his ankle. If his spirit resists, he can never be anything less than he himself believes.'

'How can you know what it feels like?' Venetia cried angrily. 'You are rich and powerful; you have never felt the lash of an overseer's whip!'

'Have I not?' An odd smile quirked the corners of his mouth. 'Let us not quarrel, lady. I cannot change what I am, though I am sorry if it offends you. Will you not speak of more pleasant matters?'

A faint blush stained her cheeks. She had pressed too hard. He was, after all, her father's guest.

'I beg your indulgence, sir. My nurse is a Morisco woman; I have perhaps said too much.'

'We shall agree to differ.' He smiled without mockery. 'Do you attend the masque at the Orsini Palace next week? I hear it is to be a grand affair.'

'I think not. My father does not approve of such affairs, and besides, we may be on our way to Cyprus by then.'

'I had not thought you... But perhaps you are right,' he corrected himself smoothly. 'I myself have business in Sicily, though I shall return to Rome to await the outcome of the conference.'

'No doubt you hope for war!' Venetia said tartly, then almost wished she had not as she saw him frown.

'I think it inevitable,' he returned, his voice suddenly cold. 'Ah, here comes your father. Your ordeal is at an end, lady.'

His thrust went home. She felt oddly chastened by his mild reproof, knowing how angry her father would be if he guessed that she had been rude to their visitor. An apology hovered on her lips, but there was no time to utter it. She wondered if he would complain of her behaviour, but then she knew that his pride would prevent him. It

26

was doubtful if her needle had even pierced his armour. He had the arrogance of all Spaniards, and she might as well have saved her breath!

Although he remained outwardly polite to her throughout the evening, Captain Domingo practically ignored her presence at the supper table. He and her father spent the whole time in earnest discussion, seeming to be very much in agreement about the formation of the Holy League, and leaving Venetia to her own thoughts. She had the leisure to observe him closely: the black hair that curled slightly in the nape of his neck, his clean-shaven jaw that was unusual in an age when other men went bearded. A beard might have hidden half his scar, she thought, and then realised that she had probably stumbled on a strange truth. No doubt he scorned to stoop to such deceit, flaunting the mark as if it were a badge of honour!

It was a long, tedious evening. She endured it stoically, knowing that there was no escape for her. Once, she caught an odd, calculating gleam in the Spaniard's eyes, and she knew that he was aware of her boredom. He bared his teeth in a flashing grin, and then turned back to her father, launching into an involved debate about theology.

Venetia felt like screaming. He was doing it on purpose, to punish her for what she had said to him earlier, and at the same time he was making a favourable impression on Marco dei Giorlandi. She could see the growing respect in her father's eyes. He liked the man! It was incomprehensible! How could a cultured, tolerant man like a ruthless mercenary? A man who had sold his sword to the devil! King Philip II of Spain was by all accounts a pious man, devoted to reforming and strengthening the Catholic faith, and for that he deserved respect; but he was also intolerant, ruthless, and often cruel. In the Low Countries the Duke of Alva had sown terror in his name, ruling by the sword and a baptism of blood. Venetia was not alone when she named him a devil, if only in her thoughts.

Captain Domingo was the devil's mercenary! She nodded to herself, determined not to succumb. She did not care if neither of the men spoke to her all evening. She would not try to change the trend of their conversation or use any of the little feminine tricks that might have drawn their attention to her – let them ignore her all night if they would! Her fingers drummed impatiently on the table.

'We forget our manners,' Domingo said suddenly. 'Forgive me, lady, such matters as these must be dull hearing for a young girl's ears.'

Now he was saying that she was an empty-headed child with no thought for anything but her own concerns! Venetia's fingers curled into vengeful claws. How she would love to wipe the smile from his face! Frustration added to her growing indignation. He was taking advantage of her inability to strike back, and she would not sit meekly by and let him make a fool of her.

Getting to her feet, she ignored the surprise in her father's face. 'I have no wish to intrude, gentlemen. You have much of importance to talk about. Please excuse me now.'

'Venetia…'

'I have a headache, Father.' She saw suspicion in his face, but dared not even glance at their guest. 'Forgive me, I must go.'

She was aware of two pairs of eyes watching her as she walked with dignity from the room. Once outside, she began to walk faster. She was breathing hard, her hands clenched at her sides. How dared that mercenary laugh at her? For she was sure that he had found something vastly amusing – and it could only be her!

Her face was an open book, if she had but known it, that mirrored her emotions faithfully for all to see. Almería was aware of her extreme displeasure the moment she stormed into her own apartments.

'That man has upset you,' she said. 'Did he insult you, sweeting?'

'He is ruthless and arrogant. I pray that I shall never have to see or speak to him again!'

'What did he do to you?' Almería's hand touched the knife she wore beneath her robe, and her dark eyes glittered. 'If he laid a hand on you, I shall kill him!'

'He had no opportunity; I have not been alone with him.' Venetia's fingers plucked restlessly at her fan. 'No, Almería, it was just as you said: he was at Galera. I asked him, and he admitted it openly.'

'I knew it. They say he is a friend of Don John.'

'The Spanish king's bastard half-brother?' Venetia took a quick turn about the room. 'It was he who turned the tide against the martyrs of Galera.'

Almería nodded, her face creased with grief. 'My brother, his wife and babes all died there. May the Prophet bring down a plague upon their murderers!'

'They will surely burn for their sins,' Venetia said, crossing herself. She knew that the siege had been carried out in the name of Christendom, but her sympathies were all with the family of the woman she loved. 'He dared to say that slavery is a necessary evil!'

'It cannot be denied that this is so.' Almería sighed deeply. 'Better to live as a slave than die of starvation.'

'You cannot mean that!' Venetia was shocked.

'But I do, child. The life of a harem slave is often easier than that of a free woman forced to labour in the fields for her bread.'

'I would rather die!'

'You will never need to make the choice.' Almería shook her head. 'My eldest sister was sold to a Turk by our own father, but because she pleased him and was of the true faith, he offered her her freedom. Yet she chose to stay in the harem. She was the lucky one. She grew fat while we went hungry.'

'My poor, dear Almería!' Venetia's temper cooled as she hugged the plump, well-fed body of her nurse. 'You shall never go hungry again.'

'Foolish one,' the nurse crooned lovingly. 'I have been blessed since I came to your father's house. Do not let the Spanish dog distress you. He is not worthy of your notice. Soon you will be the wife of the lord Giovanni...'

'Yes.' Venetia smiled, pleased by the reference to her impending marriage to Giovanni Gavelli. The match had been arranged the previous summer, and her wedding would take place soon after her sixteenth birthday. 'Giovanni will accompany my father when he returns from his trip to Cyprus.' A little frown creased her brow. 'I wish he would allow me to go with him.'

'It is too dangerous, sweeting. Your father will not risk your safety at such a time. If his ship should be attacked by Corsairs, you would present a tempting prize.'

'But surely it will not come to that? My father's flag is well known in these waters and his ships have traded safely for many years. Why should the Turks or their allies attack us now? We pay the tributes they demand each year.'

Venetia was well aware of her father's reasons for refusing to take her to Cyprus with him. Sultan Selim II had sent the Doge of Venice an ultimatum: the island must be surrendered or it would be taken by force. Since the Venetians were determined not to relinquish their possession of the island, it seemed as if it would mean war. Understanding this, the girl was still determined to have her way if a means could be found. She was reluctant to return home alone, and had several times tried to persuade her father to let her accompany him, the last only that morning. He was a fond, often indulgent parent, seldom denying his daughter, but she had found it impossible to move him on this.

'You will be safer at home,' he had said. 'I shall soon be with you again.'

'But it is so lonely without you.' She smiled at him winningly. 'Besides, I am eager to see Giovanni.'

'It pleases me that you are happy in my choice of a husband for you, Venetia, but the time will soon pass.'

There was no reason for her to be other than pleased with her father's choice of a husband. Giovanni Gavelli was a nobleman, wealthy, cultured, and not unattractive, and she knew that it was an excellent match. She respected her betrothed and was looking forward to her marriage, although he was so much older than she. Katrine had once asked her if she was in love with him, but she did not know what it was like to be in love. Besides, women of her rank did not need to love their husbands. She would do her duty to Giovanni, and he would treat her with the respect due to her as his wife. She would be cosseted and pampered by her husband just as she had been by her father. She neither expected nor wanted anything more.

She had tried pleading and sulking by turn in the matter of the trip to Cyprus, but her moods had availed her nothing. Marco dei Giorlandi could be stubborn when he chose: he would buy her pretty gowns, laces, perfumes and trinkets, but he would not take her with him. Finally she had given up the attempt, though she continued to scheme and complain to Almería as the nurse helped her to prepare for bed.

She slept soundly, undisturbed by dreams

of a black-haired Spaniard with icy blue eyes. Almería was right: he was not worthy of her notice. She would forget him. It was unlikely that they would meet again.

Having comforted herself with the thought, Venetia could hardly credit what her father was saying to her when he sent for her the next morning, to tell her that Captain Domingo would be accompanying them with his galleys for part of their journey. She stared at him indignantly, feeling shocked that he could suggest such a thing.

'But why, Father?' she asked incredulously. 'Why should you wish to sail with a Spanish war galley for company? The stench will be unbearable!'

'It will be a little inconvenient,' her father agreed, 'but a small price to pay for the reassurance of Captain Domingo's presence.'

'But why his galleys?' She frowned. 'Can we not ask for protection from our own fleet?'

'All our available ships are patrolling the waters beyond the Strait of Messina. From there on I shall be joined by our own galleys, and Captain Domingo will take you on to Corfu. You will stay with Giovanni's family there until I come for you.' He smiled at her. 'It will be less lonely for you than in Venice.'

The idea of staying with Giovanni's family would normally have delighted her, but it became irrelevant as she stared at her father in dismay. He could not mean that she was to travel on the Spanish galley?

As it dawned on her that he did indeed intend her to travel on Captain Domingo's ship, her temper erupted. She stamped her foot, her face a picture of indignation. 'I cannot – I will not – travel with that man! How could you ask it of me, Father?'

'I would not do so in normal times, but we are on the verge of war, Venetia.' He frowned at her. 'I should have left you at home. I was wrong to give way to your pleading.'

'But I have always accompanied you on your travels.' Her lip trembled. 'You always said it pleased you.'

'And so it does. Since your mother died, you have been my one consolation in life. It will grieve me as much to part with you as it does you.' He stroked her cheek. 'Please try to understand, my dear.'

Choking back her tears, Venetia hugged her father. She gazed up at him, noticing the lines of strain about his eyes, and the sprinkling of grey in his dark hair. She still could not accept his reasons for refusing to let her go with him, but her resistance was hampered by her love for him. It would only cause him more worry.

'Very well, I shall go to Giovanni's family since it is your wish, but...' She looked at him intently. 'Must I travel with that Spaniard?'

'I think you must,' Marco dei Giorlandi's face was grave as he met her earnest gaze. 'I know it will not be a pleasant journey for you, but you may keep to your cabin, and there is no need for you to notice the slaves. Avert your eyes, and you will not be distressed by their condition.'

'But– But the smell…'

'Soak your kerchief in perfume.' Her father smiled chidingly. 'Come, Venetia, this is not like you! Why have you taken such a dislike to Captain Domingo? I think him an honest, trustworthy man. I should not otherwise have employed him as your escort.'

'He is a mercenary – and a Spaniard!'

There was such disdain in her face that he laughed. 'Do not turn up your nose, daughter. I am satisfied with my bargain. In this world there is a price to be paid for everything, and the sooner you understand that, the easier it will be for you.'

'But can you trust a man who fights for money?'

'I sell silks, spices and other goods for money, and Captain Domingo sells his skills as a soldier. Where is the difference?'

Venetia felt that there was a great difference, but in the face of her father's reasonable attitude, she realised that her objections would be seen as feminine quibbles. It was very clear that this was a battle she could not hope to win.

She shrugged, giving in to the inevitable. 'You will at least let me travel with you as far as the Strait of Messina?'

'Naturally I shall keep you with me until the last moment.' Marco dei Giorlandi breathed a sigh of relief. 'We still have a few days in Rome, Venetia, and we shall spend them together. Now tell me, is there some pretty trifle that would please you?'

The official negotiations for a Holy League had not yet begun. His Holiness Pope Pius V had made many appeals to both the Spanish king and the Doge of Venice, but as yet he had not succeeded in bringing the two sides together.

The Venetians were busy building as many new ships as their famed arsenal was capable of producing – sometimes as many as five and twenty hulls in a month. Even so, they were still hoping to find a way of placating the Turks, while holding on to Cyprus. They made interested noises, but could not be persuaded to an agreement.

The Spanish king had his own reasons for delaying his decision. Venice was the only part of Italy he could not dominate. He considered the Venetians to be too free in their thinking; there were elements in their society that would benefit from the atten-tion of the Inquisition! Set beside this was his hatred of the Turks. If an alliance with the Venetians was the only way to save Christendom from the Infidels who boasted that they would hoist their banner in the Vatican itself, it might be that he must consent to help Venice. However, war was always expensive, and Philip disliked wasting money.

Frustrated by the stalemate in Rome, Domingo had decided to visit his uncle's estate in Sicily. He was too infirm to make the journey these days, and he had entrusted his interests there to his nephew. If the Turks were determined on a concentrated attack on the countries of the Mediterranean, it might be as well to make some preparation. Sicily could be attacked next.

Marco dei Giorlandi's suggestion that Domingo's galleys should accompany him as far as the Strait of Messina fitted well with his own plans. The diversion to Corfu had made him hesitate at first. Even if they made excellent time it could take ten or twelve days to reach Corfu and the same for the return to Sicily; it would delay his return to Rome for some weeks longer than he had anticipated. He had almost decided to refuse dei Giorlandi, even though the man's offer was extraordinarily generous; then he had accepted an invitation to sup, and he saw Venetia, her hair ablaze with the evening sun.

No woman had the right to be so beautiful! Roldán had felt an immediate and urgent desire to possess the divine creature standing before him. For one brief moment his passion had swept all else from his mind, but fortunately the madness had passed swiftly. He was instantly aware of the girl's hostility. Her eyes had held a cold disdain, and she had lost no time in making her thoughts painfully clear.

He was not sure why he had changed his mind and accepted the commission. It was certainly not from any romantic notion of courting the girl. He knew that she was betrothed to a Venetian nobleman – and that she disliked him personally. Besides, there was no room in his life for a woman of her status. There was always a woman ready to share his bed when he felt the need, and he had no intention of taking a wife. Marriage and children were luxuries a mercenary could not afford. Oh, he was wealthy enough – his shrewd brain had seen to that! In the ten years since he had left England he had experienced many vicissitudes, but he had been lucky. He owned two war galleys, a castle in Valencia and a large estate in Granada. He was also his uncle's heir, and had more money than he would ever need. What he could not afford was an emotional entanglement. The last time he had given his heart to a woman it had almost destroyed him. Feelings were dangerous!

So why had he agreed to deliver Venetia dei Giorlandi to Corfu? He had tried to convince himself that it was the gold her father had promised him, but he was too honest to blind himself to the truth. He had seldom wanted to make love to a woman as much as when he had first seen her. He was anticipating the chance to be near her for several days, to cross swords with her in a verbal battle – or was he hoping for more? If so, he was indeed a fool! But why not? After all, the element of risk was the breath of life to him...

Venetia stood on the deck of her father's flagship, holding her cloak tightly round her as the wind tugged at it playfully. Captain Domingo's galleys were some way ahead of them, though still within hailing distance. The merchant ships were much slower than the galleys, and every so often the Spaniard was obliged to order his rowers to stop and let the laggard vessels catch up. The little fleet had hugged the Italian coast for days, taking as little risk as possible, but now the island of Sicily was clearly visible on the skyline, and they would soon be passing through the Messina Strait. Then she would have to transfer to the *Marietta*.

For a moment Venetia wondered about the woman who had inspired Captain Domingo to name his flagship. Was it perhaps his wife or his mistress? She realised that she knew very little of the man in whose company she would be forced to travel for the next several days. Her father trusted him – but could she? She had seen the look in his eyes when he first saw her, and it had made her uneasy for a moment. No man had ever dared to look at her that way. What did it mean? She knew she had no alternative but to trust him. Sighing, she turned away from the ship's rail and saw her father coming towards her. She forced a smile to her lips, not wanting him to see how nervous she felt.

'Are you ready, Venetia? You will not want to keep Captain Domingo waiting.'

'Oh, Father,' she said, moving towards him impulsively, 'will you not change your mind and let me come with you? We haven't seen any sign of the Turkish fleet. I am sure all this talk of war will come to nothing.'

'I wish I were as sure.' Dei Giorlandi frowned. 'It may be an ominous sign.'

'You mean that the Turkish fleet could be preparing for an assault on Cyprus?' She shivered with fear. 'Then your life may be in danger!'

'Nonsense!' He dismissed her fears with a shake of his head. 'I shall fill my ships with as much as they can carry and be on my way back to you before anything untoward happens.'

If he was as sure as he sounded, he would have taken her with him. Venetia felt a stab of fear as she flung herself into his arms.

'I love you,' she whispered chokily. 'Please promise me you will take care?'

'No tears, daughter.' His look was stern, hiding the pain he felt at their parting. 'You do not want Captain Domingo to think you a weak, cowardly woman?'

She blinked back her tears. 'I am not afraid of him!'

'Of course not.' Her father smiled at the gleam of pride in her eyes. 'You can rely on him, Venetia. Now, take this and keep it safe until you reach Corfu.'

'What is it?' She looked at the leather pouch he had given her, hearing the heavy clunk of gold coins. 'You have already given me sufficient monies for my stay with Giovanni's family.'

'That gold is for Domingo. It is the price I promised him for delivering you safely to your friends.'

The purse weighed heavily in her hand, and her mouth twisted with scorn. 'Is it not rather a lot for such a simple task?'

'The journey means a delay for Domingo. Time is money, daughter. He was reluctant to make the diversion. Had he not agreed, I must have sent one of my own ships with you, and that could cost me a great deal more. My warehouses in Cyprus are packed with stores, and it is vital I move them. If the Turks were to get there first...' He paused, frowning. There was no need to tell her that he had taken out a large loan some months previously, nor that the loss of his warehouses could ruin him. 'Well, it would be a considerable loss for us, child.'

'I see...' She looked at him steadily, understanding far more than he had told her. There had been a permanently anxious look in his eyes since three of his best ships had been lost in the winter storms of 1569, and clearly things were more serious than she had previously thought. She smiled and kissed his cheek. 'Then I shall plague you no more. Do not worry about me, dearest Father. I dare say I can put up with a little discomfort for a while.'

CHAPTER TWO

The transfer from the deck of her father's flagship to the galley was not easy for Venetia. It took at least half an hour for the two ships to manoeuvre into the right position, grappled together by hooks and ropes, the wind mischievously changing direction, as the winds in this part of the world were apt to do frequently. Once the boarding plank was in position, Captain Domingo came across it to see to the loading of her possessions personally. When it was time for her to make the crossing, he took her hand, leading her along the platform from the jutting prow to the cabins in the gilded poop.

The galley was strongly built, narrow and propelled by two lines of rowers on either side. When the wind was favourable, this power was assisted by two large triangular sails. There was a catwalk between the rows of men, patrolled by an overseer with a whip. It was along this narrow plank that Venetia was forced to follow the Spanish captain.

Her father had advised her not to notice the rowers, and she studiously kept her eyes fixed on Captain Domingo's back. Yet even so she was aware of the sounds of groaning all about her, and of the stench. Most of the slaves were either naked or clothed only in a strip of filthy cloth. Since they could never leave their benches, they lived, ate and slept in their own filth. She knew that the rowers in Venetian galleys had no better conditions than these wretched slaves, but their plight affected her deeply and she could barely bring herself to look at the Spaniard as he showed her into her cabin.

It was small, but adequately furnished for her needs. Looking about her, Venetia suspected that these were Captain Domingo's own quarters. He must have given them up for her sake, and would be sharing even smaller ones with his officers. She knew she ought to be grateful, but her throat felt tight with emotion and she could not manage even one word of thanks.

'I trust you will be comfortable here? I'm afraid your nurse must share the cabin with you. Your serving-women will travel on board the second galley, since we have no more room for them here.'

She swallowed hard, her eyes avoiding his. 'Thank you. It will do for the short time I must spend on board your ship.' It was an ungracious answer. She knew it, but was unprepared for the stinging reply it earned.

'We shall make as good time as humanly

46

possible, lady. I have as little pleasure in this bargain as you.'

Her eyes flicked to his face, noting the grim lines about his mouth. In Rome she had thought him not more than five and twenty, but now he looked older. He was wearing the helmet and breastplate of a soldier, and she realised that he was prepared for an attack. It was the first time that she had really considered the possibility.

'Excuse me, Madonna Venetia, I have things to attend to. I advise you and your woman to keep to your cabin as much as possible.'

Venetia nodded, her face strained. 'I have no wish to be a nuisance to you, Captain.'

'Oh, you will be that, I dare say,' he said gruffly. 'But I shall be well paid for my trouble.'

She stared at him as he left the cabin, her foot tapping the floor angrily. He was making it quite obvious that she was no more to him than a valuable cargo he had been paid to deliver. She was not sure why his attitude made her so cross, and she was given no time to ponder her feelings.

Almería passed him in the doorway, her dark eyes glittering with a fierce hatred. She spat on the floor as the door closed behind him. 'May the curse of the Prophet be upon him and all his kind!' she muttered. 'I saw the way he looked at you, sweeting. Have no fear, I shall kill him if he attempts to seduce you.'

Surprise flickered in Venetia's eyes. 'Captain Domingo has no interest in me as a woman, Almería. He dislikes me as much as I dislike him.'

'I have seen that hot look in a man's eyes before,' the nurse said. 'Do not trust him! Given the opportunity, he will steal your maidenhead and boast of it to his friends.'

'My father believed him to be trust-worthy.'

'Your father is a good man – but the Spaniard has blinded him with fair words and smiles. That one has mischief on his mind. Do not forget, I know these Dons. I was not always a fat old woman.'

Venetia laughed as she saw the expression on her face. 'You are neither fat nor old! You have never told me just why you ran away from your home. Was it because of a Spanish Don?'

'He wanted me as his mistress. I refused him, and he threatened my family with the Inquisition. I knew that he would have me one way or the other if I stayed.'

'And so you came to Venice.' The girl's breast heaved with indignation. 'It is no wonder that you hate all Spaniards! Thank you for your warning, Almería. I shall take great care never to be alone with him. If he comes to the cabin, you must never leave

48

me – whatever he says.'

Almería took the curved dagger from inside her loose robe of black wool, showing it to the girl. 'Before I left Spain I killed the man who had threatened my family. I shall stab this one to the heart rather than let him defile you with his touch.'

Venetia stared at the weapon and then crossed herself hastily, feeling slightly sick. 'Put it away, Almería; I do not want you to think of such a thing. If you murdered Captain Domingo his men would probably kill us both! Besides, it will not be necessary. I am quite capable of dealing with him myself.'

Since she scarcely stirred from her cabin during the next seven days and Captain Domingo did not come near her, neither of the women had cause for concern. The wind had blown strongly all week, helping to speed the ships over the water and lessen the stench from the slave benches. Venetia kept a scented kerchief with her at all times and a pomander stuffed with strong spices. Despite some discomfort, she had managed to pass the time by embroidering a shirt as a gift for her father, and reading. Venice was a great publishing centre, and Marco dei Giorlandi had insisted on his daughter learning to read. She had a collection of beautiful and expensive books of her own, ranging from the Bible to the works of Tuscan, French and

English poets. She could read and speak several languages, and was accustomed to spending most of her time in study in her own apartments at the Giorlandi Palace. Although the cabin was a little confining, it had not proved to be quite the prison she had expected. There was a table for her books, and a personal cabinet for her toilette. She had begun to think that she had made altogether too much fuss about the journey, when the wind suddenly dropped.

Overnight, the conditions on board became almost unbearable. The weather had turned very much warmer, and the stench was more noticeable. The air inside her cabin was stifling, but she dared not venture outside because she knew that it would be so much worse. While the wind blew, the rowers had been able to work at a steady pace. Now the crack of the overseer's whip was more often heard as he forced the tired men to keep up what seemed a relentless speed.

'Will he never let them rest?' Venetia cried at last. 'Does he want to kill them all?'

'A man like that cares for no one.' Almería scowled. 'Even the strongest among them will crack under such treatment. Any captain of a galley must needs be a hard man – but he is a monster!'

'I shall speak to him.' Venetia stood up, her face determined. 'I cannot bear it a moment longer.'

'Think before you interfere, child. It is not your business how he treats his slaves, and he will tell you so!'

'My father paid him to deliver me safely to Corfu. If he keeps this up, the slaves will die of exhaustion before we get there. I must speak to him.'

'Shall I ask him to come here?'

Venetia was about to say that she would go to him, when she realised that it would be better if their meeting were in private. If she made her demands in front of his men, he might be less inclined to listen to her.

'Yes. And I shall speak to him alone.'

'Is that wise?' The old woman's eyes narrowed.

'Perhaps not, but I think it necessary. I hope to persuade the captain to spare his men, and it will not do to have witnesses.'

'I shall wait outside the door. Call me if you need me.' Almería's hand went to her waist, her fingers touching the knife.

'Very well. Go now and ask him to attend me here.'

As Almería left, she began to pace up and down the cabin, her pulses racing as she thought what she might say to Captain Domingo. She was taking a considerable risk, for he would scarcely be pleased by her interference, but the sound of the overseer's whip had roused her conscience. She must make some effort on behalf of the wretched slaves.

51

'You sent for me, lady?'

She had not heard him enter. A little shiver ran through her as she turned to greet him. His face was hard, his eyes cold as he met her accusing gaze.

'Yes, Captain. I – I wanted to ask if you will not let your slaves rest for a while. Surely they cannot keep up such a relentless pace for ever?'

'My men are the strongest and the fittest to be found in any galley. I chose each one myself, and they can keep up their pace for many hours at a time.'

'But surely they will die if you push them too hard?'

'They have each been given extra rations to build up their strength. I think you need have no fear that we shall not reach Corfu, although it will mean an extra day or two if the wind does not rise. I apologise for the delay, but...'

'I am not thinking of myself!' she cried, her eyes flashing with sudden temper. 'Are you a monster that you must treat these wretched creatures so cruelly?'

'It is for your own sake,' he said, making a harsh noise in his throat. 'I know how anxious you are to reach your journey's end.'

'Not so anxious that I would have your slaves' deaths on my conscience!'

'No?' He moved a little closer, his look

seeming to pierce her. 'I had thought you could not wait to leave my ship? I am aware that it is not a fitting place for a lady of your delicate nature.'

Venetia flushed, feeling guilty. If he was driving his men so hard because of her, then it was her fault. An apology was due. 'I – I have not been too uncomfortable, Captain. I would rather spend a few days longer on board than cause more suffering for these unfortunate men.'

'But I have no time to waste, madonna.'

'I know your time is valuable.' She lifted her eyes proudly to his. 'I shall pay you extra if – if you will agree to spare them.'

'Indeed?' His mouth hardened as he regarded her steadily. 'What will you give me?'

'How much do you want?' her voice quavered as she saw the strange gleam in his eyes. 'Will fifty ducats suffice?'

'No.'

'What then? A hundred?'

'Not for a thousand ducats; yet there is something I want.'

She felt her knees trembling, and she was tempted to call for Almería. 'What do you mean?'

He smiled slightly, enjoying her dis-comfort. 'One kiss, madonna. My price for the favour you ask is a kiss.'

'How dare you suggest such a thing?'

Venetia cried, outraged. 'I have never been so insulted in my life!'

'You consider it an insult?' He arched his brow. 'How highly you must value your kisses. Come, it is not such a terrible price. I might have asked much more.'

She gasped and drew back, her heart fluttering with fear. 'You would not! Not even you could behave so despicably! My father trusted you. You could not betray that trust?'

'Could I not?' His mouth was a mocking slash in his face. 'Am I not a mercenary? A creature of few morals and less mercy?'

'You may scorn me as you will. I am not afraid of you.'

'No?' His hand moved swiftly to curl about her wrist. 'I question that, madonna. Were you less afraid, you would pay the tribute I ask. Or perhaps you do not truly care what becomes of the slaves?'

She gazed up into his eyes, hating him for what he was forcing her to do. 'One kiss? No more?'

'One is all I ask.'

'Very well. I shall pay your price.'

She closed her eyes, her body rigid with tension as she waited for the awful thing that was about to happen to her. She felt his hand cup her chin, tipping her face towards him, and prepared for the worst.

'Open your eyes,' he commanded softly.

'Look at me. That's better. Do not be so frightened, Venetia.'

'I...' she began, but got no further.

His mouth covered hers. She felt an instinctive urge to pull away, but his arm went round her waist, holding her so that she was pressed hard against him, the metal of his armour bruising her. At first his kiss was gentle, seeming almost to caress her. She felt her tension easing, her eyes opening wider in surprise; then, just as she had begun to relax, he deepened the kiss, the pressure of his lips hardening as if to punish her. Feeling them grind against her own, she experienced a sharp jolt of fear and began to struggle. His arm became a girdle of iron about her waist, imprisoning her, and the kiss went on and on until she thought she would die. She was swooning when he let her go at last.

She touched her swollen lips, gazing at him in mute dismay. 'You– You exact payment to the full, Captain Domingo!'

'Always! You would do well to remember that the next time you seek to bargain with me, madonna. I may not be so generous in future.'

She lifted her head proudly, controlling her fluttering nerves as best she could. 'You will allow the slaves to rest for a while?'

'Why not?' A little smile quirked the corners of his mouth. 'The danger is passed now. It was my intention to return to a normal speed as soon as possible.'

'What danger?' She stared at him in dawning suspicion, seeing the laughter in his face.

'We were being pursued by Corsairs. They would have taken you as their prize and enslaved those of us they did not kill. Even galley-slaves understand the importance of escaping an enemy they fear more than the master they know. At least they are well fed on board the *Marietta,* and most of them will leave this ship as free men at the end of their term of servitude. As prisoners of the Corsairs, they might never see their homeland again.'

'You– You tricked me!' she cried bitterly. 'Why didn't you tell me that we were being pursued? Why did you lie to me?'

'I did not lie to you. It was for your sake as much as anyone's that I was determined to outdistance the Corsairs. My men are prepared to fight, and to die if necessary – but I gave your father my word that I would see you safely to Corfu.'

'You did not promise to seduce me!'

'A kiss is not a seduction, you foolish child! If I wished to lie with you, I should take what I wanted without waiting to argue. It was merely a jest – to teach you a lesson.'

'I hate you!' Venetia's hands itched to strike him, but she dared not attempt it. He had tricked her into yielding that kiss, and she would never, never forgive him. She heard his laughter and glared at him. 'What is so amusing?'

'Why nothing, lady. Except that I have discovered you are much as other women, after all.'

'I don't understand you.' She stared at him, piqued by his tone, which seemed to imply criticism. 'What is wrong with being like other women?'

'Naught...' There was a peculiar expression in his eyes. 'At least you paid your debt – however grudgingly. Pray excuse me now, I have work to do.'

Venetia watched, puzzled, as he left the cabin. He had seemed almost disappointed, as if he had expected something more of her. But what? Had he thought that his kiss would make her swoon with love for him? The arrogance of the man! He had asked for one kiss, but perhaps he had hoped for more. The thought made her eyes glow with pride. If she had known, she would not have given even that one kiss. He had tricked her into it and she hated him for it. She would be glad when they finally reached Corfu and she need never see him again.

Lost in her own thoughts, she was startled by a rousing cheer and laughter from the belly of the ship. Surely the slaves could not be making that noise? They sounded elated, almost as if they were pleased by something. Yet what could they have to celebrate?

She was half-way to the door when it opened and Almería came in. The Morisco woman was silent, a strange look of disbelief on her face. 'He has ordered a ration of ale for all the slaves. What did you say to make him so generous?'

A faint blush tinged the girl's cheeks, and she turned aside. 'I merely asked him to let them rest, but it was not my doing, Almería. Apparently, Captain Domingo believes in keeping their strength up. He– He actually seems proud of them.'

'Well, I must admit I have not seen much cruelty, but they are still slaves, chained by their ankles.' She scowled. 'No doubt he knows how to get the most work out of them.'

'Yes, I expect you are right.' Venetia walked to the window, gazing out at the stars as night fell suddenly around them, turning the sea to a dark midnight blue. Her fingers crept to her lips, feeling the sting of his kiss. 'Captain Domingo always knows how to get what he wants...'

Bathed in sunshine, the island of Corfu lay shimmering before them. Venetia's baggage had already been taken ashore, and arrangements were being made for her journey to the Gavelli estate. Captain Domingo had hired horses and a groom to escort them. His task was done, and she knew that he would want to lose no time. He had business of his own in Sicily, and he must return to Rome for the start of the papal conference. As she emerged from her cabin, he came towards her, obviously intending to help her to disembark.

'So we are here at last,' he said, his eyes giving no hint of his own sentiments. 'You will forgive me if I do not escort you to your friends' house, but word has been sent and I doubt not that you will be met before you have gone half-way.'

'You have fulfilled your bargain, Captain.' She held out the pouch her father had given her. 'I was to give you this when we reached Corfu, I believe?'

The Spaniard seemed to hesitate moment-arily, then he took the purse of gold and stuffed it inside his doublet. Venetia experi-enced a ridiculous sense of disappointment. Had she really expected him to refuse the money? Surely not! It was just another task for which he had been generously paid. Why should he forfeit his fee?

'My thanks to your father, lady. I trust that your journey was not too uncomfortable?'

'I would not choose to travel so again...' Venetia relented as she saw his frown. 'Yet I am grateful for a safe arrival, Captain.'

He bowed stiffly. 'I gave your father my

word, and I do not promise lightly. I hope that we shall meet again one day, Madonna Venetia.'

He waited as if expecting a reply in kind, but she said nothing. It was unlikely that his words meant anything more than mere politeness. Besides, their lives would travel in opposite directions from now on. She was not sure why that thought should weigh on her so heavily, nor why she was suddenly almost reluctant to leave his ship.

'Ah, your horses are ready. Your ladies await you, Madonna Venetia. You must go now.'

She gazed up at him, puzzled by the new, gentle note in his voice and by the tightness in her own breast. She had thought to be glad to leave him, but now it seemed almost as if she were clinging to these last moments.

'Yes, I must leave,' she said, the words catching in her throat. 'You have work to do, Captain. I must not delay you.'

She held out her hand and he touched it to his lips. 'Forgive me, madonna. It was a cruel trick I played on you.'

'You are forgiven,' she said, giving him a smile that almost blinded him with its brilliance. 'May God protect you, sir.'

Turning away, she blinked hard, surprised at her own foolishness. She saw Almería look at her oddly and ignored her. She wanted no scoldings just now. It was ridiculous to feel this way. She did not like Captain Domingo, so why should she feel as if she had been abandoned? Lifting her head, she walked towards the horses, where Isabel and Katrine were already waiting. It would not do to let them see how vulnerable she felt. She was behaving like a timid child. The Gavelli family would welcome her to their home. There was no need for her to feel so terribly alone...

The negotiations for a Holy League had finally begun in earnest when Domingo returned to Rome late in June. Cardinal de Granvelle and the other members of the Spanish mission met the Pope's represent-atives and the Venetian ambassador, Michele Suriano, in the house of Cardinal Alessandrino to discuss the dangers of a Turkish invasion.

Meeting with lesser members of the Spanish party, Domingo learned that Venice was now eager to form an alliance, though the negotiations dragged on interminably throughout July. Impatient to be at sea, he spent his time between ensuring that his galleys were repaired and cleansed, and gathering what information he could on the whereabouts of the Turkish fleet, which was known to be on a menacing cruise some-where in the eastern Mediterranean. From word brought in by a brigantine, it was learned that the offensive against Cyprus had begun, and suddenly matters became urgent.

Domingo had been supping with a friend. In the morning he would take his galleys and join the Sicilian squadron, which was to be led on behalf of Spain by Gianandrea Doria. Leaving his friend's house, he paused in the street, feeling disinclined to return to his lodgings just yet. It was a warm summer night and the scent of some sweet flower was carried on the breeze. The news of the Turks' attack on Cyprus had made him think of Venetia. Had her father managed to complete his business in time to escape or was he trapped by the invasion? If dei Giorlandi should die...

Domingo became conscious of the shadowy figure following him. He tensed, his hand moving to the hilt of his sword. If it was a cutpurse after his gold, he would be unlucky. He was carrying hardly anything of value. Still, there were vagrants roaming the streets who would kill for the price of the boots he was wearing! He turned sharply, confronting the man, who was following at a discreet distance.

'Hold, sirrah! I have nothing worth stealing save my sword, and that you may have with pleasure!' He drew the weapon as he spoke, holding it in such a way that the threat behind the words was unmistakable.

'Sheath your blade, Captain Domingo, I mean you no harm. I have come to warn you.' The man was tall and thin, and wearing a long black cloak, his face shaded by a hood.

'To warn me?' Domingo did not immediately sheath his weapon. 'Of what?'

'An attempt on your life, Captain. Do not return by your usual route tonight or you will be set upon by assassins.'

'How do you know this?'

'I know many things. Believe me when I say that I wish you only good fortune. If I had wanted to kill you, I could have sprung on your back long before you saw me!–Your thoughts were far away from Rome tonight, Roldán.'

Domingo sheathed his sword, staring at him with a puzzled frown. 'Who are you? And why are you warning me? You know me … should I know you?'

'Not by name, but you know me. We are brothers in all but birth, my friend.' The hooded stranger laughed softly. 'Do not trouble yourself over my identity. When the time is right, you shall know all. Good night, Captain. Heed my warning, for it will save your life.' He turned and walked in the opposite direction.

'Wait!' Domingo called, but his stride did not falter. 'Thank you … whoever you are.'

The stranger gave no indication that he had heard, and Domingo stared after him, frowning. Who was he, and why had he taken the trouble to warn him? Somehow he did not believe it was a trick, for it was true that he had not been as alert as usual, his thoughts far away. If the man had wished to stab him in the back, he had had ample opportunity.

The house in which he was staying could be approached in two different directions, one of which was along the bank of the river. Many a body had been disposed of in the murky waters of the Tiber. It was his habit to take the shortest route, but tonight he would go the long way round; he would also try to discover if there were really assassins lying in wait for him. He could not think of any enemies that might have it in mind to murder him, but a man in his profession could have many secret foes. There was no point in taking unnecessary risks...

'Are you sure?' Venetia stared at the man standing before her in the salon of her friends' villa. He had arrived only minutes ago asking to see her, and she had hurried to meet him, hoping for news of her father's arrival. Now it seemed that the news was bad. 'You are quite certain that my father is still in Cyprus?'

Captain Gómez nodded, his face grave.

He had known the girl since she was a babe in arms, and he felt a certain fondness for her. 'My ship was the first to be loaded. My orders were to unload and then come to Corfu and place myself at your disposal. Your father's intention was that I should take you home, lady.'

'But he said I was to wait here for him. Why has he changed his mind?' She felt a spasm of nerves in her stomach. 'You are not telling me the whole truth. What is it that you fear to say?'

He glanced down at the ground, obviously reluctant to speak. 'We had word that the Turkish fleet was on its way. Your father was anxious to clear every ship as fast as he could...'

'You think he was caught by the invasion, don't you?' She looked at him with dawning suspicion. 'You must tell me the truth!'

His face creased with concern for her. 'I know it, Madonna Venetia.' He saw the agonised expression in her eyes and stared at his feet once more. 'We passed the Turkish advance in the night. I thought they would attack us, but they were intent on their purpose. One merchant ship was too insignificant to attract their attention...'

'And there is no chance that my father got away?' Her hands curled into tense fists as she waited for his answer. Her father was at the mercy of the Turks!

'None. He was determined to see all his ships loaded. He would have been the last to leave.'

A sob caught in her throat. Tears sprang to her eyes, but she brushed them away. This was not the time for tears: she would give way to her grief when she was alone. She looked at Gómez, her face pale and strained. 'Perhaps it will be a peaceful landing. The Governor will surely sue for peace? Venice has never desired war with the Turkish Empire.'

'Perhaps you are right.' He had no desire to upset her more than necessary, though he knew that there was little chance of peace now that the invasion had begun. 'Is it your wish to return to Venice, lady?'

Venetia stared at him in silence as she tried to gather her confused thoughts. Giovanni's family had made her very welcome in their home, and she knew they would be loath to part with her. Yet if she told them she was to meet her father in Venice... It would be foolish to let anyone guess what was really in her mind. Giovanni's brother would consider it his duty to forbid her if he knew that she was planning to attempt the rescue of her father. He would say it was impossible, and perhaps it was. But she knew she had to try.

'Your orders are to obey me, Captain Gómez, is that correct?'

'Yes, my lady.'

He was puzzled by her manner, but she was unquestionably the owner of his ship now. If Marco dei Giorlandi were still alive, he would certainly be a prisoner of the Turks. It might be possible to ransom him when the invasion was over – if he lived – but that could take years. Meanwhile, this young girl would have to cope with what was left of her father's business. There was little chance of her doing so successfully without a husband to take charge of her affairs, and Giovanni Gavelli was still in Cyprus. Another man might have sailed away and left her to her fate, but Captain Gómez was honest. He had served her father faithfully, and he would do as much for her.

'Let your ship be provisioned and ready, Captain,' Venetia said, making up her mind. 'I shall come aboard in the morning. You shall have your orders then.'

He nodded, bowing correctly before turning to walk away, his boots echoing loudly on the tiled floor of the Gavelli villa. Venetia stared after him, her mind still whirling in confusion. She did not truly know what she ought to do. Sometimes the Turks were willing to ransom their prisoners, so if she could somehow send a message to their leaders, perhaps there was a sheltered cove where the ship could anchor while negotiations went ahead? Her father had always told her that his trading relations with Constantinople were good, so why should she not trade his life for money? How much would they demand for his release, she wondered. How could she raise the money if a bargain was struck? Oh, if only there was someone to advise her! Someone she dared to confide in...

Suddenly a vision of Captain Domingo came to her, and she was sure he would know what to do. Her feet paced restlessly up and down the long room as the evening shadows began to creep across the floor and the sun faded from the sky. There was a fortress on the island, but the soldiers were busy preparing to defend themselves. They would have no time to listen to a foolish female's schemes of rescuing her beloved father. They would immediately inform Gavelli, and he would prevent her from leaving.

She decided that she would take only her nurse with her. It would be unfair to risk the lives of her two serving-women, especially as Katrine's parents were trying to arrange a match with a wealthy merchant for her. She would miss them, for they were lively companions, and sometimes Almería's grumbling became tedious, but she could not ask them to put their own lives in danger for her sake. In a moment, she would go and tell them they were to stay here. She could think of some excuse…

She wondered if Captain Domingo were still in Rome. Would it be wiser to try to find him? She was sure that he would help her – for a price. But she was willing to pay whatever she must to save her father.

'Venetia, where are you?'

That was Katrine's voice. No doubt she had been sent to find her. It was nearly supper-time and she had not changed her gown.

'I'm coming,' she called, hurrying to meet the girl.

She was still turning the problem over in her mind when she entered her own apartments, to be scolded by her nurse. She did not know what to do for the best, but one thing at least was certain: she could not stay here and do nothing.

It was late August when the Sicilian squadron kept a rendezvous at Otranto. To Domingo's disgust, the Venetian galleys were poorly equipped and undermanned. Their boast of having the largest fleet in the Mediterranean was shown by a brief inspection to be hollow. The red hulls and gilded prows looked impressive when drawn up for inspection, but most had lain on a slipway for years, and though they were manned by free men, the crews were weak and too few in number. The small papal fleet was even more pitiful.

Marcantonio Colonna had overall command of the League's fleet, but his task was thankless, if not impossible. Having loyalties to both Spain and Venice, he had been especially chosen for his great tact and courage. Unfortunately the papal squadron was the smallest contingent, and this weakened his authority. Colonna was eager to confront the Turks, but Gianandrea Doria was less willing. He personally owned several of the war galleys, and would lose a great deal of money if they were sunk in battle. He argued that the Venetian ships were not fit for combat, and that, therefore, the fleet was not strong enough to confront the powerful Turks.

'Doria is afraid of the Turks,' Domingo said angrily to the captain of his second galley. 'He will waste the fine weather in talk, Carlos, and then say that the venture must be abandoned until the spring.'

Carlos Quirini nodded his agreement. 'It will be a miracle if we move from this spot, let alone attack the enemy!'

Domingo paced the deck of his ship impatiently. The leaders of the expedition were in his opinion wasting too much time in discussion. If they were to do anything this year, they must move now, before the winter storms began. Once the weather deteriorated, the ships would be hard put to it to fight their way home.

'The devil take Doria!' he cried. 'I almost believe his enemies when they say his last brush with the Turks broke his nerve!'

'If he has anything to do with it, we'll be here until spring,' Carlos said gloomily.

'And that will be too late for the poor devils in Cyprus.' He was thinking of Venetia. Both her father and her betrothed were in Cyprus, unless they had managed to get away before the Turkish fleet blockaded their escape route. If they died, she would have no one... His thoughts were curtailed by a shout from his comrade.

'Look, sir! That fregata passing among the ships! There must be something in the wind.'

A fregata was a light pinnace, which could move swiftly and easily. Often used for carrying news, it was now the bearer of fresh orders for the galley captains. A decision to move eastwards had been reached. There was to be an attempt to harass the Turks by attacking their base on the island of Rhodes.

It was not what Domingo had expected or hoped for, but it was at least a start. If successful, it might cause the Turks to stop and think. It might not yet be too late to bargain for the lives of the unfortunate people trapped in Cyprus. It might even delay the invasion. He had his own ways of communicating with the enemy, and thought he might be able to arrange for certain ships to slip through the Turkish lines. He had once been a Turkish galley-slave, chained to his oar for two long years, until an accident of fate secured his freedom. He knew how the minds of these men worked, and if there was a way of ransoming Marco dei Giorlandi, he would find it. He was not sure why he felt a sense of responsibility towards the man, though they had become friends in Rome. Even so, there was no reason why he should try to help him. He had warned dei Giorlandi of the danger of being trapped at the start, yet he could not forget the look in Venetia's eyes when he had left her at Corfu. For one brief moment she had looked so vulnerable.

Resolutely he dismissed her from his thoughts. He would do what he could to help her, but in the meantime there were other matters on his mind.

'It is madness to think of attempting it!' Captain Gómez said, staring at the girl in dismay. 'Even if we reach Cyprus safely, we could do nothing to help your father – if he is still alive, and that's doubtful.'

'Don't say that!' Venetia stamped her foot. 'We may be able to get him away under cover of darkness. You don't know that the invasion has begun. You only saw the Turkish fleet in the distance. Besides, we can ransom him if he is a prisoner.'

'How?' He saw the determined line of her mouth, and sighed. He believed that the Turks had been about to invade the island when he left, and if that were so, it was more than likely that her father was already dead. The governor had not even started to reinforce the island's defences, for most of the inhabitants refused to believe that an attack was imminent. Even if dei Giorlandi were a prisoner, his captors would demand a huge ransom. 'Why don't you let me take you home, Madonna Venetia? We can send out envoys to make enquiries, and perhaps begin talks with Constantinople if your father has been captured. The Sultan or his Grand Vizier might be willing to negotiate.'

She knew that what he said made sense, but she was desperately afraid that it would be too late. If Nicosia should fall into Turkish hands… Her eyes glittered with pride as she met his steady gaze.

'I am determined to find my father, Captain. If you are not prepared to sail under my orders, I shall find someone who will.'

She had more courage than many a man! Knowing that she was being reckless, he could still admire her spirit. He shrugged his shoulders, a wry smile twisting his mouth. 'Since you are determined on it, lady, I'll follow your orders, though I doubt not that your father will have my head for it if we succeed in our mission.'

Venetia laughed, her eyes sparkling. 'If we succeed, my father will pay you a thousand ducats, Captain Gómez. You have my word on it.'

'Then I'm with you to the last, my lady.' He smiled at her, feeling a surge of optimism. Maybe she was right and he was a cautious old fool. 'I've dealt with the Turks for many a year – and there are some who can be trusted to keep their word. We'll see what can be done to find your father.'

'We must find him,' Venetia said, her face suddenly strained and pale. 'We must!'

CHAPTER THREE

The sails drooped limply, and the fat-bellied merchant ship lay dead and heavy in the water, unable to move for lack of a wind. Captain Gómez stared anxiously at the cloudless blue sky, hoping for some sign that the weather would break soon. It was so still and calm that he could almost hear the beating of his own heart.

'Ship on the horizon!'

The look-out's cry had an ominous ring to it, as if he too sensed danger. Gómez tensed, straining his eyes as he tried to guess the identity of the vessel that was just a tiny spot between the blue of sea and sky. It was a galley, he knew that immediately, for it was moving at a fair pace, but was it Venetian, Spanish or perhaps an enemy? A prickle of fear ran down his spine as other black shapes appeared on the horizon. He watched in growing apprehension as the ships came steadily closer and he saw that they were flying blood-red banners. Corsairs! It could only be a raiding party. If anything, Gómez feared these allies of the Turks more than their masters. They were ruthless fighters, intent on plunder, and no city on the

Mediterranean coast was safe from their raids. Their quarry was human flesh, prisoners who could be ransomed for large sums or sold in the slave-markets of Algiers.

If there had been any chance of escape, he would have fled from them, but he was caught like a rat in a trap. All he could do was to assemble his men on deck and give them the choice of dying like men or submitting to the yoke of slavery. He knew in his heart that resistance was useless: they would be overrun within minutes of being boarded. Yet there were the women to consider. He cursed himself for ever agreeing to this mad venture. With no hope of a ransom, Venetia would be sold as a harem slave. A young virgin with her looks would fetch a high price from some elderly Pasha. The older woman would likely find herself in the kitchens of one of her own people, not a slave, but poorly paid and little better off than her mistress. It would be kinder to kill the girl, Gómez thought. He was appalled by the idea, but the alternative would be worse.

'What is happening, Captain?' She had come up on deck to escape the stuffy heat of the cabin, and was looking anxious as she walked to join him at the rails.

'Corsairs,' he muttered gruffly, knowing there was no point in trying to spare her. 'If we could run from them we might stand a chance, but…'

His face was grey. Venetia sensed the fear in him, and her heart began to pound. He had warned her of the dangers that a lone merchant ship might meet in these waters, but she had not really believed him … until now. As she saw the size of the Corsair fleet – two war galleys and nearly a score of galliots – she suddenly understood why Captain Domingo had thought it wiser to outdistance them than to risk a fight. Even his crew would have been outnumbered. As for hers – it would be a wanton waste of life to resist.

'You will surrender the ship, Captain,' she said, her lips white. 'It could be better for your men to live as slaves than to die uselessly trying to defend us.'

'But what of you?' he asked, his fingers straying to the hilt of his sword. 'The men may take their chances, but do you understand what is in store for you?'

'Giovanni's family will ransom me,' she said, sounding much more confident than she felt. 'Besides, I have no choice; they will not kill me. I can be sold as a slave. I am valuable to them.'

'I could end it for you quickly if you wish?' He looked at her gravely, feeling pity tear at his heart. She was so young and lovely. It would grieve him to plunge his sword into her heart, but he would do it if she asked him. 'It might be easier for you, madonna.'

The Corsair fleet was closing in swiftly. Venetia's heart was beating so fast that she could scarcely breathe, let along think clearly. Supposing the Gavellis did not ransom her, or supposing she was forced to live in the harem of a Turk? Now she could see the bright robes and turbans of the men crowding the war galleys. They had fierce eyes and cruel mouths. She was suddenly very afraid, and she turned to Captain Gómez, a look of mute appeal in her eyes. He knew that she was asking him to save her from the horror of being captured by these brutes, though she could not bring herself to utter the words.

'It will be swift,' he promised as he drew his sword. 'I beg you to forgive me, lady...'

Nicosia had fallen to the Turks. The Governor had been unprepared for the attack when it came, and after a siege of forty-six days, he surrendered to Lala Mustafa, the commander of the Sultan's army, on the understanding that lives would be spared. It was the ninth day of September when the end came, but the news did not reach the leaders of the League's fleet until much later in the month. Now that the capital of Cyprus had fallen, there seemed little point in harassing the enemy's base on Rhodes.

'So we are to simply turn tail and go home?' Domingo growled when he heard the new orders. 'So much time wasted in useless talk, and now this!'

'It would be something if we wintered nearer to Cyprus ready for an early offensive in the spring,' Carlos agreed with his captain. 'What will you do now – follow Doria to Sicily?'

'No, I think not,' Domingo said slowly. 'I believe it would be better if you accompanied the fleet, however. I shall join you there later. I have business elsewhere.'

The blue eyes were remote, and Carlos knew better than to ask questions, though he had a shrewd idea as to what his captain's business was. There had been something different about him of late, and he suspected that it had to do with the red-haired beauty they had ferried to Corfu. Still, it was not his affair. He saluted smartly.

'I shall await your orders, sir.'

Domingo nodded, watching as he transferred to the second ship. It was better that Carlos should winter in Sicily, avoiding the risks that he himself was preparing to take. The fleet was gradually dispersing, making its separate ways home. Late in the autumn, the weather was apt to change suddenly, storms blowing up from nowhere. Galleys were fast fighting ships, but flimsier than the fat-bellied supply ships that sailed in their rear. Normally, Domingo's ships wintered at their home base, but this year he had decided to make for Corfu.

It is simply that I feel responsible for the girl, he told himself a hundred times. Now that Nicosia had fallen, it is possible that her father has been taken prisoner. Please God, he is not already dead! The Turks could not always be relied upon to keep their word, sometimes slaughtering their captives without mercy. The girl was vulnerable, even though she must be safe enough in Corfu for the present, but where would the Turks strike next? Any Venetian territory was likely to be considered fair game once Cyprus was completely in Turkish hands. It could do no harm to enquire if she needed anything. Perhaps he could be of service in some way...

He gave the order to change direction, then went to his cabin in the poop. Entering, he thought he caught the faintest trace of her perfume. At first it had lingered tantalisingly in the bed hangings, haunting his dreams and reminding him of the moment when he had held her in his arms, and of the taste of her lips. The dreams had kept him restless through the night, torturing his body so that he groaned aloud and woke to find himself bathed in a fine sweat. The scent had faded now, but the memory of her face lived on in his head no matter how hard he tried to banish it. Finally, he knew that he had to see her again. She was beautiful, but a woman like any other. What he felt for her was purely physical. He should have bedded her when he had the chance and eased the grinding ache inside him. Until he had exorcised her ghost, he would never be at peace again.

Vaguely, he heard the cries and shouts from forward. Something was causing excitement among the crew. He looked up as the door of his cabin was flung open after a perfunctory knock.

'What is it, José? Are we being attacked?' he asked, half annoyed by the intrusion into his thoughts.

'It's the wreck of a ship, sir. There's a man in the water, and we think he's alive. Do we have your permission to attempt a rescue?'

'Yes. I'll come now.'

He got to his feet and followed the man outside, along the narrow catwalk to the forecastle. The rowers had upped oars, taking advantage of the brief respite while some of the officers were pointing at something in the water just ahead. The half submerged hull of a merchant ship, that looked as if it had been torn apart by some kind of an explosion, was drifting a short distance away. A man was clinging to it. As they watched, he moved his arm feebly.

'May I volunteer to get him, sir?' The speaker had been released from his chains. Stripped to the tiny loin-cloth, his tanned body rippled with cord-like muscles.

Recognising him as a particularly strong

slave, Domingo nodded, approving his courage. He had noticed him before, liking the way he set about his work without complaint.

'Be careful, Pedro, these waters are infested with sharks. If they attack, your orders are to leave him and save yourself. Do you understand me?' The man nodded grimly, and Domingo grinned. 'If you succeed, you will earn your freedom at the end of this tour.'

The man's dark eyes glinted with pride, and a sudden surge of emotion. 'Thank you, sir. I'll get him.'

He stood on the curved prow, his body tensed for a moment before he dived into the sea. Then he was cutting through the water with strong, even strokes. He reached the sailor quickly, but it was several minutes before he could pry him free of the wreck, for the half dazed creature fought to keep a hold on his refuge. At last the slave punched him on the jaw, seizing him as he flopped forward, and began his swim back to the galley.

'Sharks! There's a shark!'

Domingo looked towards the wreck, seeing the unmistakable shape of a dark fin breaking the surface of the water. He hesitated, and then beckoned to one of his officers.

'Make ready your arquebus. Hold your

fire until I tell you.'

The man stared at him, but prepared his musket, holding it steady with the barrel lodged against his shoulder. Another man stood by with the match. The dark fin was gaining on the men in the water. Soon they would be so close that it would be dangerous to fire for fear of hitting the wrong target.

'Light your musket,' Domingo commanded, his eyes narrowing as he concentrated on the desperate race for life. 'Take aim! Fire!'

The shot sounded loudly in the tense stillness, every man on board watching as the ball sped towards its target. The arquebus was a precarious weapon at the best of times, and fired from a ship's deck at a moving target that could not be clearly seen, they had little hope that it would be successful. There was a smothered sigh of disbelief when the sea began to turn red and the distance between that menacing fin and the two men grew gradually longer. But now more dark fins were closing in, attracted by the blood of the wounded shark.

Several other officers had fetched muskets and were firing at the mass of sharks swarming about the writhing body of their wounded fellow. But now the men in the water had reached the galley, and a dozen hands reached down to pull them over the ship's side. A cheer went up from the slaves on their benches as they recognised the hero of the hour. There was not one of them who did not know that he had been promised his freedom, and because of his bravery, it gave each man hope that he too might find a way of earning his own freedom one day.

Pedro was panting, water dripping from his bronzed body as he bent over the sailor he had saved. 'I believe he still lives, Captain Domingo. He is coming round again...'

'You have done well,' Domingo said. 'You are needed at your oar, so you must return to your place – but you will not be chained again. When we reach land, you will be free to leave this ship or to stay as one of my fighting men. The choice is yours.'

'I have no family and no home,' Pedro said, an odd gleam in his eye. 'I should be honoured to serve you.'

'Good. Your pay begins from today. Now take your place. We must make up for lost time.'

'Water...' The cry was feeble, but Domingo heard it. He beckoned to one of his officers, then took the cup that was swiftly brought and bent over the shipwrecked sailor himself.

'Sip this, sir,' he said. 'Gently now, for it will be difficult at first. You have been in the water for some days, I think.'

The sailor's lips were cracked and swollen.

He sipped the water, choking as it touched his throat. 'Corsairs,' he whispered. 'We were becalmed. They took those who did not resist – including the women...'

Domingo frowned, feeling a prickling sensation at the back of his neck. There was something familiar about the man's face even though it was blotched and reddened by the sun and salt water – something that set alarm-bells ringing in his head.

'Who are you?' he asked. 'I believe we have met before. Are you not one of Marco dei Giorlandi's captains?'

'Gómez...' The husky voice was full of pain as his hand gripped Roldán's wrist urgently. 'I tried to save her, but they knocked me senseless... You must help!'

His hand fell away and his eyes closed. Domingo felt for his pulse, frowning. By a miracle he was still alive! He had merely fainted from exhaustion.

'Take him to my cabin.' Domingo stood up, his eyes bleak. If he was right, this man was one of dei Giorlandi's employees, and that could only mean... And yet it could not be true. She was safe in Corfu, unless she had tried to reach her father. An icy hand seemed to grip his heart. She would not be so foolish! Yet he knew that she was capable of recklessness. If she were a prisoner of the Turks there was only one course open to him. He must find her! 'Watch over him, and tell me the moment he wakes. I must speak with this man urgently.'

Venetia stirred as the door of the cabin opened, blinking in the sudden light. She had been kept in darkness during the night, and given only a piece of coarse brown bread with a jug of water. Otherwise, she had not been harshly treated, except for those first, terrifying, moments when the prow of the Corsair galley rammed the merchant ship. She had been standing with her eyes closed, expecting the sword-thrust that would end her life at any second. But for some unknown reason Captain Gómez had hesitated, and then it was too late. She felt a terrible jarring sensation, and then the scarlet and green robed pirates had come pouring over the side of the ship. She had screamed, and her scream brought a huge swarthy-skinned brute bearing down on her. Captain Gómez had rushed in an attempt to save her, and then she was surrounded by wild-eyed Corsairs. The last time she had seen Gómez, he had been lying motionless on the deck. After she and the other prisoners had been transferred to the galleys, her ship had been fired on by the Corsairs' guns. She was sure that her faithful captain had been left for dead on board, and she mourned his loss. He had been a good man; his death was a bitter blow, since she had only herself to blame for it.

'Are you hurt, sweeting?'

'Almería?' Venetia sat up eagerly as the dark shape approached. She had thought it was one of the guards come to check on her, and her relief was immeasurable. 'Thank God you are still alive!'

Almería placed her lanthorn by the mattress on which the girl had been lying, bound by the wrists and ankles. 'The savage brutes!' she exclaimed angrily. 'There was no need to bind you! You could not escape.'

'It was because I bit and kicked my captor,' Venetia said ruefully, rubbing her wrists as the Morisco woman cut her free. 'I was warned what would happen, but I wouldn't listen.'

'You would do better to behave meekly,' Almería said. 'An obedient woman is usually treated well enough. Resistance will only result in punishment. You must learn to act humbly, even if you rebel in your heart.'

'Will they really sell me as a slave?' Venetia looked at her fearfully. 'I tried to tell that brute who carried me off that my family would ransom me, but he refused to listen.'

'It takes time to arrange – and things are different now that your country is at war with the Turkish Sultan. It may be that they will decide to follow the simplest course. You would fetch a high price in the market.'

'What about you?' Venetia wrinkled her brow. 'Will you be sold, too?'

'I am of the true faith, so I cannot be owned by a believer. I shall be given work in the kitchens of some rich Moor – unless I can find a husband.' Almería smiled oddly. 'It seems that I am neither as old nor as fat as I had thought. Mustafa has taken a liking to me, and it was he who allowed me to come to you.'

'Mustafa? Who is he?'

'Second-in-command on this ship. I told him that I had been your slave, and that you were good to me. In return for … certain favours, he has granted me the task of looking after you on the journey. I shall bring you food and water every day.'

'Oh, Almería.' The girl choked on a sob, flinging her arms about her nurse. 'I should never have brought you into danger. It was all my fault, and now you are being forced to – to…'

'Hush, it does not matter.' Almería wiped the tears away with her sleeve. 'Mustafa is not so bad. I even like him. Besides, he did not force himself on me. I offered myself to him in return for the chance to look after you. I think he may keep me as his wife. He told me he has none at the moment, for she died in childbed a year ago.'

'Do you really not mind?' Venetia stared at her doubtfully. 'You ran away from Spain rather than submit to that Don.'

'I was young and foolish then.' Almería

smiled wistfully. 'Mustafa is one of my own people. Like me, he was driven from his home by the Inquisition. We shall suit one another well enough, so do not worry about me. It is your future we must discuss. If you are to survive, you will need to curb your temper.'

'I know you are right.' Venetia caught her bottom lip between pearly teeth. 'I shall try, but...'

'The Turks have ways of breaking a harem slave's spirit. Their whips inflict pain without spoiling the beauty of soft skin. If you remain stubborn, you will die – but slowly. They are masters of cruelty. You must learn to accept what cannot be helped, child.' Almería stroked her bowed head. 'You know I would willingly die for you, but I cannot kill them all.'

'Then kill me,' Venetia said, looking up suddenly, her eyes blazing. 'Captain Gómez meant to do it. I should be better dead than living in a harem.'

'If I thought that, I would do it now, but while you live, there is hope.' Almería gave her a hard look, compelling her to listen. 'You may be lucky. You could become the favourite of a young, handsome master, and surely it would not be such a terrible life? If you bore him a son, you would rule his household.'

'And if I am not lucky? What if I am sold

to a fat old Pasha who is riddled with disease?'

Venetia smiled bitterly as the older woman was silent. She could not explain why she felt such horror at the life Almería had just described. It would not after all be so very different from that which had been planned for her by her father. She did not love Giovanni any more than she would the unknown master she was destined to serve. Yet within her breast there was still a tiny spark of hope.

'Could we not find a way to escape?' she asked eagerly. 'Not while we are on the ship, of course, but when we reach wherever it is they are taking us.'

'Algiers.' Almería sighed as she looked at the girl. 'You have not listened to a word I've said! Any attempt at escape would be bound to fail and severely punished. Put all such thoughts from your mind and accept your fate.'

The sharp note in her voice made Venetia bite back the words of protest. Obviously there was nothing to be gained from discussing it with Almería, but she was determined to take the first opportunity that came her way.

'I must go.' Almería picked up her lanthorn. 'At least you will be more comfortable now. I shall come back later with food. Try not to be afraid, sweeting.

Nothing is as bad as it first seems. In time, you will learn to accept what must be.'

As she went out, taking the light with her, Venetia hugged her knees to her chest and stared into the darkness. She was not ready to give in yet. For some reason the picture of a man's face came into her mind: a man with piercing blue eyes and a mocking smile. If only she could get a message to Captain Domingo, she was sure he would know what to do, but she did not know where he was or even if he were still alive. These were precarious times, and anything might have happened to him.

Suddenly, she felt terribly alone. Bowing her head, she wept silently. For herself, for her father, and for something she did not really understand...

'You are certain they were Corsairs?' Domingo asked, nodding thoughtfully as Gómez confirmed his earlier statement. 'Then they will take her to Algiers. Since Venice is at war with Constantinople, there can be no hope of a ransom yet. She will be sold in the slave-market to the highest bidder.'

'Then she is lost.' Gómez sighed regretfully. 'I should have killed her when I had the chance. I meant to do it, but she was so young and lovely that I hesitated. Then it was too late. They rammed us, and in the confusion my only thought was to save her.

Instead, I failed her.'

'Not necessarily. There may just be a way to save her from the harem. It is dangerous, but not impossible.'

Gómez stared up at him from the bed. He had begun to recover his strength, and was eager to be of help to the man who was responsible for his rescue, but he could see no way of saving Venetia other than by arranging a ransom.

'I fear I do not understand you, sir. We could never hope to seize her and escape with our lives.'

'No, that would be a foolish waste of life.' Domingo smiled wryly. 'It is not commonly known, but I was a galley-slave for two years. I learned the Corsairs' language, and their customs. The one certain way to rescue Venetia is to buy her from her captors.'

'But you would be discovered as soon as you set foot in the city, and likely end as a slave yourself!'

'Do you not think I could pass for a Moor if my face were stained with walnut-juice?'

'A blue-eyed Moor?' Gómez shook his head doubtfully. 'You could not hope to pass unnoticed.'

'So my mother was a Christian slave! There are others walking freely in the city who were born of such parentage. You forget, I know how to behave as they do. I can pass for a believer as well as any man.

Besides, I have a friend there who will help me.'

'A friend in Algiers?'

'Ali is a Corsair captain. He was once my master, but we learned to know and like one another. I have spent many a night in discussion with him on the works of the Prophet.'

'Yet you are a Christian. Would you trust him with your life?'

'Why not? I once saved his. It earned me my freedom, even though I would not accept Islam. Ali is his own man. I would trust him as much as any I know.'

Gómez shook his head in wonder. 'I think it will be very dangerous, even if this man does not betray you.'

'I did not say that it would be easy.'

'No, you did not.' The sailor's eyes narrowed as he studied Domingo's face. 'I can see that you are determined on this course of action. What can I do to help you?'

'You have already done more than you know, my friend. If you had not clung so stubbornly to life when all was against you, I should have wasted many months in futile searching. Now, at least, I know where to look for her.' The blue eyes glinted with some powerful emotion. 'Now, you need do nothing but rest. If I have a need of your services, I shall ask.'

Venetia paused, blinking in the sunshine as she was brought out of the cabin, and stared in bewilderment at the city of Algiers. She was not sure what she had expected the Corsairs' stronghold to look like, but the handsome white-walled city of villas surprised her. The harbour was thronged with people of a variety of origins: Moors expelled from Granada, Jews, renegades from Christian countries who had repudiated their religion in return for the chance to live freely in this prosperous environment.

'Move, woman, or you shall feel my whip!'

Venetia glanced up into the face of the huge Moor who had captured her, a stubborn gleam in her eyes. He had made it plain that she was his property, and that he would stand for no nonsense from her. If only she had been taken by the smaller, kinder Mustafa, who was even now watching her with some jealousy. He had tried to trade some of his own captives for her, Almería had said, but his offer had been brusquely refused. It seemed that she was considered to be the most valuable prize taken on this trip, and her owner was guarding her closely against any who might try to snatch her from him.

His fingers gripped her arm cruelly as he forced her to climb over the side of the ship. He had not bound her wrists or ankles this time, probably because he did not want any bruising to show on her skin when she was put up for sale. Walking at his side along the harbour, Venetia's eyes darted from side to side as she looked for an opportunity to escape. If she could only disappear into the crowds thronging the narrow roads leading away from the seafront, maybe she could hide and...

Hearing the noisy disturbance just ahead, she took in the situation quickly. A group of men and children were squabbling over some stolen fruit, and there was a lot of screaming and shouting. As one of the children broke away and came running towards them, her captor made a grab at him with his free hand. The movement weakened his hold on her, and she delivered a sharp kick at his shins. He gave a howl of rage and let go of her. In that moment she was off, running down one of the narrow alleys for all she was worth.

'Stop that slave!'

She heard the cry, but took no notice. She had a good start, so surely it was possible to lose herself in the maze of streets before he caught up with her? She had reckoned without the crowd. There were indignant cries all around, and then she was being pursued by men, women and children. They all shouted abuse at her and waved their arms angrily.

She was panting for breath, looking about

fearfully as they closed in from all sides. Where could she go? It seemed that every alley held an unfriendly face. She ran and ran, halting abruptly as she saw that her flight was cut off by a high wall. She was trapped. There was no way out. She turned, trembling, to meet the angry crowd. The women were yelling abuse, and one of them picked up a stone. She was about to throw it when the tall Corsair forced his way through the mob.

'She belongs to me,' he said, scowling fiercely. 'I don't want her damaged, it will make her price less.'

'She should be whipped!' a veiled woman cried vindictively. 'A runaway slave is useless. You must teach her to obey, or she will fetch nothing like her price.'

Venetia was almost glad when the Corsair's fingers curled possessively over her wrist, and she made no protest when he tied a rope round her waist. She did not believe that she was in danger of being beaten while he continued to think of his profit, but she doubted not that she would be made to go hungry for a while.

'Now behave, or I shall beat you,' he muttered as he dragged her away from the mob. 'Try that again and you will wish you had never been born!'

'I would rather be dead than the slave of an evil old man!' Venetia cried passionately.

The Corsair's grin had a twist of malice as he looked down at her. 'You are of no use to me dead, girl. That old witch told Mustafa that you are a virgin. If that is the truth, you will fetch a high price. If not, I may decide to keep you for myself.'

Venetia's chin went up, but she made no answer. Since he had realised that she could understand Spanish, he had seemed to take pleasure in taunting her with her fate.

He kept a tight hold on the rope as they moved through the streets of white-walled houses past the fruit and vegetable markets and a sinister-looking building that he pointed out to her as the bagnio. The slave prison! For a moment she thought that he meant to take her there, but instead he turned away, coming at last to a pleasant villa surrounded by gardens and a high wall, set in a quiet situation.

It was cool inside after the fierce heat of the sun, and Venetia breathed a sigh of relief as she looked about her, seeing that she was in the house of a wealthy man. She knew that her captor was the captain of one of the galleys, but she had not realised until now how powerful he really was. Now she understood why his claim had not been disputed by the others. At least it meant that she would not be thrown into one of the slave-barracks with the other prisoners. Obviously, she was considered too valuable.

The Corsair clapped his hands loudly, and at once a beautiful dark-skinned woman came hurrying into the room. She went down on her knees before him for one moment, her velvet-brown eyes straying towards Venetia as she got to her feet, the smile of welcome dying as she saw how beautiful the newcomer was. She re-assumed the smile almost at once as she turned to her master.

'Your safe return gives me much joy, my lord Mahomet.'

'I give this slave into your keeping, Zahara,' he replied, seeming to take her homage as his due. 'Take her to the harem and see that she is well cared for.'

'Yes, my lord.' The woman's face was sulky. 'Is it your wish that she be brought to your bed tonight?'

'You will have her examined by the old women. If she is a maiden, I shall sell her. If not, see to it that she is prepared for me tonight.'

'As you wish.'

Zahara bowed before him, accepting the rope from his hand. She pulled on it viciously, giving Venetia an angry look as she led her away. They passed through several connecting rooms, and then through a garden with olive-trees and a tinkling fountain. Once they were safely beyond her master's domain, she turned on Venetia furiously.

98

'Do not imagine that you will replace me as Mahomet's favourite. He will tire of you soon enough!'

'I have no wish to be his favourite,' Venetia replied coolly. 'Besides, he intends to sell me.'

'Are you a maiden?' Zahara's dark eyes lost some of their hostility. 'If that is so, you will bring my lord a rich prize.'

'I have a family and friends who would ransom me,' Venetia said, giving her a pleading look. 'Could you not persuade him that it would reward him more to sell me to my friends?'

Zahara's eyes were calculating as she stared at her. If she were instrumental in helping her lord to gain a rich reward, he would be pleased. Set against that was the danger the green-eyed slave represented to her. 'A ransom takes many months,' she said at last. 'My lord might be tempted to keep you, after all. It is better if he sells you at once.'

It was obvious that Zahara saw her as a rival. She would get no help from her, but perhaps there might be other women in the harem who had influence with Mahomet. Somehow she had to persuade him to ransom her to Giovanni's family!

In the main sala of the harem, there were four girls lying on divans. They were eating fruit and laughing as the newcomers entered, but they paused in their chattering to stare at Venetia. To her relief, she saw that they appeared to be more curious than hostile.

'This slave is to be examined by the old ones,' Zahara said. 'Leila, go and fetch them. The rest of you will see that the bath and clothes are ready.'

A fair-haired girl with pale skin got to her feet and left the room at once. It was clear that Zahara was in command here.

'May I not keep my own clothes?' Venetia asked.

Zahara's eyes were scornful as she looked at the girl's full-skirted gown. 'That depends on whether or not you have been telling the truth. My lord will not want you in that ugly thing.'

Venetia looked down at her gown of dark blue brocade over a silk petticoat several shades lighter. It was a fashionable dress with ribbons on the bodice, and she thought it suited her well. It certainly concealed the shape of her body better than the flimsy harem trousers and bodice that the other girls were wearing. She would feel naked in those!

'Perhaps it would be better if your lord never saw me dressed as you are, Zahara. He might decide to keep me anyway, then.'

'If you are a maiden, you shall keep your clothes,' Zahara said with a shrug of her shoulders. 'But they must be washed. You smell, and so does your dress.'

'That is hardly my fault. I was kept confined for many days without water to wash or a change of garments.'

'All Christians smell until they learn our ways!' Zahara's look was scornful. 'Here comes Leila with the old ones. Go with them and do as they say. If you resist, you will be punished.'

There was no escaping the humiliating ordeal. Venetia accompanied the three women into a small room, where the older ones shooed Leila away. She gave the girl a sympathetic smile behind their backs. The women did not speak to Venetia, making their wishes known by signs. She realised that they meant her to take off all her clothes, and shook her head, but they advanced on her determinedly and she hurriedly obeyed, slipping on the thin silk wrap they gave her. Fortunately they were experts in their task and the examination was brief, though it made her cheeks flame with embarrassment.

Afterwards her clothes were taken away and she was led into what was obviously the bathhouse. Completely tiled from ceiling to floor, it had an oval pool that was filled with warm, scented water. The two old women accompanied her into the pool, ignoring her protests that she could wash herself. They soaped her skin thoroughly and her hair, rinsing her by pushing her under the water several times. Spluttering and coughing, she fought against the rough treatment, guessing that this was Zahara's way of getting revenge.

At last it was over, and she was allowed to dry herself on the pile of soft towels. The two old women went away, and Leila came in, carrying a pair of yellow silk trousers and a brief bodice.

'You are to put these on for now,' she said, and her smile was friendly. 'Your own clothes will be returned to you later. Would you like me to finish drying your hair?' She picked up a dry towel. 'It is still damp at the back. You have lovely hair! It looks pretty now that it has been washed.'

'Thank you.' Venetia looked at her curiously. 'How long have you been here?'

'Three years. I was taken when Mahomet's men raided my village.'

'Was there no one to ransom you?'

'No. My family were all killed or enslaved. I had been married just three months. My husband was killed trying to defend me.' She laid down the towel. 'There, I've finished.'

'I'm sorry about your family,' Venetia said, looking at her with pity. 'It must have been terrible for you.'

Leila shrugged. 'It was very frightening at first, but my husband was old and bad-tempered and I did not like him. Mahomet was not unkind to me. I was his favourite before Zahara came here. I seldom see him now, though. If I had not borne him a son, she would have persuaded him to sell me. So I must consider myself lucky to be allowed to remain.'

'Yes, I suppose so.' Venetia shivered. 'I may not fare as well as you.'

'Put these clothes on,' Leila said. 'I heard the old women telling Zahara that you are a maiden. She was pleased, because it means that Mahomet will sell you.' She cocked her head to one side, appraising the girl's figure. 'If he saw you like this, I think he might change his mind. You would be happy enough here once you settled down, but I don't suppose Zahara will give you a chance to influence him. She is very jealous of the rest of us. She hates it if he sends for anyone but her. It's a pity, because it would have been pleasant to have you here. The others are all under Zahara's domination.'

'You–You couldn't speak to Mahomet for me, could you?' Venetia asked eagerly. 'I have friends who would pay a great deal of money for my release.'

'I don't think it would help.' Leila frowned. 'I seldom see my lord these days, but if I do, I shall ask him for you.'

Clearly Leila was trying to cheer her without any real hope of succeeding, but at least she was friendly. 'Thank you.' Venetia finished dressing. 'I am ready now. What must I do? What are my duties?'

'Come and meet the others.' Leila laughed, as she looked puzzled. 'We none of us do anything. Except when Mahomet sends for us, of course.'

'Then how do you spend your time?'

'Talking, eating, walking in the gardens – or preparing ourselves in case my lord wants us.' A wistful look came into Leila's eyes. 'Sometimes I am allowed to see my son. The old ones take care of him now that he is weaned, and naturally, Zahara is in charge of the nursery. She tells me when I can visit him.'

'But that's not fair!'

'She is the favourite.' Leila sighed. 'When he is old enough, he will go to Constantinople to become a janissary. The Sultan has promised Mahomet. It is a great honour, though I shall never see him again, but until then, I can see him when Zahara permits. If only I had kept my place as my lord's favourite, or you...'

Venetia understood at once. 'If I were the favourite, I would let you see him whenever you wished, Leila.'

'Perhaps there is a way.' Leila's eyes gleamed with mischief. It would settle many an old score if she could help this beautiful girl to supplant the favourite. 'Our garden is overlooked from Mahomet's window. If he should chance to see you as you look now...'

Venetia stared at her doubtfully. She did not wish to become the Corsair's concubine, but if he did send for her, she might be able to persuade him to ransom her. The price she would have to pay would be heavy, but she had little choice. If Mahomet sold her, she might find herself even worse off.

'I doubt if it will change his mind,' she said, 'but I suppose it's worth a try.'

Leila laughed and took her hand. 'It will be wonderful to have a friend at last! I can't wait to see Zahara's face if he sends for you tonight. If he does, I can tell you things that will please him and ensure that you take her place…'

Behind the wall, the favourite drew back from her spyhole, an angry glint in her eyes. That scheming cat Leila would beg on her knees before she saw her son again. And as for that red-haired witch, the sooner she was sold to a new master, the better!

'So you have come back to Algiers.' The two men looked at each other in the dimly-lit room, and Ali Ben Sahid stared into the blue eyes of the man who had once been his slave. 'But you dress as one of us. Have you become a believer, or are you here as a spy?'

'Neither.' Domingo grinned as he saw the other man's eyes narrow in suspicion. 'I have come on business of my own. A woman was captured on a merchant ship. I want her back. It's as simple as that.'

'A woman?' Ali's black eyes glinted with mirth. 'A woman! You stain your face like a Moor and risk being taken as a spy for one woman? I'll give you a dozen of them.' He threw back his head and roared with laughter, thumping the table hard. 'You always were a soft-hearted fool, my friend.'

'I want her, Ali … and I'm willing to pay for her.'

The Corsair scratched his chin, nodding good-humouredly. 'Assuredly you will pay. This woman must be beautiful, and her price will not be cheap.'

'I have gold enough.' Domingo placed a heavy purse on the table between them. 'This is to pay for information. There will be more when the girl is found.'

'So the slave has become a rich Don.' Ali's glance was shrewd. 'You offer this money to me?'

'No, to the men I am asking you as a friend to employ on my behalf. If I were to try, it would arouse suspicion, but you have ways of discovering what I need to know.'

'Yes, I have ways.' Ali nodded, his eyes seeming to pierce the other's mind. 'Then we are still of one blood?'

'We are brothers, Ali, though we do not share the same God. I owe everything I am to you. You gave me my freedom.' He laid his hand on the table so that the huge

106

emerald ring caught the light. 'I wear the ring you gave me still.'

'I see it.' Ali's teeth bared in a mocking grin. 'And you gave me my worthless life, for which I am forever in your debt.' He paused, his eyes gleaming in the light of a lanthorn. 'So, my brother, tell me about this woman. There are many slaves in Algiers, so she will not be easy to find.'

'I must find her, Ali.'

'She is important to you, this woman?' Ali looked into his face, and nodded. 'I see that it is so. Then we shall see what can be done...'

CHAPTER FOUR

'You are to come with me,' Zahara said, her dark eyes glinting with malice. 'But first you must take off those clothes and put this on.'

'Why?' Venetia stared at the garment the girl was thrusting at her. 'That is only my petticoat. Where are the rest of my clothes?'

'They had started to wash them. Stop arguing, and do as you are told. And as for you...' Zahara rounded on Leila. 'Get out of here and speak of this to no one! I heard you plotting against me.'

'We were only talking,' Leila said, her face grey with fear. 'I – I meant no harm.'

'You will regret this, you little cat. Now go before I change my mind and send you to the bagnio too!'

'You wouldn't dare...' Leila stared at her in horror. 'I bore my lord a son.'

'I, too, am to bear his child.' Zahara's face was proud. 'When I told him, he granted my wish. She is to leave this house at once.'

'I don't believe... Oh!' Leila shrank back as the other girl administered a sharp slap to her face.

'Don't trouble yourself about me,' Venetia said quickly. 'Think of yourself, Leila, and your son.'

'She will not see him again until she begs my pardon on her knees,' Zahara said spitefully. 'You are ready? Good. It will be better for you if you do not make a fuss. I can have you whipped, if I choose.'

'Goodbye, Leila. Thank you for trying to help me.'

Venetia smiled slightly before following Zahara from the room. She was not really sure what was happening. Why had everything changed so suddenly? Could it be true that Mahomet had decided to send her to the slave-prison after all? Surely he would not do that simply because his favourite had asked him?

It seemed that he had. Zahara led her through high-walled gardens to a little gate at the rear of the villa. She could see a tall, fleshy man standing outside, apparently waiting to receive her. Zahara nodded to him and unlocked the gate with a key she wore on a chain about her neck.

'This is the slave?' He looked at Venetia in surprise. 'I understood it was an old woman that was to be sold?'

'There has been a change of plan. This girl is wilful, and my master has decided he does not want to keep her. You will need to keep a careful watch over her.'

He nodded, taking a thin rope from inside his loose robe and fastening it securely

110

about Venetia's waist. 'Tell your master that she will be sold tomorrow morning. I shall bring the gold in the evening, as usual.' His narrow-set eyes squinted at Venetia. 'Is she a maiden? There are those who will pay highly for one such as this, provided that she has been with no other man.'

Zahara hesitated. If she said No, he would no doubt pleasure himself with the girl, and she was amused by the idea of the proud Venetian being subjected to his coarse advances; but then she would be ruined and fetch only half her true worth. Besides, she was counting on the girl fetching a high price to sweeten Mahomet's temper when he learned what she had done. It was true that she was to bear her lord's child, but she had not yet told him. It was her hope that it would please him so much that he would not punish her for her wickedness in disposing of a slave without his permission. She would never have dared to do such a terrible thing if she had not been driven to it by jealousy.

'Yes, she has been examined,' she said reluctantly. 'Take care of her, or my master will be angry.'

'I have never failed him yet. I value my life!' The squinting eyes turned on Venetia. 'Come, girl, and behave yourself!'

Venetia felt the tug of his cord, and winced. She saw the gleam of malice in

Zahara's eyes as she was led away. Lifting her head proudly, she tried not to show the fear she felt inside. Somehow she was more afraid of this slave-master than she had ever been of Mahomet.

Keeping her eyes downcast, she followed in the man's wake through the shadowed streets. It was no longer as hot as it had been earlier in the day, and night was falling fast. A kind of numbness was seeping through her limbs. Until now, she had not really believed that she was doomed to a life of slavery. Mahomet was not a particularly cruel man by his standards, and she had hoped that he would eventually consent to seek a ransom for her. Now that hope was ended.

'Here we are, girl.' The slave-master halted outside the sinister building she had noticed earlier. It had an air of oppression hanging over it, making her shiver. Her captor saw the look on her face, and smiled horribly. He called to another man inside, and a door was opened to admit them. 'She belongs to Mahomet. She's virgin flesh, so take care she comes to no harm, or you will pay for it!'

The second man merely grunted, grabbing hold of the rope and dragging Venetia further into the interior of the gloomy building. He unlocked a door and shoved her roughly inside, slamming it behind her.

The sound was chilling, causing her to shudder violently. Her tiny cell was dark and airless, the stench of human odours almost unbearable. She could hear moaning and weeping all around her, though she was alone in her windowless cell. Sinking down on to the dirt floor, she covered her face with her hands, the tears slipping silently from beneath her lashes.

'Oh God,' she whispered. 'Please help me!'

She remained empty and alone. Prayers could not help her in this terrible place, nor could tears. She wiped her face, and stood up. She was a slave now and there was nothing she could do about it, but they had not broken her spirit. As her eyes became accustomed to the gloom, she saw that there was a thin mattress in the corner. She lay down and closed her eyes. For a long time sleep eluded her, but when at last it came, she dreamed strangely of a blue-eyed Spaniard.

'You have found her?' Domingo got to his feet eagerly when his friend entered the house. 'Has she been sold yet?'

'She arrived in Algiers only today.' Ali grinned as the blue eyes caught fire. 'You are fortunate, my friend. She was taken early in the raiding venture, and kept on board Mahomet's galley. Had it been otherwise, he might already have sold her. Knowing of his return, I went to his house. We have done business before, and he will sell her for a price.'

'How much is he asking?'

'Five thousand ducats.' Domingo pursed his lips in a silent whistle, and Ali laughed. 'I will sell you a hundred women for the price. He did not wish to part with her. It seems he had planned to keep her for himself.'

'I shall pay him what he asks.'

'She must be very special?'

'I feel responsible for her. Her father once placed her in my care.'

'So it is merely a matter of honour?' Domingo nodded, but the Corsair shook his head. 'I think you deceive yourself, my friend ... but no matter. It is all arranged. You can collect her in the morning.'

'Why not tonight?'

'Such impatience for honour's sake!' Ali chuckled. 'The hour is late. Mahomet has been away for many weeks and will be with one of his women now. If you disturb him, he may change his mind about selling her. Oh, do not look so alarmed, my friend! She will not be in his bed. I told him that you would not pay if she had been spoiled.'

'Then he hasn't... Thank God!'

Ali threw back his head and laughed loudly. 'For a man who cares only for his

114

duty to her father, you look mightily relieved. Sleep now, my brother, and dream of your green-eyed houri. Tomorrow night you may not have time for sleeping!'

Domingo's mouth twisted wryly. 'You do not know Venetia dei Giorlandi!' he said, but the words were only in his mind.

Venetia blinked as the door opened, letting in a stream of light. A man came in, and she saw it was the one who had taken her from Mahomet's house the previous night. He beckoned, but she shrank back against the wall, terrified.

'Come, girl,' he ordered, giving a sigh of exasperation as she hung back. 'It will be the worse for you if I have to drag you out.'

Her fear of the unknown made her resist. 'Please! My friends will pay for my safe return.'

'I warned you!'

The slave-master came into the cell. His fingers clutched her arm as she tried to move away, digging into the soft flesh cruelly. Suddenly his eyes gleamed and he pressed her back against the wall.

'If you were not virgin flesh...'

He was breathing hard, his face twisted by an ugly lust. His free hand plunged beneath the bodice of her petticoat, grabbing clumsily at her breasts, then he fastened his mouth greedily on hers, thrusting his body

115

against her several times as though he would vent his passion on her as she stood there. She flinched from the stench of him, the vomit rising in her throat. If this was a taste of what she must endure from now on, she would kill herself!

'You will get me a flogging!' he muttered throatily. 'If I could afford you, I'd buy you myself.'

Venetia was trembling from head to foot as he dragged her through the prison to an open square. Here, she saw that she was not the only woman to be brought out for sale. About twenty were herded together, most of them standing silently, too numbed to cry. They stood dull-eyed, waiting their turn, not even bothering to look as she was thrust into their midst.

A dark-skinned girl of scarcely twelve years had just been sold. Her eyes were empty, as if she were unaware of what was going on around her. Looking at the wiry little man who had bought her, Venetia felt a pang of sympathy for the girl. He was old enough to be her grandfather, his teeth blackened and rotting in his mouth as he leered at his prize. The sickness swirled in Venetia's stomach as she watched him lead the child away. It was wicked and inhuman that such a thing could happen!

The next to be sold were a mother and her daughter. Fortunately, the girl was too young to be a concubine yet. At least she would grow up in the harem, and by the time her turn came she would know nothing else. It was easier for those women who were trained to please their masters from an early age, Venetia thought. She would find it much harder to obey. There were only two others before her now. She moved closer to the platform where she must soon take her place, surprised as the slave-master grasped her arm, pulling her back. She had not heard him come up behind her.

'Not you,' he said gruffly. 'Praise be to the Prophet that I did not give way to temptation! That she-cat Zahara lied to me: you were not supposed to come here. They say Mahomet was furious. I hope he flogs her!'

Relief flowed through Venetia. Mahomet had changed his mind, and perhaps she was to be ransomed, after all.

'Am I being taken back to the lord Mahomet's house?'

'No. You have been sold privately. Your new master has come to fetch you.'

So she had already been sold! Her heart sank. She had been saved from the humiliation of the auction-block, but the reprieve was short lived. She was the property of an unknown man.

'Am– Am I going to Constantinople?'

The slave-master leered at her. 'How should I know? Your new master is Ali Ben

Sahid. He may keep you for himself or sell you again. You are his property to do with as he will.'

Venetia closed her eyes as the dizziness swept over her. She saw two men waiting for her, both wearing rich robes and silk turbans, but which was her master? Their faces were no more than a blur as she swayed uneasily on her feet. She had been standing too long under a hot sun, and it was some time since she had either eaten or drunk anything. The world was spinning madly as she took another step forward and then halted, clutching her head.

'I – I cannot...' she whispered.

'No more of your tricks, girl!'

The slave-master tugged angrily at the rope, anxious to be rid of her. Venetia tried to respond, but the ground seemed to veer away. Suddenly, there was a roaring in her head and everything went black. She gave a little sigh and crumpled to a heap on the ground.

She was mercifully unaware of what happened next, remaining serenely unconscious as the grim-faced Corsair shouldered his way through to her, his blue eyes glittering with anger as he glared at the unfortunate slave-master.

'If you've harmed her, I'll break your neck!'

'She has but fainted, my friend,' a calmer

118

voice said at his elbow. 'Come, we shall take her to my house. Here, slave-master, this is for your trouble.'

The squinting eyes gleamed with greed as he caught the small purse, his curiosity dulled by the sight of the gold inside. 'May the blessings of the Prophet be upon you.' He touched his forehead, and bowed. When he looked again, the two men were striding away, the tall stranger carrying the girl in his arms. Those eyes were startlingly blue for a Moor, but he seemed to be a friend of Ali Ben Sahid, a man well known and respected in the city. The slave-master considered reporting his suspicions to the lord Mahomet, but remembering the unfortunate circumstances of the girl's arrival at the bagnio, he decided against it. It would be wiser to stay away until the Corsair captain's temper had cooled. Besides, he had been well paid. It was nothing to do with him...

The sound of water slapping on wood awoke Venetia. She opened her eyes, staring at the ceiling in bewilderment. Where am I? Her mind was confused. She had been at the slave-market... She had fainted when she was being taken to her new master!

Vaguely, she remembered waking in a strange house. She had been lying on a silken couch, and a woman had brought her something cool to drink. She had slept after

119

that. It must have been drugged! Tasting the bitterness in her mouth, her suspicions were confirmed. Why had the woman given her that drink? And where was she?

The cabin was very similar to the one in which she had been confined after her capture, but more luxurious. It obviously belonged to a rich man. She was being taken to Constantinople, probably for the harem of a pasha. They had drugged her to make sure that she could not try to escape. Mahomet must have told them that she was a wilful slave who was likely to cause trouble.

How long had she been asleep? Surprisingly, she felt refreshed, and much better than she had after her night in the slave-prison. Had there been something in that drink that healed her as she slept? Scrambling across the bed to gaze out of the small window, Venetia saw that the sun was shining brightly. At least her window had not been shuttered this time. She supposed that her master had decided that there was no longer any danger of her trying to run away. They must be far from Algiers, for she could see nothing but sky and sea.

Hearing the door open behind her, Venetia tensed, a tingle of fear running through her. It could only be Ali Ben Sahid, her new master! She turned slowly, still kneeling on the bed, her eyes downcast. Determinedly, she stilled her trembling limbs. She must not show him how scared she really was.

'So, you are awake at last! Forgive me for having you drugged, but Ali assured me that it would help to calm your nerves.'

The tiny hairs at the nape of her neck prickled as she heard his voice. She must be dreaming! Her head came up disbelievingly. Staring at the man in the doorway, she was still unable to fit the face to the voice. It sounded like … but it could not be. Yet the eyes were his!

'Who are you?' she whispered, feeling as if she were in the grip of a nightmare. 'Are you Ali Ben Sahid?'

'Ali is my friend.' He chuckled softly. 'Do you not know me, Madonna Venetia?'

'You!' she breathed, her head whirling. It was he – but… There were so many questions buzzing in her head. 'How? Why? What are you doing here – and dressed like that?' Her body was seized by a sudden trembling, and she felt a little lightheaded.

'It was the only way to find you. I bought you from the man who had captured you. At least, Ali did the bargaining for me. He tells me Mahomet wanted a thousand ducats, but I told him that I would only pay half. We settled on…'

'Ohhh!' The tension had built up to bursting-point as she gave a scream of indignation and launched herself at him, pounding at his chest with her fists in a storm of emotion

121

that was half anger and half relief. 'So I am worth only five hundred ducats. You beast! I hate you!'

Domingo caught her wrists, grinning as he saw the fury in her face. Thank heavens! He had feared that her ordeal might have broken her spirit, but quite clearly it had not!

'Well, you could hardly expect me to pay a thousand ducats for you, could you?' he asked mockingly. 'Why, that's almost a fifth of a quarter's revenues from my estate!'

'My father will double whatever you paid,' Venetia said, her eyes glittering with pride.

'If I choose to ransom you.' Domingo held her as she renewed her struggle. 'Cease fighting me, madonna, or I may put you across my knee. This show of temper will not help your cause. I may decide to release you, *if* you behave properly. You have, as yet, not even thanked me for rescuing you.'

'I am not afraid of you!' she snapped, failing to see the gleam her defiance brought to his eyes. 'Why should I thank you? You have made it plain that I am no more than a piece of merchandise to you. I dare swear that you decided to buy me only because you saw a handsome profit in the transaction.'

'Naturally.' The blue eyes danced with amusement. 'Why else should I bother with you? What other reason could there be?'

'None, I suppose.' Venetia's bottom lip

trembled, and she caught it between her teeth. 'Perhaps I – I should thank you.'

'Do not bother, lady. I shall take my own reward when I am ready.'

'What do you mean?'

'I told you that I should not be satisfied with a kiss next time. Had you forgotten?'

Her eyes flew to his. He was merely taunting her, or was he? 'You– You are mocking me!'

One hand curled possessively round her wrist. 'It is time to transfer to my own ship. Come and say goodbye to Ali, lady, and curb that shrew's tongue of yours. I advise you to thank him for his trouble. Without his help, you would probably be Mahomet's concubine by now ... unless that bitch Zahara had managed to poison you.'

'She hated me from the first.'

'She guessed that her master meant to keep you for himself, despite his threats to sell you, so she sent you to the bagnio instead of a woman from the kitchens. If Ali had not gone early in the morning to complete the sale, you might have disappeared into a harem. Even he could have done nothing then.'

'Will Zahara be punished?'

'Do you want revenge, Venetia?'

'No. Her only crime was to love her master too much. I pity her. She imagined that I wanted to be his favourite.'

'And did you?'

'Of course not!' Venetia blushed as she felt his piercing eyes on her. 'At least... It would have been better than...' She faltered as the ice gathered in his eyes. 'He was better than some of the evil old man I saw at the slave-market. I would have taken my own life rather than submit to them.' She squirmed beneath the contempt in his face. 'Almería told me that I had to accept my fate.'

'The foolish old witch!' Domingo said angrily. 'Had I known, I would have left her in Algiers.'

'You have rescued Almería too?' Venetia stared at him, puzzled. He could not hope for a rich reward for ransoming a servant? 'That was thoughtful of you.'

'She was a loyal servant. No doubt your father will pay me something for my trouble?'

'Yes.' Venetia glanced at his profile. She had forgotten her situation for a while. Remembering that her father might still be a prisoner in Cyprus, she wondered how soon she could broach the subject of his ransom. How much more could she expect this Spaniard to do for her and her family?

Following him out into the brilliant sunshine, it suddenly struck her that she had not asked how he had known where to look for her. He had made her so angry... Her cheeks flushed as she realised how

124

ungrateful she had been. Until he had looked at her in that insulting manner, she had felt like weeping in his arms. It occurred to her that he might have mocked her on purpose, but she dismissed the idea almost at once. Why should he want to make her angry?

She had no time to ponder the question, for a dark-skinned Corsair was advancing on them. Staring at him curiously, she was surprised at the humour in his brown eyes. She discovered that he had a warm smile. He stopped before her, his twinkling gaze resting on her face, then he touched his fingers to his lips and forehead, bowing before her.

'Welcome to my ship, O green-eyed houri! In your arms a man might find his paradise on earth. Now I understand many things. A man might buy a hundred women and lie alone if he had once seen you. Perhaps you were worth your price, after all.'

'I am worth more than five hundred ducats,' Venetia replied, glancing angrily at her companion. He was not looking at her, but seemed to be conveying a silent message to the grinning Corsair.

'Five … hundred. Ah, I see.' Ali looked at her assessingly. 'Assuredly, you are worth twice that sum. I would give as much for you myself.'

'Then perhaps I shall sell her to you.'

Domingo's words made her look up at him in alarm. Surely he was not serious?

'You don't mean that! My father will pay you whatever you ask for my safe return.'

'Naturally, he does but jest, lady.' Ali's lips twitched as her eyes sparked. 'Such fire! I envy you, Roldán. She will be enchanting to tame. I thought you mad, but a little madness can be pleasurable sometimes.'

Venetia could not but be aware of his meaning. Her cheeks flushed, but she controlled her temper. She believed Captain Domingo was merely teasing her, but she could not be sure. Five hundred ducats was not a great deal to a man like him, but it was a profit. If she annoyed him too much, he might decide to take it!

'I – I believe I have you to thank for my rescue, sir?' Venetia looked at the Corsair, trying hard to hide her nervousness. 'I should like to say how grateful I am for all you have done.'

'It was naught… A favour to a friend.' Ali's face was grave as he glanced at the man beside her. 'I owe my life to Roldán. Many galley-slaves would kill their master, given the chance. He risked his own life to save mine. You also have reason to be grateful to him. Had you returned to Mahomet's harem, his favourite would have had you killed.'

Venetia shivered. 'I know. I am grateful.'

'Then you are a fool!' Domingo's voice was harsh. 'My ship is ready, and it is time for us to leave. Ali, you have my thanks for everything. You now have a claim on me. Ask, and it shall be honoured.'

'I shall remember if the need arises, my brother.'

The two men clasped hands. Venetia watched them, feeling oddly shut out and almost jealous as she saw the warmth in Domingo's face. She was puzzled by Ali's reference to galley-slaves. Surely he could not mean that Captain Domingo had once been his slave? And yet there was an obvious bond between them. Had he really saved Ali's life?

'Venetia! My lady!'

Almería's cry made her look round, and she moved to embrace her with a smile. 'I have missed you. I thought I should never see you again!'

'I thought you already in Mahomet's harem.' Almería hugged her, sobbing. 'When Mustafa told me I had been sold to a friend of his, I thought I was to be sent to Constantinople.'

'So he did not take you as his wife, then?'

'Men!' Almería glanced maliciously at the two captains, her eyes glittering. 'They are none of them to be trusted ... least of all that Spaniard!'

'Hush, Almería.' Venetia frowned at her.

'You do not know what you are saying. Captain Domingo has rescued us. If he had not come when he did, I would have been sold in the slave-market. We must be grateful to him.'

Almería's eyes narrowed in suspicion. 'Perhaps, but I do not trust him. Does he know that your father must be ransomed before he can repay any debts?'

'No. Say no more now. He will hear you.' She smiled as Domingo turned towards her. 'We are ready, sir. Do not let us delay you.'

His brows went up as he heard the change in her tone. 'Longer than you already have?' he asked. 'How thoughtful you are all of a sudden, lady.'

The sarcasm in his voice made her flinch. Why was he so angry? Until now, she had believed his harshness was feigned merely to taunt her, but now he was really annoyed. What had she done? She tossed her head defiantly. The man was impossible. He laughed when she raged at him – and became icy cold when she smiled. She simply did not understand him!

'But why will you not take me to Venice?' Venetia stared into the Spaniard's hard face. 'It will be easier to arrange a ransom for my father at home. I realise now that I should have listened to Captain Gómez when he told me that a rescue was impossible.'

'I have told you that I have business in Rome, madonna. I shall make enquiries on your behalf there.'

'But I do not wish to go to Rome!' Venetia pouted sulkily. It would actually be easy for her to contact her father's lawyers in Rome, but for some reason she felt like being contrary. They had been at sea for several days, and she was restless. Without her precious books, the long hours she spent alone were proving tedious. Besides, they gave her too much time to think – and thinking was dangerous. She had found herself wondering about Roldán Domingo too often. Just who was this man, and how many secrets were there in his past? He had been a galley-slave – Almería had made her own enquiries – Venetia could scarcely believe it. What else was there to know about this man? The thin scar on his cheek tantalised her, and she was sure that there was some mystery concerning it. She had noticed that he sometimes stroked it with his finger when he believed himself unobserved.

'For the moment, your wishes are not my first concern.'

His voice broke the pattern of her thoughts. She gazed up at him, her heart jerking in her breast. Sometimes she wondered why he had this strange effect on her.

'When have you ever cared what I wanted?' she demanded, her annoyance more at herself than at him. Why was it that he seemed to dominate her thoughts? She felt an urge to push him as far as she could, to see that sudden flash of fire in his eyes. 'I am nothing to you but a hostage. I have merely exchanged one master for another.' It was not true, but she was driven by a strange emotion that she did not understand. 'You are no better than Mahomet!'

'Am I not?' His eyes glinted, and a shiver of anticipation went through her. 'What do you want from me, Venetia – this?'

She gasped as he pulled her against him, a feeling of excitement shooting through her as his mouth possessed hers. It was as if she had exposed her flesh to a searing flame. She felt it burn through her veins, making her dizzy with some strange new sensations. She was terrified by what was happening to her body, but she was still driven by that inner devil. She had to know how far she could torment him before that iron reserve crumbled. His first kiss had been meant to tease and punish her, but she sensed that this one was very different. He was breathing hard, and she felt him shudder, as if he were struggling to check some fierce emotion. She had touched the inner man! Her body arched against him as his lips moved feverishly down her throat to the pulsating swell of her breasts. She was still wearing only her petticoat, for there was nothing else suitable on board, and she could feel the heat of his body through the thin material. She glanced up at him, a look of triumph in her eyes as she saw his features contorted by passion. He was not made of ice, after all!

'You are exactly the same as Mahomet,' she said mockingly. 'He could not keep his hands off me, either.' She was smiling as she lied, but in the next moment she wished the foolish words unsaid. A murderous expression entered his eyes as he gripped her wrists, holding her away to look at her. She saw a pulse beating in his temple, and caught her breath. He had never been so angry with her before. He looked as if he might kill her!

'You little wanton!' he growled. 'Did you lie with him? Is that why Zahara tried to get rid of you?'

'Y– You are hurting me,' she whispered, afraid of the savage fury she had unleashed. She had been playing a game, but it had rebounded on her badly.

'Answer me!' he thundered.

'No! No, he never touched me! I thought he meant to sell me,' Venetia cried. 'I said it because ... because I wanted to hurt you.'

'You wanted to hurt me?' He was breathing deeply, his face strained with the passion that had flared out of control. 'Yes, I understand that, Venetia. You have despised me from the beginning. You cannot bear to be even a little grateful to me, can you?'

'You kissed me to punish me that first time!' she yelled, angry again. 'I wanted to see what you are really like behind that stoical mask.'

'You wanted to know what I think about you, didn't you?' His mouth curved in a sneer. 'Like all women, you need flattery to feed your vanity. You were annoyed because I took money from your father for seeing you safely to Corfu – because I expect payment for rescuing you.'

'I am not vain...' His bitter words flayed her like the lash of a whip. 'It– It was just a game!'

'Oh yes, a game! A game women have played since the dawn of time. You play it well, Venetia. Almost too well for your own sake.' He let go of her so abruptly that she staggered back. 'You want to know what I think of you, madonna? It will be my pleasure to tell you: you are a spoilt bitch! You have some beauty, and I have thought it would be pleasant to lie with you, but now that I know you for what you are, I despise you. You are vain and empty – a heartless shell of a woman who worships at her own shrine!'

'No...' she whimpered, retreating before his terrible anger. What had she done to deserve this? His eyes were glazed as if he were looking through her, seeing something in his past that haunted him still. 'I didn't mean ... I didn't think...'

The searing anger gradually faded from his face. 'Did you not?' he asked, a flicker of contempt in his eyes. 'Are you not an avenging Venus then, but merely a silly child?'

Somehow his contempt was harder to bear than his anger. She turned away, fighting a foolish urge to weep on his shoulder and beg him to forgive her. She had provoked this scene, but she had not expected this. Yet it was her own fault. She had wanted... She was not sure exactly what she wanted. For a moment, in his arms, her body had cried out for something, but what? She had wanted the kiss to go on – to become something more. No, that wasn't true. She despised and hated him. He was a Spaniard and a mercenary. She could not like such a man. She had wanted to hurt him, but not so much. Not so much...

'I – I am sorry,' she whispered. 'I did not think you would be so angry. Please forgive me?'

She found the courage to face him, and turned to discover she had been speaking to air. Had he heard her apology before he left? Somehow she did not think so.

What had she done? He must hate her now, and she needed his good will so badly. She suddenly knew that she would feel desperately alone if he were to abandon her to her fate. What had possessed her? Why had she wanted to prick him with her thorns of spite? She ought to be grateful to him, and in her heart she was, so why the urge to hurt?

The knowledge that she had somehow hurt herself was little consolation. She hunched up on the bed, staring into space as she tried to understand her own feelings. She had hated him from the moment they met – or had she? Was this strong emotion he aroused in her hate or something far different?

A single tear trickled down her cheek and she brushed it away. He had said such terrible things to her. She was not vain and empty, though she knew she had been spoilt by her father. But she was not heartless! She was not heartless, for she felt that her heart was breaking...

'I hope that you will be comfortable here, lady. It is the home of a friend of mine, and his wife will take good care of you while you are in Rome,' Domingo said.

Venetia looked at the large whitewashed villa with its shaded terraces, flower gardens and marble statues. It was a peaceful, pretty place where she could recover her spirits after the ordeal of recent weeks.

'I know I shall like it here. It is very kind of your friends to invite me.'

'Maddalena and Paolo have no children of their own. They enjoy filling their house with guests.' Domingo smiled as he took her arm, leading her towards the house. 'It may not be for too long. I shall do my best to discover your father's whereabouts. Do not give up hope yet, Venetia. He may have managed to leave Cyprus.'

'You–You are generous, Captain. I do not deserve such kindness after what I did.'

'Your father was my friend.' Domingo frowned as he heard the subdued note in her voice. He stopped walking and turned her towards him, studying her face.

'It is I who should apologise for losing my temper, Venetia. I was angry with you when I had only myself to blame. It was not really you who…' He paused, a wry smile curving his mouth. 'In truth, I lost my head. You are a charming little wretch despite your shrew's tongue, and I wanted to make love to you. There, I have confessed it. Will you forgive me now?'

She saw a gleam of mischief in his eyes, and her heart lifted. Perhaps he did not hate her, after all. He might even like her a little.

'You said I was vain…'

'And so you are, a little, but perhaps you have good reason. You are reasonably pretty.'

'And heartless? Am I heartless, Captain Domingo?'

'If you pursue this, I shall not be account-able for my actions. Be warned, Venetia.'

'Will you...' She had been going to ask him if he meant to kiss her again, but she was prevented by the arrival of a tall woman with smiling grey eyes.

'We shall continue this conversation another time. Here is Maddalena come to greet you.'

'Roldán! How good it is to see you again.' She held out her hands, smiling warmly as he kissed her cheek, then she turned to the girl. 'I am so glad Roldán brought you to us, my dear. You are very welcome to stay for as long as you wish.'

Venetia found herself being embraced in a haze of sweet perfume as Maddalena gathered her in her arms. 'You are very kind.'

'It is kindness to us.' Maddalena brushed away her thanks. 'Now come into the house. My husband is out, but he will welcome you later.' She glanced at Domingo. 'Will you stay for a glass of wine?'

'Not this time. I have urgent business, Maddalena.' He turned to Venetia. 'Enjoy your stay here, madonna. You will be quite safe. I hope to have news for you soon, so try not to worry too much for the moment.'

His smile made her heart catch. Since their quarrel, he had spoken to her only when necessary, and for several days she had been living in fear of their parting. Now it seemed that she had made too much of it all. He was behaving as if nothing had happened.

She watched as he turned and walked away, feeling puzzled and a little piqued. Had the wretched misery she had endured been all of her own making? How could he say such terrible things to her and then tease her as though they had never quarrelled?

'Come inside, Venetia.' Maddalena glanced at the pale grey gown she was wearing, pulling a face. 'I see my clothes almost fit you, but I am sure we can do better than that old thing!'

'I could hardly walk through the streets of Rome in my petticoat! I was glad to have it.'

'Well, now that you are my guest, I shall see to the matter of your wardrobe. You must leave it all to me, Venetia.'

'I – I think I should explain...' Venetia bit her lip. 'Everything I had was lost when the Corsairs attacked my ship. I cannot pay for new clothes until my father's lawyers arrange...'

'Oh, do not worry about such trifles. Roldán will see to everything.' Maddalena squeezed her arm. 'We all want you to be happy, my dear. We shall help you to forget all the terrible things that happened to you. Now, you must tell me exactly what you need.'

Venetia smiled at her reflection in the mirror. She was wearing a pretty lilac gown with silver trimmings, and a beautiful ruby pendant set in gold and pearls. The pendant was valuable, and she had at first been reluctant to borrow it from Maddalena.

'It is far too valuable,' she had said on being shown the necklace. 'I should be afraid of losing it.'

'It is a gift, my dear.' Maddalena smiled. 'To replace a little of what you have lost. Please accept it. It would please ... me so much.'

'I couldn't possibly take it, but I would like to borrow it.'

'Then wear it if it pleases you.' Maddalena studied the ring on her finger, pretending unconcern. 'It will look very pretty with your new dress – the one you will be wearing when Roldán dines with us this evening.'

She had not seen him for ten whole days. It seemed much longer, even though her stay at his friends' villa had been so happy. She was excited by the prospect of seeing him again, and it showed in her eyes as she finished dressing for the evening.

'Do I look pretty, Almería?' she asked, turning to surprise a speculative look in the nurse's eyes.

'If you mean, will he think you look beautiful, you are a foolish girl. That man has only one thing on his mind as far as you are concerned, and he won't care what you are wearing!'

'You have no right to say that,' Venetia reprimanded her sharply. 'We should both be grateful to him. If he meant me any harm, he had ample opportunity on board his ship. He brought me here so that I could be chaperoned by his friends.'

'For reasons of his own, no doubt! You are a considerable heiress, lady.'

Venetia felt annoyed by her insinuations. It was wrong of Almería to harbour such suspicions. She herself was inclined to trust him, but her nurse seemed determined to put fresh doubts in her mind.

'If he intends to ask for payment for his trouble, it is only just. He spent a lot of time and money on rescuing us.'

'It's not the money that one wants. At least, it's not all he wants from you!' Almería sniffed. 'But there's no use in saying more. Plainly, he's turned your head.'

'Be quiet, Almería!' Venetia snapped. 'I've had enough of your grumbling. Captain Domingo is my friend.'

Her nurse was silenced at last, but the look on her face said more than a thousand words. Venetia ignored her, leaving the room without speaking again, and feeling cross with her.

She wanted to trust Roldán. She had

missed seeing his tall figure these past few days, and her heart was beating faster than normal as she made her way towards the main sala. Would he smile when he saw her? She wondered if he had by chance missed her, too. The sound of men's voices made her pause by an open window. Paolo and Roldán were taking a stroll in the garden. As she hesitated, a fragment of their conversation reached her.

'Don't you think it would be best to tell her the truth, Roldán?'

'No, not yet.' Roldán's voice sounded harsh to her ears. 'She is stubborn and proud. If she knew the facts, she might...'

The men moved on, and she could hear no more. A cold chill ran down her spine. They had been talking about her, she was sure of it. What was it that he did not want to tell her? She pressed her trembling fingers to her lips as a feeling of disappointment swept through her. He had called her stubborn and proud, so he had not really forgiven her for that quarrel! The feeling of anticipation died within her. She had been looked forward to being with him again, but now she felt as if he had plunged a knife into her heart. How could she trust him when he was planning to deceive her? Almería was right! She had allowed him to take command of her thoughts, but from now on, she would be on her guard.

Controlling her emotions, she began walking towards the main sala again, the anger fermenting inside her. She was proud and stubborn – and heartless! Well, in future, she would be exactly what he thought of her. He was a cold, unfeeling mercenary and she had been a fool to believe otherwise, even for a moment. Yet she would not let him know she had discovered his treachery. For now, she was dependent on his help, but as soon as something was known of her father's whereabouts... Her heart pounded and she paused for an instant. Of course! It had to be something to do with his ransom. Roldán must have discovered something. He was keeping it from her, because he thought she might act rashly...

Her mind was churning in a confusion of speculation as she walked into the sala. Roldán was speaking with his hosts, his back towards her. Maddalena said something and he turned, his smile of welcome dying on his lips as he saw the hostility in her.

'Madonna Venetia,' he said flatly. 'You look ... rested.'

'Thank you. I trust you are well, Captain Domingo?'

'I have perfect health, as always.'

She clenched her fists, wanting to strike out at him, but knowing that she could not before her hosts. 'Have you news of my father, sir?'

Maddalena glanced at him as he hesitated, then at her. 'Not of your father, my dear...' She paused, as both men looked at her as if in warning. 'But we do have something to tell you.'

'Maddalena!' Her husband frowned as he spoke, but she shook her head at him.

'Venetia must be told the truth.' She walked to meet the girl, a look of sympathy in her eyes. 'I told you that Nicosia had fallen to the Turks, and we have just learned that the terms of the surrender were not honoured. They– They murdered everyone within the city.'

'Everyone?' Venetia's face drained of colour, and she swayed as the room and the people in it seemed to fade away. She was seeing her father's face as he kissed her goodbye. It could not be true that he was dead. It could not! 'M– My father,' she whispered.

Roldán moved towards her. 'We don't know yet, Venetia. He might be in Famagusta. We believe they are still holding out against the enemy there. No one can be certain what the situation is as yet.'

He was holding out his hand to her, but she would not accept it. She ran to Maddalena, burying her head against the woman's shoulder. She could trust her. Maddalena had told her the truth. With an effort she held back the tears, and in a little while was able to stop shaking. She glanced up at her hostess.

'Thank you for telling me.'

'I saw no point in hiding it from you. Will you forgive me for hurting you, my dear?'

Venetia forced a smile to her lips, in control of her emotions once more. 'Of course. I am glad you told me.' Her eyes met Roldán's for a moment, accusing him. 'I am not a child. I know what this means.'

'I would have told you, once I was sure.'

'Would you?' She looked at him coldly, wondering if there was anything more that he was concealing. 'I think it's time I went home to Venice. I must speak to my father's lawyers. If you were to escort me, Captain Domingo, I could make arrangements to pay what I owe you.'

His eyes glittered strangely, then he bowed his head. 'I am at your service, lady. We shall leave in the morning.'

'Thank you.'

She turned back to Maddalena, missing both the startled glance Paolo shot his friend and the warning look in the Spaniard's eyes.

'I – I have a headache, Maddalena,' she said. 'Would you think me very rude if I did not dine with you this evening?'

'No, of course not, my dear. It's best that you get some rest if you are to leave tomorrow. Would you like me to send

143

something up to your room?'

'I do not feel hungry.' Venetia glanced at Paolo, and then, briefly, at Roldán. 'Forgive me. I shall see you tomorrow.'

She walked away, the tears burning behind her eyes. It seemed as if the whole world was falling to pieces around her. If her father was dead, she would be completely alone. Giovanni's home had been in Nicosia. She was sure that he must have been killed. The thought saddened her, though she had never loved him. His family might still be willing to take her in, but she would rather go home.

Somehow, she must find the courage to wait alone for news of her father's death...

CHAPTER FIVE

'You are taking me where?' Venetia stared into the blue eyes, her temper mounting. 'But you promised to take me to Venice. Why have you deceived me?'

They had been on board his ship for some days, and her suspicions were aroused when her nurse told her they were passing the island of Sardinia.

'I told you he was not to be trusted,' Almería said with a smirk of satisfaction. 'Why would he not take you overland as you asked if he was not planning to abduct you? You are on your way to Spain, my lady.'

'He would not dare!' Venetia said, jumping to her feet. 'I shall speak to him at once.'

She had found Domingo on the poop, just forward of the cabins. He came to meet her, frowning slightly, intending to warn her of the coming storm. Her first words were sharp and accusing.

'Where are we bound?' she demanded furiously. 'That island is Sardinia, isn't it?'

'Yes.' He met her furious gaze calmly. 'I've been ordered to Madrid. I'm taking you to my castle in Valencia.'

'Where?'

'You will be safer in Valencia while I am in Madrid,' he said, ignoring the sparks in her eyes. 'You can do nothing to help your father or yourself alone in Venice and had much better leave everything to me. When Marco dei Giorlandi's fate has been ascertained, I shall do what must be done.'

'How dare you assume control of my affairs?' she yelled, aware of the curious stares of his officers, but too angry to care what anyone thought. 'I demand to be taken to Venice immediately!'

'Unfortunately I cannot obey you, madonna. This time, I am under orders from King Philip. You will just have to be patient for a while.'

'Why did you not tell me the truth in Rome? I could have gone home some other way.'

His eyes narrowed. 'Why will you not trust me? What I have done is for your own good.'

'You abduct me … and then you ask me to trust you?' She stared at him incredulously. 'You are beyond belief, sir! I could never trust a man who would lie to me.'

'When have I lied to you?'

'You promised to take me to Venice.'

'No…' His eyes glittered with pride. 'I said that I was at your service, and I am. No harm will come to you, Venetia. You are under my protection until your father comes to claim you.'

'And if he cannot claim me, what then?'

'We shall see what happens.' He met her outraged gaze with a slight smile. 'Do not imagine that this gives me any pleasure, lady. I had hoped to collect my reward and have you taken off my hands, but...'

'Of course! You were afraid that you would not be paid if you let me go home alone.' Her lips twisted with scorn. 'Do not be anxious, Captain. I shall see that you are paid every penny you are owed.'

'Good!' He was infuriatingly calm, refusing to rise to her taunts. 'If you have finished venting your spleen on me, Venetia, you may go to your cabin. A storm is about to strike, and I have no time to waste on your tantrums.'

'Ohhh!' She clenched her hands into tight fists, wanting to wipe that smug look from his face. He was so pleased with himself because he had outwitted her. 'I hate you!'

'Then nothing has changed. Go below at once, or I shall take you there myself!'

The look that accompanied the threat had her scampering back to her cabin. She was smarting from the verbal battle, which she had somehow lost, though she did not know why. He had deceived her, but he did not seem at all ashamed of himself; indeed, he was mightily pleased about something. She appeared to have lost her power to make him angry. It looked as if Almería had been right all the time. Perhaps he had never intended to let her go.

Almería glanced at her as she entered the cabin, but was wise enough not to say anything.

'We are going to Valencia,' Venetia said haughtily. 'It is a temporary arrangement. Captain Domingo thinks it will be safer for me at the moment.'

'Is that what he said?' Almería's eyes slid away from her mistress's angry gaze. 'Safer for...'

What she was about to say was lost as a huge wave crashed against the ship, almost causing it to capsize. She gave a scream, looking at Venetia fearfully.

'Mercy on us! What was that?'

'There's a storm coming.'

Almería clung to the bed-rail. 'We shall all be drowned!'

'Oh, I shouldn't think so,' Venetia said bitterly. 'That wouldn't fit in with Captain Domingo's plans at all... And he always gets his own way!'

It was almost dark when they arrived at the castle. Domingo had taken Venetia up before him on his own horse, ignoring her caustic remarks that he was afraid she would run away. His good humour was remarkable, for she had done nothing but complain since the day of the storm. They had weathered it with no more than the loss of some rigging, just as she had expected. Obviously, the Spaniard bore a charmed life!

Riding through the dusk with his arms about her was extraordinarily comforting, so much so, that Venetia had no reason to feel nervous about what was happening to her. She had accused him of abducting her at every opportunity, but she had no fears that she was to be a prisoner in his home. When he showed her to her rooms himself, brushing aside the offers of his housekeeper – an attractive Morisco woman – Venetia was not surprised to see that they were those normally reserved for the mistress of the house. He stood back, watching as she wandered about, touching the polished surfaces of heavy, carved tables, stools and a huge four-poster bed hung with silk.

'I trust everything is to your liking?'

She turned to see an odd, almost vulnerable expression in his eyes. 'It is well enough,' she said coldly. 'I do not intend to stay here for longer than I must.'

'You will stay here until I permit you to leave.'

'Indeed? Am I your prisoner, then?'

'You are being childish, Venetia, and you know it! I have brought you here for your own good. Nowhere is safe while this war drags on, but I do not think the castle will be attacked. I keep sufficient men here always to defend it. None of my people will ever be carried away to become slaves of the Turks – or anyone else.'

There was a ring of pride in his voice, and she looked at him curiously. 'Your ship is manned by slaves, isn't it?'

'Yes. Most have been condemned by the Inquisition. I choose each man personally, and they all know that they have the chance to earn their freedom. Besides, I normally spend only the summer months at sea. For the rest of the year they are given light duties in the gardens – or work on my estate in Granada.'

'Is that what happened to you when you were Ali's slave?'

'I wondered when you would ask that question.' He smiled slightly. 'So Almería could not ferret out the whole story? Christian slaves can usually earn a measure of freedom from their Turkish masters only by converting to the Moslem faith, but I refused to do so. I lived in the hope of escaping, but when the opportunity arose, I could not take it. We were working in the gardens when one of Ali's slaves seemed to lose control. He had been acting strangely for days, and I think his mind had cracked. Anyway, he attacked Ali while he was taking a stroll in the courtyard, and some of the other slaves followed his example. I went to my master's assistance. Ali had not treated us cruelly, and we had spoken a few times in the gardens. I could not stand by and see him murdered.'

'And then he gave you your freedom?'

'Not at first. He invited me to eat with him, and we talked. Gradually, we became friends. He told me that he would make me a rich man if I would change my religion, but I still refused. At last he saw that I wanted only my freedom...'

'Then how can you deny that same right to me?' Venetia cried.

'Are you so unhappy, madonna?'

The very quietness of his voice made her pause. She looked up at him, her heart beating fast. 'No, I am not unhappy.' His eyes seemed to see into her very soul. 'You know I am anxious about my father. I feel so – helpless.'

'Trust me,' he said. 'Is that so much to ask?' Wordlessly, she shook her head. He smiled, bending his head to brush his lips gently over hers. 'I wish I could stay and kiss away all your fears, my green-eyed houri, but I have important business elsewhere.'

She smiled at the memory his words evoked. 'You should have taken Ali's thousand ducats. It would have saved you so much trouble!'

His soft laughter sent little tingling sensations down to her toes. He was so attractive when he smiled like that! 'What would you say if I told you that I had paid Mahomet five thousand ducats to save you from his harem?'

'You must be jesting? No one would pay that much!' She gazed up into his eyes. 'You are teasing me, aren't you?'

'Perhaps.' He touched her cheek with the tip of his finger. 'We shall discuss this another time, when I return from Madrid. In the meantime, I want you to give me your word that you will not do anything foolish while I am away.'

'You want me to promise that I shall not try to run away?' She looked up at him, puzzled by something in his manner that she did not understand.

'Yes. I do not want to have to place a guard about you, Venetia, yet I must protect you for your own sake.'

'I shall not run away. Where would I go? I have no money and no family. You know I must rely on you for everything until my father's whereabouts are certain.' She blushed and flicked down her lashes. 'I taunted you with abducting me only because I was angry. You should not have tried to hide the situation from me; I am not a child.'

'I have never thought of you as a child. If I hesitated to tell you things that would hurt you, it was for another reason.'

Her heart felt as if it was being crushed in her breast. 'What reason?'

He smiled and shook his head. 'Do not

tempt me, Venetia. Be patient until I return.'

'But...'

'When I return. Until then, this must content you.'

He reached out and drew her into his arms, kissing her so sweetly that it set her body trembling. She clung to him, staring up at his face in bewilderment, unable to understand what was happening to her. Why did she feel so weak, as if she would fall if his arms did not support her? Letting her go, he shook his head when she would have spoken. She stood in silence as he walked from the room.

Why did she want to run after him and beg him not to leave her? What was this strange feeling inside that made her want to shout for joy and weep at the same time? Her fingers moved over her lips in wonderment. Every time Roldán kissed her, it was different. This time, it had set her heart singing. Could it be...? Was she falling in love with him? She had read poetry about men and women who had willingly died for love, but she had never understood how that could happen in real life. A child must love its parents, but was it possible to feel so much for a stranger? A man she had thought she hated, until... Or was it only Almería's image of the man she had disliked? Was it not true that her heart had acted strangely from the first moment that she had looked into his eyes? In her innocence, she had perhaps mistaken hatred for love. She believed that the dividing line between the two must be very fine. It would explain her frustration at being unable to break through the indifference he had shown after rescuing her – and the pain their quarrel had caused her.

Venetia turned away as Almería came into the room, afraid that her nurse might be able to read what was in her mind. These new feelings were very fragile, and she could not bear to have them exposed to her scorn. Nor did she want fresh doubts put in her mind. She needed time to think about her discovery...

The castle gardens were small, but it was pleasant to walk in the sunshine. There was not a great deal of warmth in the air as yet, but Valencia's gentle climate was never really cold, and Venetia hardly needed her cloak as she stopped to pick a tiny pink flower and held it to her nose, inhaling the perfume. She turned as a woman left the castle and came towards her. Perhaps there was news from Roldán!

'Is there word from Captain Domingo?' she asked, her heart quickening in antici-pation.

'No, my lady.' The woman's dark eyes held a certain hostility that puzzled her. 'He will scarcely have reached Madrid as yet. I came only to tell you that food has been prepared.'

'Thank you…' Venetia looked at her curiously, wondering how she had come to the castle. 'How long have you been here, Mirhmah?'

'It was just after the siege of Galera ended. I was one of the four thousand who took no part in the fighting, and Don John spared my life. I was to have been sold into slavery, but Captain Domingo brought me here.'

'Are you not a slave, then?' Venetia was surprised. She had thought all the Morisco men and women in the castle must be slaves.

'For his bravery at Galera, my master was allowed to select his choice from among those captives who were to be sold. When he brought us here, he told us that we were free to stay or to go, as we wished. If we stayed, we must outwardly accept the Christian faith, but we were promised that we should not be harassed if we kept our own religion in private.'

Venetia nodded, understanding the compromise. It had been the accepted practice in Spain and other countries for many years. It was only since King Philip II had succeeded his father, that the Inquisition had begun to persecute the Morisco people. Yet the discovery that Roldán was so tolerant of their religion made her think deeply. She was learning so many new things about him. When she had first met him, it had seemed to her that his hands were freshly stained with the blood of a persecuted people; for he must have come to Rome straight from his success at Galera. Almería had condemned him as a murderer, but now it seemed that he had actually saved some of her people from slavery. He had been able to help only a few, of course, but that was surely worth something. It was true that he had fought at Galera with Don John's troops, but his profession was that of a soldier – that did not necessarily make him evil.

'You were fortunate to find a home here,' Venetia said, feeling vaguely uncomfortable beneath the older woman's hard stare. 'Captain Domingo is unusually tolerant for a – a Spaniard, these days.'

'Perhaps because he is only half Spanish. His father is an English baron and a Protestant.' Mirhmah's eyes gleamed. 'You did not know that, did you? There is much that I could tell you.'

'What do you mean?' Venetia sensed the hostility in her, almost wishing that she had not begun this conversation. They had kept a distance between them until this moment, and now she thought that might have been for the best.

156

'I have lived in his house for a year now. I know all his secrets.'

'Indeed?' Venetia looked at her haughtily. 'I suppose you have shared his confidences?'

'Perhaps. When a woman shares a man's bed, she learns much.'

A cold breeze seemed to pass around Venetia's heart. She felt betrayed, though she knew she had no right to feel anything. 'You were his mistress before he left for Rome?'

'Yes.' There was triumph in Mirhmah's eyes. 'And when he returned. He came to my bed before he set out for Madrid.'

'I do not believe you!' The words were out before Venetia could stop them. She saw the scorn in Mirhmah's eyes, and flushed. 'H-He was in haste to reach the Court. He told me so.'

'Yet he did not leave until dawn. He would not have gone then if I had not thrust him from my side.'

'You are lying! He would not have left me to come to you.'

'No?' Mirhmah's mouth curved slyly. 'You think he loves you, but you are wrong. He will never love you – or any other woman. There was a woman he cared for once, but she betrayed him. He will never give his heart again.'

'How can you know that?' Venetia asked. 'You may have lived in his home for a year, but for most of that time he has been at sea or in Rome. I have been with him more often than you.'

'You have seen the scar on his face?' Mirhmah smiled as she saw the girl's attention was caught. 'He was whipped by the Englishwoman's husband. It is the reason he left his home to become a mercenary. He will never love a woman – but he needs one in his bed, and I make him happy for a while. You are cold and proud. You only remind him of the woman who betrayed him.'

'How dare you insult me?' Venetia cried angrily. 'You are merely a servant. I shall not listen to you any more.'

She turned away, hearing Mirhmah's mocking laughter as she walked towards the castle. Her mind was whirling in confusion as she tried to sort out the truth from the lies. She did not doubt that the Morisco woman had been Roldán's mistress for a short time before he left for Rome, but that could have been only a matter of days. Galera had fallen in February, and she had met Roldán in April. She was sure he had not been back to Valencia until the night he had brought her to the castle. How could the woman know so much about him? There was always gossip among the servants, of course, but she could surely not know his innermost feelings – unless he had told her himself!

He had told Venetia nothing of his past, except to confirm Ali's story. The only time she had managed to break through his reserve, they had quarrelled bitterly. Yet Mirhmah knew all his secrets. The fact that his father was English, the scar... Had he whispered them to her as their heads lay side by side on the pillow? The realisation that he must have done so was a bitter blow. He had kissed her and then gone to the arms of his mistress! Probably they had laughed together behind her back. The pain twisted inside her as she knew herself a fool for imagining that his kiss was more than a moment's pleasure to him.

He had told her to be patient, and she had believed he meant to speak to her of love when he returned. What a blind, innocent child she was! She had let her dreams lead her astray. He could not love her, because he was incapable of love. She remembered how he had called her heartless and vain – like all women! So Mirhmah was not lying. He despised all her kind, wanting nothing more from them but physical pleasure. His smiles and kisses were all false; he wanted only to seduce her. Almería had been right all the time!

Making her way through a maze of passages and small dark rooms to her own chamber, Venetia curled up on her bed, hugging her arms about herself in a silent agony of grief. Her pain was too sharp for tears, mixed as it was with shame and humiliation. She had come so close to submitting to his lovemaking. She had wanted that last kiss to go on and on... If he had stayed with her, she would have... But he should never deceive her again!

She sat up, her face cold as she stared blankly in front of her. She had wanted to trust him, to believe that he really cared for her, but now she knew that he was cold and ruthless – a man with no heart. She had thought she was falling in love with him, and she had hoped that he loved her, too. Now she hated him. When he returned, she would demand to be taken back to Rome. From there she could make her own way home.

'Mirhmah says that her master wishes you to dine with him.' Almería paused in her task of brushing the girl's hair. 'Perhaps it would be wiser to hear what he has to say before making any demands, my lady.'

Venetia's fingers played restlessly with the ruby pendant at her throat. Maddalena had insisted that she keep the gift, and rather than offend her, she had given in. She was wearing it tonight because she wanted to look like the daughter of a wealthy Venetian noble, to remind Roldán that she had relatives and friends. He had brought her to Valencia against her will, and now he must make arrangements for her journey home. If he could not take her himself, he must pay her passage on a merchant ship. She would see to it that he was generously repaid for his trouble when she contacted her father's lawyers. It was time that she took control of her own affairs.

'It cannot benefit Captain Domingo to keep me here,' Venetia said, pretending to a calmness she did not feel. Her heart had been fluttering nervously ever since she had heard of his return to the castle. 'Besides, you have been warning me against him from the first. Surely you are not suggesting that we should stay here?'

There was an odd, half-shamed look in Almería's eyes. 'I believe I may have mis-judged Captain Domingo. My people are allowed to live freely here. It would not be such a terrible place to settle down. He is a strong man, and we should be safe under his protection.'

'Then you may stay here alone!' Venetia jumped to her feet, sending the stool she had been sitting on clattering to the stone floor. It was too much! That Almería should change sides now, when she had finally discovered the truth!

'I am only saying that perhaps you should listen to Captain Domingo.' Almería stared at her angry face. 'Mirhmah may have been lying.'

'He did not leave here until after dawn. You discovered that from the other servants yourself.' Venetia's face hardened. 'He spent the night in her arms after asking me to trust him. I told you, he cares for no one but himself. You were right, Almería. He wants only to seduce me, and then he will sell me to my father.'

Almería shook her head. 'No, he cannot do both. He wants either you or the money. Your father would never pay if you had been ruined. He would probably challenge him to a duel. Besides, no one knows where...'

'Enough!' Venetia stamped her foot angrily. 'Do not make excuses for him. I know he has only evil in his heart.'

'Are you sure that the evil is not the jealousy in your own heart, child?'

'Be quiet! You forget your station.' Venetia's temper made her forget the love between them. 'You are a servant, and you would do well to remember it! I can have you whipped if I choose.'

'Yes, my lady.' Almería looked at her resentfully. It was the first time she had ever spoken to her so harshly.

Venetia regretted the hasty words as soon as they had left her lips, but she was too angry to retract them. Her nurse's change of heart had hurt and bewildered her. Just when she needed her support, Almería had gone over to the enemy's side!

'You need not wait up for me. I can manage to undress myself.'

Ignoring the pained expression on her nurse's face, Venetia swept from the room. This evening she was wearing a full-skirted gown of grey brocade encrusted with silver embroidery and pearls, a ruff of exquisite grey lace framing her pale face. Her long titian hair was combed loosely on to her shoulders, held in place by a twisted silver band. She felt that she was looking her best, and it gave her the courage to face Roldán. She had to make him see that she was not one of the waifs and strays he seemed to collect. He had rescued her from the Corsairs, and he would be rewarded for it with money. If he imagined that she was so grateful that she would fall into his arms as Mirhmah had, then he was much mistaken!

She could hear his voice as she neared the great dining hall. Her foot paused on the twisting stairway, and she was seized by a fit of trembling. Why was it that the sound of his voice could make her feel so weak? With an effort, she controlled her emotions. He was a liar and a cheat, and she must remember that! She must harden her heart against him.

Rounding the bend of the stairwell, she saw him standing in conversation with Mirhmah, laughing at something the woman had said. As she paused, the Morisco woman turned and noticed her standing there. She smiled maliciously, then curtsied to her master and murmured something. Roldán looked up, his eyes meeting Venetia's. She watched the eagerness die from his gaze as he sensed her anger.

'Venetia.' He came towards her, unaware of his servant's departure. 'You look lovely this evening.'

'You flatter me, sir,' she replied coldly. 'I trust your urgent business in Madrid was satisfactorily concluded?'

'Yes, thank you.'

He eyed her warily, taking her arm to draw her nearer to the fireplace. Although the spring days were warmer, the evenings were always chilly in the castle. Indeed it was warmer outside than in this vast, high-ceilinged room – though it was not the chill that made her shiver as he touched her. He glanced down at her white face.

'Are you cold – or ill?'

'Neither, thank you.' He looked so handsome in his black velvet doublet, his face framed by the white lace of his ruff. She drew away from him quickly, to hold her hands to the flames. 'I wish to return to Rome as soon as it is convenient, sir. I shall write to my father's lawyers from there and make arrangements to pay you what is owed, and for my journey home.'

'And may I ask the reason for this haste, madonna? I had thought you content to stay here until your father's whereabouts were certain.' He frowned as he saw the stubborn look on her face. 'Has something given you a distaste for my home?'

'Not for your home. I have been very comfortable here.'

'I am glad to hear it.' His eyes seemed to pierce her. 'If it is not your situation you dislike, it must be the company. What have I done this time?'

His tone was calm, but there was a distinct glint in his eyes. Venetia's toe tapped the floor. He was hinting that it was her fault if she was dissatisfied! He had kissed her and asked her to be patient – then spent the night in the arms of another woman! How dared he look at her like that? As though she were the unreasonable one!

'Why should you have done anything?' she asked, her lips tight with suppressed temper. 'I merely asked to leave. If you recall, you brought me here against my will, so is it surprising that I should want to go?'

'After the way you behaved when we parted – yes.' He glared at her, becoming angry despite his efforts to remain calm. 'You are an impossible child, Venetia! I warn you, I have had nearly enough of your tricks.'

'I am not a child,' she cried. 'I was sixteen while you were in Madrid.'

'It was your birthday?' He seemed puzzled. 'Are you angry because I did not send you a gift? I did not know.'

'Pray do not insult me! Why should you send me presents? I was merely telling you that I am a woman now...'

'Then why do you not act like one?'

'Oh, I hate you!'

Anger swept through Venetia. Without realising what she was doing, she struck him across the face. He had not been expecting it, and he stared at her, seeming stunned. She felt a surge of misery. Why did he not shout at her or strike her back so that she could feel justified in what she had done? Suddenly the hot shame welled up in her belly and she was unable to face him. She gave a cry of agony and ran from the room.

The tears were burning behind her eyes as she fled up the stairway to her own chamber. Thankfully, it was empty. She could not have borne Almería's critical gaze just now, with her own thoughts in turmoil. She had meant to be calm and cold towards Roldán, but instead she had lost her temper and behaved like the child he had named her. It was because of the way his eyes accused her – and the foolish way her heart behaved when she was near him. She had felt like weeping in his arms and begging him to forgive her, but that was something she must never do! He would take it as a sign of weakness.

Dashing the unspilled tears from her eyes, she began to struggle with the lacings of her bodice. Her fingers were made clumsy by distress, and she gave a cry of annoyance. Was she capable of nothing?

'Shall I do that for you?'

Roldán's voice made her whirl around in alarm. She had not heard the door open, but he was there, standing in the doorway, watching her.

'What are you doing here?' she demanded, her heart suddenly pounding wildly as she saw a strange gleam in his eyes.

'I came to talk to you, Venetia. It's time we discussed all this nonsense.'

He turned the key in the lock, placing it inside his doublet. The very deliberateness of his action made her gasp. He was making very sure that she would not escape this time.

'Why have you locked the door?'

'I want to be certain that we shall not be disturbed, my sweet.'

'Don't you dare to call me that!' Venetia felt her knees tremble as he smiled at her. He was mocking her trying to frighten her as a punishment. He would surely not actually do anything?

'What shall I call you, then?' he asked

pleasantly, almost as if passing the time of day. 'It seems that, whatever I say, I am wrong. I called you a child and you denied it. I have come to find out if your claim to be a woman is true, Venetia.'

Her cheeks flamed as she saw his look, and she gave a little squeak of fright. 'Don't you dare to touch me! I shall scream if you take one step towards me.'

'No one will answer your cries for help. Have you forgotten that I am the master here? I can do whatever I please with you, my green-eyed houri!'

'I am not your slave. I know you bought me from Mahomet – but that was a ransom. You will be paid as soon as I can raise the money. So the sooner you let me...' Her words trailed away as she saw the burning look in his eyes, and she ran the tip of her tongue over lips that were suddenly dry.

'But I do not want your money. I have all I need, and more.' He grinned at her, his teeth white and strong like a shark's. 'I lied when I said you were lovely, Venetia. You are breathtakingly beautiful. I have wanted to make love to you from the first moment I saw you standing there with the sun setting fire to your hair...'

'No!' She backed away, her heart thudding so furiously that she felt as if she had been running very fast. When he looked at her like that she could feel her limbs turning to water and her resistance ebbing. 'You– You think to deceive me with soft words, but I know you for what you are.'

'What am I?' he whispered.

He had been slowly advancing as she retreated, and now was within an arm's length of her. She knew that one more step would be too many. Her back was against the wall, and she could not move away. His eyes seemed to draw hers like a moth to a candle-flame, and she was trapped just as surely. She felt her will to resist being sapped as she met his mesmerising gaze. He was dominating her by the power of his will.

'You are a…'

Her words were lost beneath his kiss. His mouth covered hers at the same moment as his body pressed against her, holding her captive against the wall. She could feel its coldness through the material of her gown, contrasting with the heat of his body. She raised her hands as if to ward him off, but he put them round his neck, catching her to him, and suddenly her fingers were curling in his hair and she was responding to that searching kiss. She felt herself go limp as he bent to scoop her up in his arms, carrying her to the bed. Looking up at him in dazed bewilderment, she could only whimper a protest as he laid her down and bent over her again. His blue eyes were burning her with a combination of fire and ice. She shivered as his hand caressed her cheek, pushing the hair back from her eyes. She was like a bird plucked from the tree, trembling yet acquiescent as he stroked her. His mouth came down to brush her lips lightly once more.

'No! Please do not...' she whispered, but she had ceased to fight. Whatever this feeling was inside her, it was too strong.

She lay motionless as his lips touched her eyelids, her cheek, the tip of her nose, trembling as the featherlight kisses trailed the arch of her white throat. Her body was pulsating with a delicious new sensation, making her feel weak with something she vaguely recognised as desire. Now his fingers were unlacing the bodice of her petticoat. His hand slipped inside, encircling her breast.

'You want me, too, don't you?' he whispered, a note of triumph in his voice. 'Why else did you run away if it was not because you wanted me to follow you?'

She froze at his words, suddenly realising what was happening to her. She was being seduced by a very skilled lover! A man who took women to his bed just for the pleasure it gave him. It must not happen, even though her body ached for his touch. If she gave in to this heady sensation spreading through her body, she would belong to him as surely as if she were really his slave. She would be like Zahara – a wretched thing at the mercy of her master's whims. Loving him even when he tired of her, so desperate for his attention that she would do anything rather than risk being cast aside.

'No! I shall not let this happen,' she cried, rolling away from him, her eyes blazing with anger. 'I am not a slave to be used for your pleasure, sir! Go back to Mirhmah. Go to your mistress…'

She was on her feet, clutching her bodice to cover herself, staring at him wildly as she fought for control. Her face was turned from him.

For a moment he neither moved nor spoke, then said, 'Did she tell you?'

'Yes. I know you lay with her the night you left for Madrid.'

He was silent a moment more, then murmured, 'And, of course, you believed her? You did not even wait to ask if it was true. I should have known there was something…'

'Are you saying that she lied?'

He got up and turned to face her. She was shocked by the expression on his face. He looked tired, grey – almost defeated.

'Would it matter what I said?' he asked bitterly. 'You have never believed anything I say. I knew you despised me from the start. I had hoped to win your trust, but it was a wasted effort. From now on, I may as well 'treat you the way you seem to expect.'

'What do you mean?' She looked at him uncertainly, and he gave a harsh laugh.

'Your meals will be served to you here so that we are not forced to meet too often. You will be allowed to walk in the gardens during the day, but only under supervision.'

'So I am to be a prisoner, now?'

'You have left me with no other option, Venetia.' He sighed, running his fingers through tousled black hair. 'I have been ordered to place my ships at Don John's command. There is to be a new offensive against the Turks, and he is to lead it. I shall be absent for several months. Since I cannot be sure that you will not try to run away, I must keep you secured for your own safety.'

'But, why?' She stared at him helplessly. 'Why will you not let me go home?'

'If I told you, you would not believe me.'

'If you think I shall submit to being your mistress...'

'Had I wanted only that, I might have taken you months ago. You were always at my mercy, Venetia. Your nurse was certainly aware of it.'

He looked so cold and angry that she shivered. She knew that much of what he said was true, but still could not grasp his meaning. He did not care for her. Surely he could not expect her to believe...

He had read her thoughts, and his mouth

twisted into a wry smile. 'Do not torture yourself, madonna. You know why I will not let you go. You have always known that all I care for is money, have you not? Why should I let a wealthy heiress slip through my fingers? You would pay me a paltry reward, but I shall have it all. If I marry you, everything your father owned will be mine.'

'No!' She shook her head, blenching at his cruel words. 'My father will never let you marry me.'

'If Marco dei Giorlandi lives, he is a prisoner.' Roldán frowned as he saw her face. 'You said that you were not a child, Venetia. Now I am treating you as a woman. You must accept the facts. Even if your father is in Famagusta, his chances of escape are small. King Philip is prepared to send his galleys against the Turks, but we could not hope to reach the rendezvous at the Strait of Messina by April. It will take weeks to supply and man the ships. Famagusta has been under siege all winter. By the time any relief could come...'

'Stop! You have made your thinking clear, sir. Now I shall make my answer just a plain.' She raised her eyes to his proudly. 'I shall never marry you. Never!'

'No?' A light flickered in the blue eyes. 'I believe I know how to change your mind.' He smiled as she gave a gasp of horror. 'Do not be anxious, my sweet. I shall make no further attempt on your virtue for the moment. I am more interested in my dinner.'

'You– You…' Words failed her, and seeing her predicament, he laughed.

'What? Can you not think of anything to say? Well, I am sorry to wound your vanity, Venetia, but I am very hungry. At the moment I am more concerned with the excellent dinner waiting for me than seducing you – though I might consider it later.'

He took the key from his doublet and unlocked the door. She considered making a desperate effort to escape, but the steely glint in his eyes deterred her. She had won a respite from his disgusting attempt to seduce her, but the next time she might not be so lucky.

'Very wise, madonna.' He grinned at her. 'I may send you some supper later if you continue to be sensible.'

'Do not bother. I am not hungry.'

'Are you not? Then I shall not waste the food.'

As the door was firmly closed and locked behind him, Venetia sank down on the edge of the bed, all the resistance draining out of her. She was very hungry, but her pride would not let her admit it. If she was to be starved into submission, so be it. She did not care any more. He was as cruel and as heartless as he had once named her. How could he use her fears for her father against her like that? What he had said was no more than Maddalena had already told her, she could not deny that even to herself. She knew that she must accept that her father was probably dead, but only an uncaring brute would have thrown the words at her like that. And after he had declared his intention of marrying her for her fortune!

He was completely ruthless; far worse than even Almería had suspected. It must have been in his mind when he bought her from Mahomet. Now she understood why he had abducted her instead of taking her home to Venice, why he had tried to charm her into trusting him. He was determined to have her, one way or the other.

She would never, never consent to be his wife of her own free will. A look of determination settled over her features. He thought himself so clever – but she would find a way to outwit him yet. If he imagined that she was going to wait here tamely while he went away to war, he was deluding himself!

CHAPTER SIX

'If Captain Domingo is determined to keep you here, I cannot see how you can hope to escape,' Almería said, frowning, as she finished brushing the girl's hair. 'Even if you could leave the castle, you have no money to buy your passage on a ship.'

'Why have you turned against me?' Venetia asked. 'Is it because I threatened to have you whipped? You know I did not mean it. I was just cross because you were on his side.'

'I knew that,' Almería said with a little sniff. 'I have not turned against you. I've simply changed my mind about Captain Domingo.'

'But I told you what happened!' Venetia screwed her head round to look at her in annoyance. 'He tried to seduce me – and then he had the effrontery to say that he intended to wed me for my fortune!'

'If he had wanted to rape you, you would not have been able to stop him. I think he wants to marry you.'

'For my father's wealth!' the girl cried indignantly.

'Giovanni Gavelli wanted to marry you because you were an heiress,' Almería reminded her.

'That was different.'

'Was it?'

Her nurse's steady gaze made Venetia hesitate. 'Well, I know my dowry was part of the agreement between my father and Giovanni, but – but he was fond of me, and I liked him. He would have taken care of me, and...'

'And spoiled you, as your father did? Now you have met a man whose will is as strong as yours, my lady. Perhaps it will be good for you.'

'I shall not marry him!'

'You were willing to accept a marriage of convenience with Giovanni, so why are you so set against it now? Captain Domingo is younger and better looking. You will be happier as his wife than as a harem slave.'

'So I should be grateful enough to marry him?' Venetia stared at her incredulously.

'Why not?' Almería's serious eyes studied her face. 'Besides, I think you are lying to yourself. You are in love with him, but you won't admit it.'

'Nonsense!' Venetia's mouth twisted with scorn. 'How could I love a man like that? I despise him.'

'Well, have it your own way. At least I have the courage to admit that I was wrong. I thought him a murderer and as intolerant as his master, but I was a foolish old woman who did not know what she was saying. He is a fair-minded man, and I would be content to serve him for the rest of my life. My advice to you, my lady, is to cease fighting him. If you apologised politely, you might find that things are not as bad as they seem. You might even enjoy being his wife.'

'Me! Apologise to him?' The girl's foot tapped the floor impatiently at the very idea. 'Never!'

'Then you will continue to be locked in your room at night, and under constant supervision in the gardens. Until you show you are willing to be sensible, he will not relent. He is as stubborn as you, my lady, and he has the advantage. I believe you must give in in the end.'

'And you think I should marry him!'

Venetia shot her a darkling glance as she flounced from the room. Almería was unkind to chide her in that fashion, especially now that she needed a friend. Her confinement had not proved to be unbearable. She had certainly not been starved, and she was able to move freely about the castle and gardens during the day, though she knew herself to be under constant supervision by the servants. Once she had wandered towards the gates, only to find her path blocked by two burly guards. They had said nothing, merely staring at her with blank faces. She had turned aside, realising

179

that their orders forbade them to let her pass. At night, Mirhmah came to lock the door of her chamber, and it was this that irritated her the most. That he should appoint his mistress as her gaoler!

It seemed that escape was impossible. She could not even rely on Almería's help, for it was clear that her nurse believed she was fortunate to have an offer of marriage from her captor. It was so infuriating! Was it supposed to make everything as it should be just because he was prepared to marry her? As far as Venetia was concerned, it was the worst thing that could happen. To be married to Roldán, knowing that he was interested only in her fortune, would be intolerable. She would be bound to betray herself. His very touch made her melt into submission, so how could she hope to hide her feelings in the intimacy of marriage? Almería thought it should be easy to wed him because she loved him, but it was just because of her feelings that she could not accept her fate. To love a man who did not love her would be humiliating. She could not bear it if he discovered her secret and used it to humble her pride. She had to escape... But how?

She had been walking in the gardens for nearly an hour, her thoughts still in turmoil, when she saw Roldán coming towards her. He had avoided her company as much as possible for the past week, and she was surprised that he had deliberately sought her out this morning. Her heart quickened as she saw that he was dressed simply in a white shirt and black Venetian trunk hose. It was a fashion that he quite often adopted, less fussy than many men were apt to follow, and it underlined his vital masculinity. His shirt was open at the neck, revealing a glimpse of tanned skin and a sprinkling of black hair on his chest. She felt a spiral of desire fan through her, and clenched her hands in a desperate attempt to control her emotions. How could she hope to win when even the sight of him made her long to be in his arms? She was a weak fool!

'Good morning, Venetia.' His smile sent the blood racing through her veins. 'May I walk with you awhile?'

'If you wish.' She did not return his smile, though it had set her pulses dancing with excitement. 'I can hardly stop you.'

'You have only to say, and I shall leave you in peace.'

He seemed as if about to turn away, but she laid her hand on his arm. 'That was rude. Forgive me; I have no wish to quarrel.'

'Nor I, madonna.'

'Then we shall enjoy the sunshine together.' She avoided his gaze, afraid that he would be able to read too much of what was in her mind. 'Did you wish to speak to me particularly, sir?'

'I came to say goodbye.'

She stopped walking, her eyes flying open in alarm. 'You are leaving? When?'

'At dawn tomorrow. My ship is provisioned and ready. I shall join the fleet under Don John's command when he calls at Rome. I have some unfinished business there myself.'

'Will you not change your mind and take me with you?' she asked, a note of unconscious pleading in her voice. 'I know I have made you angry many times, and I beg you to forgive me. Please let me go home?'

'I cannot.' He seemed to hesitate, as if there was more he wanted to say but could not. 'Soon I may be able to explain my reasons, Venetia, but for the moment I believe it safer for you to remain here.'

He would not change his mind; she realised that as she gazed up into his face and saw the determination there. She was to remain a prisoner in the castle while he went off to war! The frustration made her frown at him. Even when she tried to be reasonable, he would not listen. Why should she listen to him?

'You have made your reasons plain enough, sir.' She glared at him, angry again. 'Excuse me; I prefer to be alone.'

She turned away, leaving him to stare after her in exasperation. 'If only you could go home,' he muttered. 'I swear I am almost

182

tempted to leave you to your fate. I must be mad to waste my time with a shrewish witch!'

She had not heard, for he spoke his thoughts softly, and only out of frustration. For a few moments he stared after her, wondering whether to follow and tell her the truth. If she knew… But the knowledge could only hurt her and humble her pride. He could not win peace of mind for himself at her expense. If things went well in Rome this time, he might manage to keep the worst of it from her. At least until she had come to terms with his plans for her.

'Will you want anything more tonight?' Almería asked, as she turned back the bed-covers. She looked curiously at her mistress. Venetia was standing at the window, staring out into the darkness. She had been very subdued all evening, hardly touching her supper and sighing deeply. 'You are not ill, I hope, my lady?'

The girl turned and smiled. 'No, I am not ill, Almería. Go to bed now and do not worry about me. I shan't want anything more.'

'If you should need me…' Almería's face was anxious. Something was wrong, she was sure of it.

'Please, go now. I – I have a little headache, that's all.'

The ache was in her heart, not her head,

but she was too proud to confess it to Almería. Ever since she had left Roldán in the garden, she had been regretting it. Even though he was wrong to keep her here against her will, she could not bring herself to hate him as she should. The truth was that she had come to love him, despite herself. Now he was going away to war, and he might be injured or ... killed. If she truly hated him, the thought would have given her some comfort, but as the long day passed, she had realised that it filled her with dismay. Supposing he died and she had not even said goodbye to him! He had come to take his leave of her, and she had acted churlishly. They could not part with anger between them...

She moved towards the door instinctively, knowing that she must speak with him before he left. He had saved her from a life of slavery, and she had never really thanked him. She must at least do that and try to heal the breach... She stopped abruptly as the door opened and Mirhmah came in. Panic swept through her. She was to be locked in, and her last chance to see him would be gone!

'Please do not lock me in yet!' she cried.

'Hush.' Mirhmah placed a finger to her lips. 'I have come to help you.'

'To help me?' Venetia stared at her in surprise. 'Why should you do that?'

'You want to leave here, don't you?'

'Yes, but…'

'I can help you to go aboard my master's ship. If you stay hidden until after he sails, he will be forced to take you as far as Rome. When you get there, you can make your own way home.'

'Yes, I could.' Venetia felt suspicious of the woman's offer of help. 'Why are you doing this? How do I know I can trust you?'

'Because I want you to leave this house.' Mirhmah's voice was sharp with dislike. 'You know he does not love you; he wants the fortune you could bring him. If he cares for any woman, it is me. With you gone, he might marry me.'

Mirhmah was deceiving herself, Venetia thought. Roldán would never marry a woman who had no dowry, but she did not say so, for it would be pointless. If the housekeeper was willing to help her, she was prepared to take a risk on Roldán's anger when he discovered she was on board.

'How can I be sure you do not intend to trick me?' she asked. 'I know you hate me. This might be a plot to have me killed!'

Mirhmah snorted with disgust. 'Why should I risk my own neck? You are not worth it. He will never love you. Even if he weds you, he will come back to me as soon as he tires of you. Besides, I am not an evil woman. You must trust me or not as you

185

wish. I came here to show you a way of escape, but if you do not want to take it...'

'Very well, I believe you.' Venetia's eyes took sudden fire as a surge of excitement went through her. 'How do I escape? I am watched every time I leave the castle.'

'Captain Domingo's personal belongings are to be delivered to the ship tonight. I have arranged for an extra chest to be loaded on the wagon. You will be inside it, dressed in a youth's clothes. There are several new recruits on this voyage. If you are careful, you can slip out of the trunk and mingle with the others. Keep out of the way for as long as you can. My master will not put back to the harbour and waste several days' journey; he cannot afford the time. He will be forced to leave you in Rome – and he cannot keep you a prisoner there!'

'Yes... It might work.' Venetia felt her spirits lift. She was not to be left at the castle, after all. She would see him again before they finally parted. She was not sure why that made her feel happy, but the prospect of being on board his ship again was exciting.

'Come with me.' Mirhmah placed a finger to her lips. 'And be quiet. If we are discovered, we shall both be punished.'

'Just a moment; I must take a few things with me.' Venetia flew about the room, gathering personal items and rolling them in her cloak. 'I cannot take all my clothes, but

I must have at least one gown. It would be too much to expect Maddalena to provide me with another wardrobe.'

'I have already packed some of your things. You will find them in the trunk.' Mirhmah beckoned urgently from the doorway. 'We must hurry, or the men will finish loading and go without you.'

'I must have this.' Venetia swooped on the ruby pendant. 'I am ready now.'

She followed the housekeeper from the room, her heart beating erratically as they walked cautiously through the narrow passages, Mirhmah's candle showing a pale yellow light. If one of the other servants should see them, their plan might be discovered and reported to Roldán. He would immediately see to it that Venetia was locked in her room once more. Every creak or rattle set her nerves jangling, and twice they were forced to stop and flatten themselves against the wall as doors opened and closed near by, but they reached their destination without discovery. Mirhmah unlocked the door and beckoned her inside the tiny storeroom.

There were two large leather-bound trunks standing on the floor, one of which she had often seen in Roldán's cabin. Mirhmah opened the lid of the other chest, showing her the iron lock.

'I shall give you the key, so that you know

I mean you no harm. It is easy enough to open from inside. See, you simply press this lever and push up. It's quite safe; you cannot be trapped inside. If you wish to test it, I shall get in first and you can close the lid on me. Meanwhile, change into those clothes.' She pointed to a pile of clothing. 'I think they will fit you.'

Venetia nodded, hastily slipping off her nightrobe and putting on the shirt and breeches Mirhmah had provided. She closed the lid as instructed, watching to see if it really was easy to get out of the trunk. She had been tricked by Zahara, but she was wiser now and there was no reason why she should trust Mirhmah.

'There...' Mirhmah said as she climbed out, 'it is simple. I have cut a little hole at one side so that you can breathe. At the moment the opening is covered, but as soon as the trunk is loaded on the wagon, you can push...' She glanced over her shoulder. 'I hear someone coming, so you must get in now. Take your things with you!'

Hastily Venetia did as she was told. It was very dark inside the trunk once the lid was closed, but the pile of clothes on the bottom was soft to crouch on, and it should not be for too long. Once she was on board, she could find somewhere more comfortable to hide. The men had arrived now. She held her breath as she heard their voices.

'Are these the master's trunks?'

'Yes. Both of them. Be careful.'

'You've no need to worry. We've handled them before.'

The voices sounded muffled to Venetia, whose heart was beating so loudly that she was afraid they would hear it. She heard the scrape of booted feet close by, then the trunk swayed as it was lifted from the floor.

'This one's heavy! What's in it?'

'That's none of your business,' Mirhmah said sharply. 'Just be careful with it, that's all.'

'We're always careful.'

She was being carried from the room. Each man had hold of an iron handle at the end, and they were finding it hard work. Venetia felt the bottom of the chest scrape the floor several times. When they reached the stairs, they slid it from one step to the next, jolting her so roughly that she almost cried out. Only the fear of discovery kept her silent as the trunk slid the last few steps and came to a halt with a bump.

'You fool! If we've broken something... Mirhmah said we should be careful!'

'Who's to know it was us? Keep your mouth shut and pick up your end. We've another to fetch after this has been loaded on the wagon.'

The trunk was lifted again. A few moments passed, then some grunting and groaning from the men as they pushed it on to the back of the wagon. During the silence afterwards, Venetia searched the inside of the trunk until she found the loose chunk of wood. It was beginning to get warm and stuffy, and, pushing the plug out, she gratefully inhaled the air let in. Mirhmah had thought of everything.

Hearing the men return, she crouched very still, feeling the wagon shake as the other trunk was loaded. There was an exchange between them, and then the wagon began to move forward slowly. A thrill of excitement ran through her. She was on her way. It was going to work!

After a while, the excitement of having made good her escape gave way to a feeling of acute discomfort. There was not much space in the trunk, and she was lying awkwardly on one foot, which was gradually becoming numb. It was also stuffy and hot, despite the airhole Mirhmah had cut. Venetia could breathe, but it was a most unpleasant way to travel, and she could hardly wait to reach her journey's end.

Fortunately, it did not take too long to reach the harbour. Venetia caught a breath of salty air, and eased her aching body. Soon she would be able to get out of her tiny prison. She heard the wagon-driver shout to his horses, and the jolting motion ceased at last. Then there were men's voices all around her, and the trunk was being dragged from the wagon.

'You'll have to rope that,' someone said. 'You'll need to winch it on board.'

Venetia's heart jerked with fright. If they bound the chest with ropes, she would be trapped inside. For a moment she considered making her presence known, but then decided to wait. Surely they would untie the ropes once the trunk had been delivered to Roldán's cabin? She was so close to achieving her goal that she might as well take another risk. After all, she could always bang and shout for help if the worse came to the worst.

The trunk was being winched on board the ship. She could feel it swaying precariously on the end of a rope as it was swung through the air. It made her stomach feel peculiar and her heart lurched. Supposing the rope broke and she went crashing to the ground? Sweat was trickling down her back, and she gulped mouthfuls of air to help calm her nerves. This was not quite as easy as she had imagined. Supposing the trunk fell into the water! There was a bump as it landed on the deck. She would be covered in bruises! Now they were carrying her again. She could hear their groans and moans at the weight of the chest. Surely she was not so heavy? Thank goodness her ordeal was almost over! Once the trunk was deposited in Roldán's cabin, she would… Ah, they were putting it down. And none too gently! If she had been made of glass, she would have been broken by now. The footsteps retreated. She must wait for a while, until she was quite certain that no one was around. Her heart was thumping so loudly that she could hear it in the stillness.

There had been silence for some time, so it must be safe. Cautiously, Venetia reached for the lever, releasing it carefully the way Mirhmah had showed her. It clicked open, and she pushed against the lid, eager to get out. Nothing happened. The lid seemed to be stuck. She pushed again, harder this time; then she realised what had happened. They had not bothered to untie the ropes. She was trapped! Panic swept through her as she strained against the unyielding lid. Suddenly the trunk had become a fearful prison. Every part of her body ached, and the air was becoming stale. She had to get out, even if it meant being taken back to the castle in disgrace. She began to beat against the sides of the trunk with her fists, shouting at the top of her voice. She had to get out! She was frightened now, her mind conjuring up all kinds of awful pictures. She screamed for help despairingly. Yet, even as she did so, she knew that it might be hours or even days before anyone heard her cries for help.

He could not leave without making one

more attempt to heal the breach between them. He had hoped that she might relent and seek him out, but it was clear that she was still angry. Roldán pushed aside the papers he had been staring at blankly for the past hour, and got to his feet. It was no use, fight it as he might, she had somehow become a part of him, worming her way under his skin so that her face haunted him day and night. There was anger mixed with the burning ache in his loins as he pictured her in the garden that morning, seeing again the defiance in those wonderful green eyes. No other woman had ever affected him this way; no, not even Marietta, though he had thought himself mortally wounded at the time. He had been a green youth then, but now he was a man and, as such, should be capable of fighting his desires – or having the determination to do something about them! Perhaps he should have carried out his threat the other evening. It was certain that he would have no peace unless he bedded the wench.

God knows, he had tried to put her out of his mind often enough these past few days, telling himself that this burning in his guts would cease once he was at sea and no longer had temptation near at hand. That was surely what he needed! He had no time for a woman in his life. Especially one who had such devastating power over his senses.

She was always with him whether sleeping or waking, and he could taste the sweetness of her lips and smell her perfume in his dreams. He had vowed that no woman would ever do this to him again, but the red-haired witch had scratched his heart and he could feel himself bleeding inside. His desire for her was almost like a sickness that he had to fight with all his strength, because if he did not... He had held back from telling her the truth about things that would be better openly discussed because he did not want to hurt her, but now he knew that he could not leave without clearing the air. She could not go back to Venice alone. It was impossible. He had wanted to spare her, but it was time she learned to accept the truth. He had been too gentle.

He pushed back his chair with a scrape. He would go to her. He would force her to listen to him, make her understand that this nonsense could not go on. His anger flared inside him as he pictured her standing before him with her eyes blazing defiance, and then he knew that he was deceiving himself. What he really wanted was to quarrel, so that he could force her to accept his kisses.

'You fool...' he said softly. 'You blind fool...'

He must talk to her, but gently. The hour was late. She might be sleeping, but he would wake her without frightening her. No doubt she would accuse him of trying again to seduce her, but he must not lose control. After she had heard what he had to say, she might begin to understand. He wanted her. Yes, he wanted her badly, but only on his own terms.

Walking towards her room, his heart quickened at the thought of her lying in bed with her glorious hair spread out on the pillow, the soft flush of sleep on her cheeks. He smiled at his thoughts, knowing that much of the blame for their quarrels lay at his own door. Another man might have taken an easier path to his goal, but it had amused him to see the fire in her eyes, and he had hoped... But perhaps it would be better this way. If she understood why he had acted as he had, she might learn to accept what the future held.

He had reached the door to her room. Mirhmah had given him the key as usual before she retired, and now he took it from a pocket inside his doublet. Hopefully, this would be the last time it was used. It had gone against the grain with him to keep her a virtual prisoner this past week, and he did not wish it to continue while he was away. He turned the key and entered.

'Venetia,' he whispered. 'Do not be alarmed! I only want to talk to you.'

The light from his lanthorn shed a yellow

glow over the room as he walked softly towards the bed, not wanting to startle her. It was not the first time he had crept in to see that she was resting peacefully. She looked so lovely when… He stared in disbelief at the empty bed. 'What…!' His eyes moved swiftly round the chamber, hoping to find her still. He saw a single glove lying on the floor. Her combs and trinkets had been swept from the side-table where they usually lay. She had gone! It was impossible! How could she escape from a locked room? Where could she go? A glint of anger lit the blue eyes. She could not have escaped without help. Someone had betrayed him!

'Mirhmah!' he shouted as he ran out into the hall. 'Almería! Where the hell is everybody? Raise the house! Come here. Damn the lot of you! She's gone – and when I find out who helped her…'

Where had she gone? The foolish wench! Roldán's fists clenched angrily as he began to shout again, banging on doors as he ran through the house. She was stubborn and proud – and when he found her… Pray God he did find her before something happened to the wretched girl!

It seemed that she had been trapped inside the trunk for ever. Her foot had no feeling in it, and her neck hurt terribly. She had shouted until she was hoarse, but no one came. Her fingers clawed the wood in helpless frustration and tears ran down her cheeks. She had tried to sleep, but it was impossible; her mind was filled with fearful pictures. Supposing no one ever came near her again! She would die slowly of starvation...

'Oh, please help me,' she murmured weakly. 'Please find me...'

It was to Roldán that she was speaking. She would rather be his prisoner than locked in this trunk. The sudden bang, as of a door being thrown open, roused her from her apathy. She knocked against the side of the trunk and shouted as loudly as she could, but her throat was dry and it came as a whisper. No one would hear her.

It seemed that her cry had been heard, however, for there was an answering shout, and then the noise of the ropes as they were swiftly disposed of. The trunk was being opened. Thank God! She felt the rush of air as the lid was lifted, gulping it gratefully. Blinking in the sudden light, she gazed up into the face of her rescuer, unsurprised to see who it was. She might have known that he would come. Uncurling with an effort, she found herself unable to rise.

'I cannot...' she whispered. 'I'm too stiff.'

'It's a wonder you are not dead,' he said, his voice harsh with emotion. 'You foolish, stubborn wench!'

He bent to lift her from the trunk, gathering her in his arms to carry her to the bed. She clasped her arms about his neck, the tears slipping down her cheek as she wept helplessly.

'I was so frightened,' she sobbed. 'Thank you for coming. Please don't be angry with me. I know I shouldn't have done it, and I'm sorry for the trouble I've caused you.'

He sat beside her on the bed, gazing at her with serious eyes. 'I'm not angry with you,' he said, and his tone was gentle. 'I'm angry with myself. It's my fault. I made you so desperate that you were willing to risk your life to escape from me. Forgive me, Venetia. I had no right...'

'No...' She shook her head as the tears choked her. 'I – I am such a fool. I thought I wanted to run away, but I was hurt and angry. If you hadn't come, I should have died, and now you'll despise me. I'm stupid, stubborn and spoilt ... and I've done nothing but cause you trouble! It will be my own fault if you send me back.'

He reached forward to wipe the tears from her cheeks with the tips of his fingers. 'No, I shan't send you back to the castle, Venetia. If you would do this to escape, you deserve your freedom. Since it means so much to you, I must let you go home.'

'No!' She caught his hand as he would have left her. 'I – I don't want...' Meeting

198

his steady gaze, she faltered, choking. 'I – I don't know what I want. I'm so confused.'

'We shall talk about your future when you are feeling better,' he said, bending to stroke the hair from her forehead. 'Try to sleep now, and don't torture yourself with foolish thoughts. None of this was your fault. I should have told you the truth before we left Rome. If I had, you would not have tried to run away.'

'What do you mean?'

'There is nothing for you to worry about. Your father placed you in my care, and I shall not betray his trust. Whatever I do is for your own good, Venetia. Remember that; it is all that matters for the moment.'

She knew that there was no point in asking more questions for the time being, so she merely nodded. He had said that he was not going to send her back to the castle, and that meant she would be with him until they reached Rome. She was too exhausted to think beyond that for the moment. As he left her, she closed her eyes, snuggling down beneath the covers. Her body still ached from the hours of confinement, but somehow her spirit felt lighter. Almería had been right when she had said it was time to stop fighting him. Tonight's ridiculous escapade had shown her clearly that she could rely on no one except him. She must simply trust in him to do what was right.

'I've never seen such fury in a man's face,' Almería said, as she fastened her mistress's gown. 'When he finally forced the truth from Mirhmah, I thought he was going to kill her!'

Venetia cast her eyes down. She knew he did not like to be thwarted, and she pitied Mirhmah. 'I – I hope he wasn't too harsh with her. I agreed to the plan. I did not think it would be so unpleasant.'

'It was dangerous and reckless! If you had been locked in there for several days, you would certainly have died.' Almería tweaked the strings of her bodice crossly. 'How could you do it? To run off without so much as a word to me! I knew there was something wrong, but I never guessed what was in your mind.'

'That's because it wasn't,' Venetia replied, sighing. 'It was Mirhmah's plan. She thought Roldán might turn to her if I was no longer there. I suppose she did it because she cares for him.'

'More likely because she hates you!'

'She couldn't have known what would happen. If the trunk had not been left tied like that, her plan would have worked. I don't believe she really meant me any harm. She just wanted me to leave his house.'

'Perhaps.' Almería frowned. 'We shall never know. When Captain Domingo discovered what she had done, he gave her her wages and sent her packing.'

'That was not kind of him. She will find it hard to get work elsewhere.'

'She was lucky that I did not have her flogged. I will not tolerate disloyalty from my servants!' Roldán's blue eyes glittered as he surveyed them from the doorway. 'You may go, Almería. Your mistress will not need you for a while.'

'Yes, sir.' Almería bobbed a curtsy.

Venetia shook a few drops of perfume on to a kerchief, keeping her face turned aside until her nurse had left, closing the door carefully behind her.

'I – I did not mean to criticise,' she said, still not looking at him. 'But I deserve to be punished as much as Mirhmah. I agreed to the plan. It– It was very wrong of me. I hope you will accept my apology.'

'I have already said that I was to blame for the whole. Had I not made you my prisoner, you would not have needed to escape. I had not realised how desperate you were until last night.'

'I was not desperate.' Venetia's fingers shook as she pleated the lace of her kerchief. 'You have often told me that I am spoilt and vain. Well, I fear that you were right, sir. My father gave me everything I asked for, and I have been used to having my own way. It has made me thoughtless and selfish.'

'Do not condemn yourself so harshly, madonna.' He stared at her as she sat there, her head bent, frowning as he saw the pallor of her cheeks. 'Almería told me that Giovanni Gavelli was as indulgent as your father.'

'He was like an uncle to me. I was fond of him, and he liked me. Or he seemed to enjoy my company...'

'I am sorry, Venetia, but he will never marry you. He is dead. I discovered that the last time we were in Rome. He was one of those killed at Nicosia. I should have told you then, but...'

'You thought it would distress me? I am saddened by his death, but – but I never loved him. The marriage was arranged by my father.' She kept her eyes downcast.

'Yet you were content to wed him? The idea of such a union did not upset you?'

She looked up then, surprised by the intensity of his gaze. 'It was my father's decision. He thought Giovanni suitable. I saw no reason to question it.'

'Then why should the idea of another marriage of convenience be so repulsive? Do you dislike me so much?'

'No – it is not that.' She hid her hands in her lap because she could not control them. Surely he must see the effect his questions were having on her? She made a determined effort to hide her emotions. 'I thought I

202

despised you when we first met, but I know now that I was wrong to do so. Even Almería has admitted that you are not the blood-stained murderer she thought you.'

'Then why did you try to run away?'

Her heart was hammering wildly in her breast. With all her heart she longed to confess her love for him, but she was afraid of the pity she might see in his eyes. 'I – I simply wanted to go home. Is that so terrible? I thought I might be able to discover news of my father. I still hope that he may be alive, you see.'

'And that was your only reason?'

'Yes.' She glanced down as she lied, fearing to let him read the truth in her eyes. She still had some pride left.

'You do not hate me, then?'

'No. I do not hate you.' She dared not believe that he was asking these questions because he really cared what she felt.

'Would it be so terrible to marry me, Venetia? You would not always have to live at the castle. I have a pleasant estate in Granada.'

She was silent, twisting her kerchief in her lap. It would be both heaven and hell to wed him, but how could she tell him the truth? She was no longer afraid that he would use the knowledge to hurt her, but he might feel pity for her, and that would be even worse.

'I see.' His words sounded ominous. She

wished that she dared to look up at him, but she knew that her eyes would betray her. How could he look into them and not know that she loved him? 'I had hoped that you would be content to marry me, and that I would never need to tell you...'

'Tell me what?' She gazed up at him then in sudden consternation. Seeing his grim expression, she was surprised. Had her refusal to answer made him look so grim? 'Is it my father? Is he dead?'

'I do not know yet, Venetia.' He sighed heavily. 'What I have to tell you concerns his fortune. Your father was deeply in debt. It was for that reason he made that desperate journey to Cyprus. Had he succeeded in getting his ships away...'

'What are you saying?' Venetia felt a cold tingling at the base of her spine. 'How bad is the situation?'

Roldán frowned, deliberately squashing all pity for her. She would not want sympathy from him. 'The Giorlandi Palace was mortgaged in the winter of 1569. It is now the property of those who lent your father money. There are some small debts still outstanding, but you will have a small income when I have managed to settle your affairs – perhaps five thousand ducats a year.'

'I have no home...' The colour drained from her face. The sum he had named was sufficient, but nothing like what she had

204

been used to. 'Then why should you wish to marry me?' She looked up at him in bewilderment, hope flaring in her heart. It surely meant that he cared for her!

'I gave your father my word that I would protect you, and that means something to me.' His eyes narrowed as he saw that she was still shocked. 'Besides, five thousand ducats is a useful sum, and, who knows, your father may yet be alive. If he has managed to save something...'

She shook her head. 'No. I believed once that it was my fortune you wanted. Now I see that you were pretending to save my pride. You knew that my father would be lucky to escape with his life. Everything he had in Cyprus is lost.'

'Then believe me when I say that I would be proud to wed you. You are beautiful and intelligent, Venetia. I am of an age when thoughts of marriage and an heir attract me. Since I need a wife, why not the daughter of a friend? Your father was my friend, though for only a short time. We found much in common. It would please me to take care of his only child.'

Each word was like a knife-thrust in her heart. She would rather that he had really wanted her for her fortune. This was humiliation indeed. If only he had made her angry, so that she could fly into a temper and pretend to hate him! He was offering her kindness – charity! He would marry her for her father's sake. She wished that she could die instantly. Yet she knew that she would never have the courage to take her own life.

'It– It is good of you to make me this offer, sir, but I…'

'You do not wish to accept it.' Roldán's face was expressionless. 'Well, I cannot force you, madonna. I thought it would be the lesser of two evils, but…'

'You misunderstand,' Venetia said miserably. 'This has all been a considerable shock. I need time to decide.'

'Then I shall give you time.' Roldán smiled slightly. 'Do not look so nervous. I have done threatening you. It was a game I played and expected to win, but now I see there is no hope of that. I must settle for less than all.'

She gazed up at him then. 'What do you mean?'

'Perhaps I shall tell you one day.' He touched the scar on his cheek with the tip of his finger. 'I, too, need time. I should have learned my lesson years ago. I am no longer an impetuous youth. I sought perfection, but perhaps that is an impossibility.'

'You speak in riddles, sir.'

'Should I speak more plainly, Venetia? No, I think not. I may be a fool, but I still hope to win.' His lips twisted wryly. 'Shall I leave you with Maddalena again?'

'If– If she will have me. I should like that.'
She smiled shyly at him.

'Then it is settled.' He glanced at the book
lying open on the table before her. 'Have
you been trying to read that?'

'Yes, I found it beneath your pillow, but I
could not decipher the script. It's written in
Arabic, is it not?'

'It is a copy of the Koran.'

'Are you a believer?' Her eyes opened wide
with surprise.

'No, I have not changed my faith. I was
born a Catholic, and will die one – though
there is much I think of interest in the
Mohammedan scriptures. I try to keep an
open mind.' He smiled at her, a glimmer of
amusement in his eyes. 'I believe you will
find other books in my trunk that will please
you more. You are welcome to read them, if
you wish.'

'Thank you. It helps to pass the time.'

'You have been much at sea this past year.
In Rome you will be able to enjoy yourself.'

'Yes. Maddalena is a pleasant companion.
I liked her very much.'

'I know she became fond of you and will
be pleased to have you as her guest again.'
He paused, looking at her oddly. 'You will
find time to consider my offer while I am
away?'

'Yes.' Venetia's fingers moved nervously in

her lap. 'I shall give you your answer when you return.'

'Then I shall not press you further, for the moment.' He turned away. 'Now you must excuse me, for I have work to do.'

Venetia nodded, knowing how much was involved at the start of a journey. He would be away for many months, especially if the fleet engaged the Turks this time. Even after the door had closed behind him, she sat staring into empty space. Everything had changed so suddenly that she found it hard to accept her situation. She was no longer a wealthy heiress, yet Roldán was still prepared to marry her. He wanted a wife and a son. It would be the kind of marriage most young women of her rank expected to make, so why was she hesitating? It was foolish to hope for something that was unlikely to happen. Roldán found her attractive and thought her suitable to be his wife, so why could she not settle for that?

But she wanted so much more! She wanted him to love her, so much that the world seemed to have no meaning if they were not together. A sad smile played about the corners of her mouth. How could he love her, when he had lost his heart to a girl in England long ago?

CHAPTER SEVEN

'I am sorry, Venetia. I had not expected this. I am afraid it means that you must stay at my house.' Roldán frowned. He had been to his friends' villa, only to discover that they had gone away to their summer home. 'At least you will have Almería with you. Maddalena's servants say that she will return in a few days. I hope that will be before I am forced to leave Rome.'

'It is not your fault; you did not intend to bring me with you. I am quite content to stay with you until she returns. If she has not arrived when you leave, I shall simply remain indoors until she does.'

'Unfortunately I must leave you alone today, though we shall dine together this evening. I have a meeting with Don John that I cannot break.' He looked at her anxiously. 'Will you be content here by yourself?'

Venetia glanced around the sala of the house he had brought her to. It was smaller than Maddalena's, for he had not expected to have female company, but it was comfortable, and sufficient for her needs.

'I shall spend my time reading or walking in the gardens. It is good to be on dry land again!' She gazed up at him, a spark of the old defiance in her eyes. 'I promise you that I shall not try to run away.'

He laughed, a gleam of amusement and something more in his eyes. 'At least, not in a trunk, I trust?'

'Never again! I have learned my lesson, sir.'

'I am glad to hear it. Is there anything you need before I go?'

'No, I have all I want. Do not let me delay you. I know your meeting is important.'

'This time, I believe we shall all agree on action. A stand must be taken against the Turkish threat if they are not to over-run Christendom.'

'You are a strange man, Roldán.' She cocked her head to one side, looking at him curiously.

It was the first time she had used his given name, and he smiled slightly. 'Why? What have I said now, madonna?'

'Oh, nothing that offends me! You read the Koran, a Corsair is your blood-brother, and you allow the Moriscos to practise their own beliefs under your roof – something that could bring you to the Inquisition's notice if it were widely known. Yet you are willing, nay eager, to fight under the Pope's banner!'

'A man may be many things, but in the end he must be true to himself. I am neither good nor evil, Venetia. When you know me better, you will understand.'

'Yes, I suppose so.' She shook her head, and sighed. 'I was so wrong about you at the start. You must have thought me an ignorant child!'

'I thought you many things! Among them, the words headstrong and reckless spring readily to mind.' He was smiling, his mockery less stinging than it had once been.

'And you were right. You also called me vain and heartless.'

'For that, I beg your pardon, madonna. You made me very angry that day. You played with fire, and you cannot blame me if your wings were scorched.'

'If you marry me, I shall probably make you angry every day!'

'Perhaps. Yet I believe there is a change in you?'

'I am older now.'

'Ah, yes. Sixteen. I think you said?' His eyes danced with mischief. 'I must buy you a gift. What would you like? Something to match the pendant?'

Her eyes opened wider, and she touched the smooth surface of the ruby at her throat. 'It was *your* gift? And the clothes?'

'Yes. I thought you might refuse it if you knew it came from me.'

'I should have done so.' Venetia bit her lip. 'I do not know what to say.'

'Say nothing. My reward has been to see

how well it becomes you.' He reached out and touched her cheek gently. 'I wanted you to have it.'

'Thank you, but please do not buy me anything more. I – I owe you so much already.'

'You owe me nothing. I was well paid for my trip to Corfu.'

She shook her head. 'I may be headstrong, but I am not an idiot, sir! I know that you have spent far more on rescuing me.'

'I have never thought you an idiot. Now, I must go. I shall see you this evening.'

She watched as he walked away, her face thoughtful. She ought to have guessed that the pendant came from him. Maddalena had been so insistent that she take it, even looking guilty when she had thanked her for all her gifts.

The house seemed terribly empty after Roldán had left it, as if its life-force had somehow gone. Venetia wandered about, too restless to settle with a book or some sewing. She was trying to sort out the confusion of her thoughts. Was she being too stubborn in holding out against this marriage? In her heart, she knew that she longed to be with him always. Would it not be better to accept her fate?

Tempted by the sunshine, she wandered into the garden. She strolled through the shaded walks, lost in her own thoughts, enjoying the scent of flowers and the birdsong all around. When the man's shadow fell across her path, she jumped with fright.

'Who are you?' she cried.

The man looked as surprised to see her as she was to see him. He hesitated momentarily, then swept off his hat and made her an elegant bow. 'Forgive me lady. I did not know you would be here. I was looking for Captain Domingo. I am a friend of his. Is he not at home?'

'No, I fear not, sir. He has a meeting with Don John. I am afraid I do not know where it is being held.'

'No matter; I shall find him. I am sorry to have disturbed you.' He smiled at her, and she saw that he was attractive, though several years her senior. 'Pray forgive me if I startled you. I would not have done so for the world.'

'You are forgiven. It was just that I did not expect to see you.'

'Nor I you. Farewell, sweet lady. I hope that we shall meet again soon.'

He turned and walked swiftly away, leaving Venetia to stare after him in surprise. How had he come to be in this part of the garden, instead of entering at the front of the house? He was not an Italian, though he spoke the language easily, but his skin was too pale, and his hair was a light brown. Perhaps he was English – a friend from the past. The thought made her frown. There was still so much in Roldán's past that she did not know.

Mirhmah had said that he had once loved an Englishwoman, and it was because of her that he bore that scar on his cheek. It was because of her that he had left his home to seek his fortune in another land. Suddenly, Venetia's heart was filled with despair. She had been considering the possibility of a marriage with him, but how could she fight the memory of a woman she had never met? The ghost that haunted him still...

Would it not be an impossible task? Even if she could bring herself to swallow her pride, it would break her heart to live with the knowledge that his heart could never be hers. No, it would be wrong to wed him, feeling as she did. Even though the pain of their parting would destroy her, she must make the decision now. She would tell him tonight after they had dined together. It would be better to end it now, rather than wait until he returned from the war...

The hour was growing late. Venetia stared at the platters of succulent food spread out on the table before her, and scowled. The roasts had gone cold, the fat congealing on the plate. She had eaten nothing but an apple and a morsel of cheese. Roldán's message that he would be late had not come in time

214

to save his servants the task of preparing a meal that was wasted on her. She could not eat alone. The day had seemed so long and empty...

Pushing away her plate, she got to her feet, feeling the frustration claw at her. Where was he? It was thoughtless of him to leave her alone all this time. Surely he could not still be at a meeting! She wandered into the smaller room that led from the dining sala, her steps slow and hesitant. Where was he? Why did he not come home? Why did it matter so much to her? She stared out of the window and into the darkness. It was so lonely without him.

Something was moving out there: a shadow that lurched unsteadily towards the house... It was Roldán! He was intoxicated. He had left her alone while he went out drinking with his friends! A surge of fury went through her. How could he be so thoughtless? She flung open the door in disgust as he tottered drunkenly towards her.

'How dare you...' she cried, then faltered, something warning her that all was not as it seemed. 'Roldán, what's wrong?'

'I've been attacked,' he said hoarsely, and she gasped as she saw the blood seeping between his fingers where he was clutching his shoulder. 'Help me inside, Venetia.'

'Lean on me,' she said, hastening to his

side. 'I thought you were drunk.'

He half smiled. 'So that's why you were ready to fly at me just now!'

'Forgive me, I did not know,' she said guiltily.

He was leaning on her heavily, his un-injured arm about her shoulders. 'I am the one who should apologise. This is not what I had planned for this evening,' he said with a wry look.

'It does not matter. Nothing matters except that you are still alive. You might have been killed!' She drew a shaky breath, and he glanced at her white face.

Inside the villa, she helped him to a wooden bench. He sat down, glancing at his shoulder. The blood had soaked through his doublet, the whole length of the sleeve.

'I shall send for a physician at once.'

'It is but a flesh-wound. It looks worse than it is.'

'You are faint from loss of blood.'

'No, one of them struck the back of my head. I shall be better in a moment or two.'

'How many were there?' She looked at him in concern. 'Where did it happen?'

'Just down the road. I was on my way home when three of them jumped out on me. I drew my sword, but I was outnum-bered. If a party of late revellers had not chanced this way, I think they might have killed me.'

'Oh no!' A cold hand clutched at her heart. 'But why? Who would want to murder you?'

'I have no idea, but it is not the first time it has happened. On the other occasion, I was warned. Unfortunately my black-robed friend was not watching over me this time.' He shook his head as she looked puzzled. 'Do not bother your head with the details, Venetia. I believe I could reach my room now if you help me.'

'Of course.' She placed his arm about her shoulders. 'Are you sure you do not want a physician to bind your wound?'

'One of the servants will see to it. It needs to be cleansed and bound, nothing more.'

'Then I shall do it myself.'

'That is generous, especially as I have left you alone so long! Don John insisted that I dine with him. I am sorry, but I could not refuse him without explaining why.'

'I understand.' She gave him a self-conscious look. 'I should not be staying in your house without a female companion. Almería does not count, because she is my servant.'

One of his friends had already seen her, so his attempts to protect her reputation would be to no avail. She did not tell him so: time enough for that another day, when he was not in so much pain.

Opening the door of his room, she helped

him to the bed. He sat down on the edge of it, wincing slightly. He tried to unfasten his doublet, but made a sorry job of it and was obliged to let her finish the work. She was as gentle as possible, but it hurt him as she eased it off. His white shirt was stained crimson all down one side. Seeing that it would not be possible to remove it any other way, she fetched a knife from among his personal items on a table, ripping the fine material so that it fell away to reveal the wound in his shoulder. It was a long, slanting cut, but, as he had said, it had not gone deep.

'Hold this against it to stop the blood while I fetch bandages and water,' she said, bunching a wad of his shirt into a little pad. 'I think it has almost stopped bleeding now.'

'Cold water will do the rest,' he agreed. 'Will you pass me that jug of wine before you go, please?'

She saw the wine-flask and frowned. 'Do you think it wise?'

'Yes, it will ease the sting – and help to cleanse the wound after you've washed it.'

There was no gainsaying him. She handed him the flask, shaking her head as she watched him extract the stopper with his teeth. He grinned and raised the jug to his lips, drinking deeply as she hurried from the room. She believed that the wine might ease his pain, but might it not also increase the chance of a fever? Until now, she had had no experience of such things, having led such a quiet life until this past year. She was not sure how best to treat his wound, and her ignorance annoyed her.

Calling to Almería, she hurried towards the servants' quarters. Cold water, bandages, advice and offers of help came in quick succession. She accepted the first three and refused the fourth. This was something she was determined to do herself. It was time that she stopped being a spoilt child and learned how to be a useful woman. Returning as swiftly as she could, she found that Roldán was still sitting where she had left him, apparently content to drink his wine. She deposited her basin on a table beside the bed and wrung a cloth out in the water, looking at him measuringly.

'I think this may hurt a little.'

'Do what you have to,' he growled, taking another drink from the flask.

She dabbed at the blood, washing round the edges of the wound before daring to touch it. It gave her little butterflies in her stomach, but she quelled her nerves and pressed the cloth firmly on the open slash. A muscle flicked in his neck, but he gave no other sign of having felt anything. When she had finished cleansing the injury, he splashed some of the wine on it, smiling as she wiped away the runlets.

'It's a waste of good wine, but it may help

to prevent infection.'

'Hold this pad against the wound while I bind your shoulder.'

'Yes, my lady.' He grinned at her, but obeyed as she crossed the linen bandages over his shoulder and round his body. 'You are very efficient.'

Venetia made a little sound of denial in her throat. She was clumsy and had probably hurt him, but he would not say so. Her hand trembled a little as she saw the dark scars on his back, some of them old wounds, but others obviously lasting reminders of whippings he had received. She remembered telling him that he could not know what it felt like to be a galley-slave, and felt a little ashamed. This man had known his share of suffering.

'You have been wounded before, I see,' she said chokingly.

'Long ago – and I was not tended by so fair a nurse. Thank you, Venetia, that feels much better.'

'It– It was nothing.' She glanced away as she saw the look in his eyes, suddenly very much aware of the intimacy of their situation. While she had been concerned with his wound, it had not occurred to her that she was alone with him in his bedroom. 'I should go...'

'Must you?' he asked, his voice suddenly low and husky. 'I wish you would stay.'

Her heart jerked as he caught her wrist, turning her so that she was forced to look at him. The expression on his face was one of such longing that she stared in surprise, experiencing a fierce surge of love towards him. She felt an overwhelming desire to hold him in her arms and run her fingers through his dark, silky hair. The attack on him tonight had shocked her, making her realise that he was vulnerable. He had always seemed so strong and powerful to her, but now she saw that he was as mortal as any other man. He could be killed. It had almost happened this evening on the streets of Rome. How much more likely was it then that he would die on the deck of his galley in a war? Suddenly all the foolish doubts and jealousies that had haunted her during the day seemed to fade away. What did the past or the future matter? It was now, this moment, that was important. She loved this man, and she wanted him as a woman wants her own special man. Her claims to be a woman were now valid; she had left her childhood behind.

'Would it make you happy if I stayed?' she asked breathlessly.

He stood up, his uninjured arm slipping about her waist so that she was pressed against him, looking up into eyes that were ablaze with passion. The intensity of his gaze made her gasp, and tremble at the knees.

'Yes... But only if you want it, too.'

'I... You know I do,' she whispered, her cheeks hot. 'I have wanted to be with you in this way for a long time. I was too proud to admit it, but surely you must have known?'

He smiled, his hand moving to caress her cheek, and then the white line of her throat. 'I have hoped that something was building up between us, but you hid your feelings well, my sweet. I was never sure whether I would be met by a raging she-wolf or an ice-maiden!'

She gave a choked laugh. 'And I was never sure whether you would attack me or mock me, sir.'

'Then we were each as foolish as the other.' Roldán bent his head to kiss her lips gently, exploring them with a tenderness that set her pulses racing. Both his hands were on her waist as she reached up to wind her arms about his neck, and she felt his involuntary flinch as she pressed against his shoulder.

'Oh – I hurt you! Perhaps we should wait until...'

'I can bear it,' he muttered, trapping her against him as she would have moved away. 'It was but a scratch.'

Her hands moved over his back tentatively, feeling the contrast of smooth flesh and the rough texture of linen. The pulses in her fingertips reminded her of how close she had come to losing him before ever really knowing him, and it sent a spiral of desire curling through her. Whatever happened in the future, she would have this night to remember. She was swept away on a tide of recklessness, abandoning all her fears on the altar of love. Perhaps he felt it, too. His kiss deepened as his tongue moved inside her mouth, exploring the softness of her inner lips and arousing the new woman in her. She shivered, arching her body against him in acknowledgement of the ache within her.

'Turn round,' he whispered. 'Let me unlace you.'

She did as she was told, lifting her hair to allow him access as he began his task. It was not easy for him, hampered by the bandages, but as the bodice loosened he took his time, kissing the back of her neck and the hollow between her shoulders, then the curve at the bottom of her back. His kisses made her shiver with delight. She stepped out of her petticoat, turning to face him with a shy smile. His eyes seemed to burn her as they dwelt on her small, firm breasts, flat belly and the dark silken patch below.

'You are even more lovely than I had imagined,' he breathed. 'Let me just look at you for a while. Lie here on the bed, Venetia.'

She obeyed silently, trembling as he stood by her, feasting his eyes on the sight that seemed to please him so much. His hand trailed slowly over her breasts, navel and thighs. Then, as if understanding a need in her that she could not voice, he thrust his breeches down over his hips, allowing them to fall to the floor. His stomach was flat and hard, his thighs strongly muscled. The sudden first sight of his pulsating manhood shocked, yet fascinated her. Almería had explained the facts of life to her, but nothing had prepared her for the vitality of his thrusting maleness. Her eyes moved up to meet his, and there was an unspoken fear in them, fear of the unknown.

'Just trust me,' he said softly, bending to kiss her once more. 'I shall not hurt you. It won't happen until you are ready for me.'

'Show me how ... I don't know,' she whispered.

'Relax, and leave the rest to me. I shall teach you the joy of loving, my lovely one.'

He bent over her, kissing her forehead first. She closed her eyes and felt his lips feather along the line of her lashes, moving down her cheekbone to her jaw and then her mouth. Her lips opened beneath his easily, responding to something known and sure. Then his kisses moved on to her throat, her breasts, nuzzling gently until the nipples hardened beneath his tongue, on to her navel and the sweet silken patch between her thighs. Each new caress made her more aware of the growing need within her. His tongue stroked the soft flesh between her thighs, causing her to writhe with some strange ecstasy that flamed her entire body. Her lips parted on a sigh, and she murmured his name.

'Roldán, I...'

'Yes, my sweet?' He smiled, and touched her cheek. 'I want it, too, and I think you are ready now.' He parted her legs and slipped between them, kneeling on the bed. 'Hold yourself to me... That's right...' His hands were on her waist, lifting her hips as he began to nuzzle at her gently, seeking entry. The heat of his throbbing manhood seemed to burn her, then a sharp thrust and she cried out as he pierced her. She felt pain and then a slow spreading warmth like molten honey, sweet and thick. He was inside her, moving with a gentle rhythm that made her gasp and lift herself to meet him, anticipating each thrust with pleasure. Feeling her response, his surging became more urgent and deeper as they rose together to the climax of love.

He had spent himself inside her as she clung to him in the moment of fulfilment. She felt the weight of his body as he lay on her, momentarily exhausted. Her lips moved on his neck, tasting the salt of his sweat as he moaned and murmured her name in a voice thick with passion, his hand moving in her hair. Then he rolled over on his side, one arm still about her waist. He was smiling at her, and the look in his eyes made her bury her face in his shoulder. She was still afraid to let him see how much he meant to her. He had her body and her heart, but something must remain her own.

'So you are mine,' he whispered, a hint of triumph in his voice.

'Am I?' She raised her head to look at him with a sigh. 'I – I suppose I am. I can hardly refuse to marry you now. It is what you intended, is it not?'

'Yes, but it was not the reason I asked you to stay.' He smiled crookedly. 'You shouldn't have been such an excellent nurse, my love.'

Did he mean that her touch had aroused him? Had she so much power over his senses? She was still so ignorant of all that love meant. He had called her tender names while he made love to her, but she did not know if he truly cared for her. Perhaps men were always thus at such times. Would it have been as pleasurable with Giovanni? She had no way of knowing. She only knew that she had never known such happiness. If only it could always be this way... She suddenly became aware that he was speaking.

'We shall be married before I leave,' he said, his hand still lazily stroking her back. 'The servants will know that you stayed with me. I have dishonoured you in the eyes of the world, so I must make an honest woman of you as soon as possible! Besides, there might be a child...' He felt her jerk away and pulled her back against him, chuckling deep in his throat. 'Be still, you foolish wench. Have I not shown you why I want to wed you?'

'Did I please you?' she asked, looking into his face and wishing she could read what was in his mind. 'I am so ignorant...'

'That's as it should be.' He smiled, bending to touch his lips lightly to hers. 'You are mine. I shall teach you all you need to know of these matters. I would not have it otherwise in the woman who is to be my wife.'

He was the master and she the slave. Something in her rebelled a little. In his arms she was willing to submit to his dominance, for it was right, but she would not always be so meek. She lifted herself on one elbow, her eyes sparking with defiance.

'It is customary to ask the bride when she wishes to be wed. I have nothing suitable to wear, and...'

'You shall have all the finery you desire,' he promised, a wicked glint in his eyes. 'Have I offended your pride, sweet lady? Do you want me to go down on bended knee and swear my undying love?'

'Now you are mocking me!' she said crossly. 'I know you do not love me any –

any more than I love you...'

'Do I not?' He arched his brow and the smile left his face. 'Then I shall not waste my breath in swearing it. Instead, I shall show you what I want of you.'

His mouth took hers with a new possessive kiss. She sensed the difference at once. This was no gentle wooing as the first had been. Now he was aggressively male, demanding where he had coaxed before. He raised her arms above her head, holding her pressed into the mattress as he rolled her on to her back and covered her with his body. This time he thrust into her with no warning, battering her with a fierce ramming motion that shocked her into an angry protest.

At first she fought, arching to try and dislodge him, but his strength made that impossible. Furious at this callous attack, she gave a cry of rage, tossing her head on the pillow and yelling abuse at him.

'Stop it, you beast! Leave me be.' She glared at him. 'What do you think you are doing? I don't want this! I don't want you to...'

He did not speak, merely lowering his head to kiss her again. His mouth ground against hers in relentless passion, his breath coming hard as if he were tortured. She tossed beneath him, fighting the response that had begun to flame in her despite herself. She would not let him see that even this cruel usage of her body excited her. Was she bewitched that she gloried in anything he did to her?

'Devil! I hate you...' she panted. 'Ah...'

Her cry was one of anger mixed with passion as he drove into her for the last time and then lay still, his body slumped on hers. She turned her face away from him, breathing hard, her cheeks stained with tears. He rolled away, lying silently at her side.

'Why?' she whispered at last. 'Why...'

'Don't you know?' he asked hoarsely. 'No, I suppose not. Well, it's time you learned what men are, Venetia. Scratch deeply enough and you will find the savage in all of us. Let that be a lesson to you.'

A lesson! What had she done that he must teach her such a harsh lesson? She moved across the bed and tried to leave it, wanting to run from him before the tears broke. He caught her arm, holding her as she struggled.

'Where are you going?'

'To my own room. You don't expect me to stay all night? We're not married yet. If you do not care what the servants think, I do.' It was a weak lie, but it saved her pride.

She looked back into his eyes, seeing the angry glint there. Why was he angry? She was the one who had been abused! As she stared at him defiantly, his eyes dropped and then he let her go.

'Run away then, Venetia!' he said, a twist of bitterness in his throat. 'Escape me while you can.'

She swooped on her clothes, pulling her petticoat over her head but not bothering with the rest. All she wanted was the safety of her own room. Keeping her face averted from the bed, she fled out of the door, her mind whirling in confusion. How could one man be two people at the same time? He had changed so suddenly! What had she done to turn him from a tender lover to a savage brute?

Alone in her own chamber, she leaned against the door, panting as if she had been running hard. She had thought she was beginning to know Roldán, but there was still a secret core that remained a total mystery. How could she marry such a man? He could do anything he liked with her! He might beat her or kill her… Yet, even now, her honesty would not let her blind herself to the truth. She had been in no danger. He had not really hurt her. She had simply been shocked by the fierce passion that had possessed him. She was trembling as she stumbled towards the bed, sinking down on to the edge. He had shocked her, and yet he excited her, too. There was such a raw, savage passion beneath the veneer of stoicism he showed to the world. Just who was the real man?

Slipping off her petticoat, she saw that

there was blood smeared on her breasts and stomach. His blood! His wound must have opened again during their lovemaking. She touched the stains with her fingertips, and shivered. He had put his mark on her. She was his now, and he had made it quite clear that he was to be the master. Should she return and bind his shoulder with clean linen? No, that would seem as if she had submitted. He could call a servant if he needed one. He had sought to teach her a lesson, but now he would learn that she had a mind of her own.

They would be married, but she would never be his slave! He wanted her body. She could give him something he needed; she had learnt that much tonight. She wanted him, too, but she would not give herself so freely again.

'I'm so glad that we returned to Rome in time for your wedding,' Maddalena said.

'It's good of you to let me stay with you,' Venetia replied. 'Roldán has to leave the day after the ceremony. Had you not come home, I would have had to stay here alone.'

'It was unfortunate that we were away when you arrived. There has been some gossip, but that will not matter once you are wed.'

'Oh, people will always talk – and I have travelled with him for many months quite

231

safely.' Venetia avoided her eyes. 'Besides, Roldán has had a slight fever for three days. It wasn't until yesterday that he was able to arrange the wedding.'

She remembered the morning after that fateful night, when Almería had told her he was not well enough to leave his bed. They had needed to call a physician, after all, and though the fever had lasted only three days, it had worried her. Was it her fault for not going back to staunch his wound? But Maddalena was speaking again...

'That was a terrible business, my dear. That he should be attacked near his own house!' She looked, and sounded, shocked. 'And he has no idea who it was?'

'None. They all wore masks, you see, and they ran off when a group of young men chanced to turn into the street. If they had not arrived at that moment, he might have died.'

'Well, I don't know what the world's coming to! If a man is not safe to walk the streets of Rome! Is Roldán able to join his ship?'

'His shoulder is healing. As I said, he had a slight fever, but it has passed. Besides, nothing would keep him from this war. Don John came to see him, and I heard them talking. They seem to be of one mind on this. It will not be Don John's fault if there is no outcome to the venture, this time. He is determined on action, and I believe he will have his way. He is a very forceful man.'

'I believe he has already left Rome?'

'Yes. It is his intention to pause at Naples. Roldán will catch up with him there. That is why he must leave so soon after the wedding.' Venetia sighed. Since she had fled from his bed, her only contact with Roldán had been a few reserved enquiries about his health. He had slipped into one of his old moods, and they were almost strangers again.

'I believe the Pope was very taken with Don John,' Maddalena said. 'At last we have a leader worthy of the name! If this venture is a success, he will surely be well rewarded.'

'His Holiness seems to think he should be given some high honour...' Venetia's thoughts trailed away. She was more concerned with her wedding the next day than with politics.

Seeing this, Maddalena smiled. 'But you have more important things to think about, my dear. I have brought you this kerchief to wear as a lucky token tomorrow. I wore it at my own wedding, and so did my mother and grandmother.'

'Oh, thank you.' Venetia threw her arms about her. 'Having you there tomorrow will be like having my – my own family!'

Maddalena embraced her. 'You know I am very fond of you. It is sad that your husband must leave so soon after your wedding, but I shall try to keep your thoughts cheerful while he is away.' She looked up as Roldán and Paolo walked into the room together. 'Ah, there they are at last. Shall we dine, my dears?'

'Have you enjoyed your gossip, my love?' Paolo bent to kiss his wife's cheek, and Venetia found herself envying them. They were so obviously fond of one another.

She turned to find Roldán at her side, evidently intending to take her into supper. Walking just behind the other two, she glanced up at the grim face of the man at her side. 'Are you feeling better now?'

He looked down at her, but did not smile. 'I am quite recovered. Do not worry, I shall be there when Paolo brings you to the church tomorrow.'

'Of course. I was not concerned about that.'

'Were you not? You were certain that I would keep my promise to wed you, then?'

She flushed as his eyes seemed to scorn her. 'Why do you taunt me so? Are you angry with me?'

'Why should I be?' He sighed, and his expression lightened slightly. 'I thought you might still be angry with me, Venetia.'

He deserved that she should be, but she was not. She was puzzled and a little hurt, but not angry. 'I am not ... angry...'

He sensed that there was more. 'What, then?'

She shook her head as Maddalena glanced at them over her shoulder. 'Now is not the time, sir.'

'Will the time ever be right, I wonder?' His enigmatic look puzzled her, but he smiled as he saw her frown. 'Do not bother your head, Venetia. Tonight is to be a celebration with our friends. Be happy if you can. It is your right.'

'I am … happy.'

'Are you?' He looked into her face, seeming surprised. 'Then I am content.'

There was no more time for private conversation then. The evening was given over to laughter and gossip with their hosts. Having been away while Don John was being fêted in Rome, Maddalena wanted to hear about everything she had missed. Roldán was at his most charming, entertaining them all with witty stories about the various power struggles that went on among the leaders of the fleet.

This was yet another facet of his nature that was new to Venetia. She listened to him, finding herself fascinated by his charms and obvious intelligence. It opened up fresh windows in her mind, giving her a glimpse of what it might actually be like to be his wife. She saw herself presiding at his table, surrounded by people like Maddalena and

Paolo. She saw children's faces at her feet, and the seasons changing day by day...

'He has a habit of sweeping his hair back like so...' Roldán paused in his description of one of his commander's mannerisms to glance at Venetia. 'But you are tired, my love. Perhaps it is time I left?'

She blushed, aware that her thoughts had wandered. 'No, I was listening, truly I was. I have noticed Don John's habit of pushing back his hair when hatless. I think everything he does must be noticed.'

'Then you have felt it, too.' Roldán's eyes gleamed with pleasure. 'There is something of greatness about him. I believe we must succeed with such a leader, even though they hedge him about with petty restrictions.'

Thereafter, the talk was of the war. Venetia took little part in it, though she smiled and answered whenever a question was directed at her. For the most part, her thoughts were centred on the man who was so soon to be her husband.

They were married in a small church in a quiet corner of the city, far away from the busy squares, fountains and the crumbling remains of the Colosseum. Modern Rome was a city of beautiful buildings, teeming with pilgrims, priests and its hard-working citizens, but it was still possible to find peace and tranquillity among the cool climes of an ancient church. Here, at the very heart of the Christian world, Venetia took her vows beneath the rainbow colours of a glorious stained-glass window, and the shadow of a heavy iron cross.

Her face was very pale as she knelt in prayer before the altar. The priest's intoning hardly reached her numbed brain, though somehow she managed to answer when required. It all seemed so far away, as though it were happening to another girl in another place. She was really only aware of emerging into the sunshine and hearing the sound of birds' wings as a flock of white doves rose into the air. Their bodies were pale and silver in the sunlight, like the messengers of heaven. She smiled, and breathed deeply of the scented air.

Then everything suddenly came to life around her. Maddalena was there, smiling at her, and several more of Roldán's colleagues, faces she had come to know well from her travels on his galley. Almería was wearing a new gown given to her by her master, and a smug look about her mouth.

Maddalena and Paolo had insisted on holding a reception for them. It was a small but merry party as the guests danced in the gardens under a benign sun. There was an abundance of wine and food laid out on a shaded patio, but neither the bride nor the groom ate or drank very much. The bride was noticeably quiet, though beautiful in her gown of cream silk and silver lace. The groom smiled and joked throughout it all, accepting the taunts of his friends good-naturedly, but his eyes were seldom far from the face of his lovely wife, following her wherever she went.

'It seems you were right,' Paolo said to him as they stood beneath the shade of a tree while Venetia danced. 'I must admit I thought you foolhardy at the time, but you have achieved what you set out to do.'

'Have I? I wonder...' Roldán frowned as he watched the bride laugh up at her partner. 'You will take care of her while I'm away, Paolo? If anything should happen, I rely on you to see that she is accepted by my uncle. My affairs are in order. You should have no trouble.'

'Knowing you, there will be little for me to do. But you will return, my friend.'

'Of course. It is only that I wanted to be sure. I would not have her left alone and friendless a second time.'

'Maddalena would see to that. She dotes on her as if she were her own child.' Paolo looked at him uncertainly. 'At first, I was not sure. I thought her a little cold ... and perhaps selfish. Love has softened her, I think...'

'Love?' Roldán's eyes narrowed as he watched Venetia. Had Paolo seen something he had missed? 'She agreed to wed me only because she had no choice.'

'You cannot truly believe that!' Paolo smiled, and shook his head in mock reproof. 'Are you so blind, my friend? Don't let pride mislead you. She has hers, too, you know.'

'Undoubtedly…' Roldán grinned suddenly. 'Excuse me, I must dance with my wife.'

As she saw him moving towards her, Venetia's heart jerked to a stop and then raced on. He was smiling at her in the way that always made her knees go weak. It scared her so much that she wanted to run away. After fleeing from his bed, she had vowed that he would never have such an easy conquest over her again, but when she saw him looking at her like that, all her determination to hold out against him seemed to melt in the heat of her love for him. How could she refuse him when her whole body cried out for his?

She was trembling as he took her hand for the galliard. It was a lively country dance, meant to be enjoyed. By the time they had finished whirling and swirling, Venetia was out of breath, her eyes shining and her cheeks flushed.

'I think we should leave now,' he said. 'Say goodbye to Maddalena, my sweet.'

Embraces and kisses followed. They were showered by the good wishes of their friends

239

as they climbed into the wedding coach, which had been duly decked with flowers and ribbons and a few unspeakable objects placed there by Roldán's colleagues. In a few hours, Venetia would return to Maddalena's house, but the night belonged to her husband. He was sitting opposite her as the coach lumbered through the streets – streets that had settled under the hush of a summer evening – and watching her intently. It made her nervous.

'At what hour must you leave?' she asked, twisting a ribbon between her fingers.

'Soon after dawn.' A gleam of malice showed in his eyes. 'Don't worry, my sweet, there will be time enough for you to perform your wifely duties.'

'Must you always goad me?' she muttered, her restless hands fraying the silk in sudden frustration. 'I asked only out of politeness. It does not matter to me when you leave.'

'Does it not? Then you will not miss me while I am gone?'

'Well, perhaps…' She scowled at him. Why must he ask foolish questions? Of course she would miss him! 'I am used to you. I should not have married you if I did not wish to be your wife.'

'Would you not? You shock me, Venetia.' His brows arched. 'After I seduced you, I believed you had no choice. I see I was mistaken in your character!'

'You are a devil!' Venetia cried, furious with him now. 'It amuses you to mock and taunt me. Have done; I shall not easily forgive you for this.'

'But I enjoy teasing you,' he murmured. 'You are so beautiful when your eyes take fire like that. Besides, it is my nature, and you must learn to live with it however tiresome it may be.'

'I suppose I must.' She eyed him warily. Was she at fault for firing up so swiftly? If he was merely teasing her, perhaps it was foolish to be angry. 'I have never been teased. My father spoilt me, and I had no brothers or sisters.'

'That's better,' he said as he saw her relax. 'Sometimes one must laugh or weep – I prefer to laugh. You have more power than you know, madonna. You must use it to make me your slave.'

'You! My slave?' She stared at him in surprise. 'How could I enslave you?'

'A clever woman can always twist a man round her little finger. Have you not seen the way Paolo dotes on Maddalena?'

'He adores her.' Venetia smiled wistfully, unaware of how much of her inner self she was revealing. 'I have no such power over you.'

'Would you like to have me at your feet, begging for the favour of a smile?'

'Yes... No!' She laughed as he pulled a

face at her. 'I don't know. Since it will never happen, it does not matter. I should like…'

'What would you like?' His eyes were suddenly alert.

Her heart pounded wildly. Now was her chance to confess her love. She was certain that if she did so, he would be the tender lover she wanted. Their life would be contented and peaceful, spent in mutual respect. He would be the master in his home, generous and giving in every way but one. She would never have his heart. It was not enough.

He was still waiting for her answer as the coach lurched to a shuddering halt. They had arrived. She looked at him, her eyes sparkling with mischief. Two could play his little game!

'I should like to get out of this gown. Almería laced me too tightly, and I can scarcely breathe!'

CHAPTER EIGHT

Roldán saw the invitation in her eyes, and felt a surge of hot desire in his loins. God, but she was beautiful! She retained the innocence of a child, which combined with the sensual allure of a lovely woman to become a devastating attraction. Sometimes he felt that she used those green eyes of hers to drive him to the point of madness. She was infuriating, stubborn, carelessly cruel and yet adorable. All the things that Marietta had been... It was a woman such as this who had betrayed him years before. In his youth he had been led like a lamb to the slaughter, believing every word, sigh or tear she shed, and discovering her perfidy only when it was too late. Was he a fool to let Venetia affect him so deeply? There were times when he thought... But she had denied her love when they lay together in the aftermath of intimacy. Why she should lie at such a time, if not to torment him, was a mystery.

He offered his hand to help her from the coach, resisting the temptation to crush her to him and carry her straight to his room. He had given way to his baser urgings out of anger once; it must not happen again.

However much she provoked him, he would not let his guard slip again. She was his wife now and he must take care over their relationship if it was not to be totally destroyed. Earlier, he had felt a quick surge of jealousy when watching her dance in another man's arms, but he had hidden it beneath the mask he habitually wore. Whether she loved him or not, she was his, and he would keep her. Once she had children to fill her days, she would mature into the woman she was always claiming to be.

'Go to your room, Venetia,' he said, giving no outward sign of the clamouring of his pulses. 'I have some business to attend to, but I shall come to you within the hour.'

He thought he saw disappointment in her eyes as she turned away, and he was tempted to call her back and kiss her. She had obviously expected some reaction to her flirtatious remark and perhaps he was unkind not to pamper to her. A faint smile quirked his lips. If only she knew the true extent of her power! He wanted her badly at this moment; so much that it moved in him like a sickness, a grinding ache in his guts that would not be denied. It would take every bit of his will-power to hold back for the hour he had promised her.

Seeking the solitude of his own chamber, he took a sheaf of documents from his sea-chest. It was true enough that he had work to do, for he must make sure that his affairs were in order before he left her, though he doubted his ability to concentrate on the figures before him with the smell of her perfume filling his senses. He had thought that bedding her once might bring him peace of mind. Instead, it had lit a fire that threatened to consume him...

Clothed only in a fine silk robe that revealed more of her than it hid, Venetia sat brushing her hair and staring out of the window at the glorious red-gold sky. She had sent Almería away, preferring to be alone with her thoughts. She was married now. His wife. And he had made it clear that he intended to exercise his rights whenever he chose. He had told her once that he always exacted payment to the full, and she had no reason to disbelieve him.

Part of her was impatient for him to come to her, though a tiny corner of her mind rebelled. Was it always a woman's duty to submit to her husband when *he* chose? Should it not be a mutual need that came about through shared pastimes – a look, a touch of the hand, a smile? It would not be hard to accept his caresses, for she drew as much pleasure from them as he, but was there not something more? Sighing, she laid down her hairbrush and stood up, moving towards the open window to breathe in the scented air. Perhaps she was asking too much of life.

There was a pale moon now. She stared up at the sky, feeling a strange sadness move inside her. It was useless to yearn for something that could never be hers; she must be content with what she had. She did not turn as the door opened, standing perfectly still until he came to her.

His arms went round her waist, holding her gently as his lips brushed the back of her neck and then her bare shoulder. She felt him shudder, and a shiver of anticipation ran through her. As the hot desire surged, she knew that, for tonight at least, this was enough. Lifting her face to receive his kiss, she abandoned all attempts to deny the feeling between them. It might only be physical desire on his part, but it was strong and urgent. If she could not touch his heart, at least she could enflame his senses.

Feeling her response, Roldán's arms closed about her, crushing her against him as the ache became a fierce, burning need. 'Come to bed, my beautiful wife,' he murmured huskily. 'Let this night be an end to dissent between us. Life can be good for us, Venetia, if you will only accept me for what I am.'

'Take me and use me as you will,' she whispered. 'I cannot deny you.'

'I shall never willingly hurt you again,' he said, his voice cracked with passion. He groaned as he saw the total surrender in her, feeling her body sway pliantly against him as he bent to gather her in his arms. 'Tonight you shall be the mistress, my sweet, and I your adoring slave...'

She smiled at him as he laid her gently on the bed. When he looked at her like this, she could almost believe that he loved her.

She was swept away on a tide of passion. If she had thought his lovemaking tender the first time, tonight she learned that there was much more to the art of love. He was a master. His lips, tongue and hands adored her, seeking only to bring her pleasure. Never could she have guessed what delight he could bring, nor that she would give such joy in her turn. It was like a fevered dream, transporting her to paradise.

When at last he lay still beside her, the tears slipped down her cheeks. She drifted into sleep, not really aware of all that had passed between them or the promises he had made. Surely it was not real? This warm, tender, caring lover could not possibly be the rogue who mocked and teased her so unmercifully! Yet, if he was, she was more fortunate than she had guessed. The future gleamed golden and tantalising before her. She was half sleeping, half dreaming when she nestled her head against his shoulder.

'I love you,' she murmured, and did not know she had spoken.

He saw that she slept, and smiled, touching his lips to her forehead with a kind of reverence. 'Would that I dared believe you, my green-eyed houri,' he said softly.

It was light when Venetia awoke, stretching lazily as her eyelids flickered. Why did she feel so good this morning? Her body glowed all over and a sense of contentment filled her. Remembering what had taken place a few hours earlier, she reached out to touch her husband.

The bed was cold and empty beside her. She felt shocked, sitting up in alarm to see with her eyes what her mind had already perceived. He was leaving this morning, but he could not have gone without saying good-bye! She knew that he had. The morning was well advanced, the sun pouring through the window. Her gaze fell on a folded paper and a small casket on the table beside the bed.

She opened his letter first. It was brief and to the point. She had been sleeping, and he did not want to disturb her. He asked her to think of him while he was gone, and hoped that he would soon be with her once more. It was an unsentimental note with no words of love, no mention of the hours they had spent in each other's arms.

Venetia crumpled his letter into a ball, disappointment welling up. It had been so wonderful for her; was it no more than a night of pleasure for him? How could he leave her like this with so much unsaid between them? Surely he would not have done so if he really loved her? A terrible feeling of despair washed over her. He had gone, and she had not kissed him goodbye. She had never told him how much she loved him, never allowed him to see that the world would have no meaning for her now without him. Supposing he never came back? Her throat stung with emotion and there was a painful tightness in her breast. She could not bear to lose him – not after that wonderful night they had spent together. He was a part of her now, and she felt empty without him.

She smoothed out his letter and pressed it to her lips, smiling slightly as she began to recall some of the things he had said to her during their loving. Funny, warm, tender words that must surely mean he cared for her. She sighed and lay back against the pillows, wishing he were still by her side. She wanted to talk, to learn all the things she did not know about him.

It was some time before she remembered to open his gift. The casket was wooden and lined with velvet. Inside she found a ruby ring, earrings and bracelets to match her pendant. She draped them on herself, smiling with pleasure. It was typical of him to leave his wedding present by her bed instead of giving it to her himself. He was generous, but he did not like to be thanked. Her father had always made much of presents, expecting cries of delight and hugs from his daughter, but Roldán was almost too afraid to be seen to give lest it revealed too much of his inner self. She sat up, her heart thumping wildly. Had she stumbled on the truth? Was his mockery a form of self-defence – his icy calm a mask to hide the strong emotions beneath? Was he afraid to confess his love for fear of being hurt?

He had been hurt badly once when he was very young. She had sensed it even before Mirhmah told her of his lost love, but she had been too immature to understand what it might mean. She had felt the future was golden last night – but if he truly loved her! And surely he did? How foolish she had been to let Mirhmah's lies destroy her. All those wasted days and nights...

Her thoughts were disrupted by a tap at the door. She pulled the coverlet up to her chin to hide her nakedness as she called out that Almería might enter. It was not that she was shy of her nurse, but her flesh still tingled from Roldán's touch, and she was afraid that the marks of his loving might be visible.

'I am sorry to disturb you, my lady, but the lady Maddalena is waiting. I explained that the master's orders were to let you sleep...'

Suddenly Venetia's shyness fell away from her. She threw back the covers and jumped out of bed, her eyes sparkling with mischief.

'Very well, Almería, you need not look so pleased with yourself! You were right. I do love him – and I think that perhaps he loves me just a little.'

'I have known it from the start, or almost...' Almería had the grace to look contrite as she saw her mistress's indignant stare. 'Well, since he took us to Valencia, anyway.' She sniffed and tried to look cross. 'So you are not as miserable as you had feared, then?'

'I am not miserable at all! At least, I would not be if my lord was here with me.' She smiled brilliantly at Almería. 'But I shall not let myself pine. I mean to ask Maddalena to teach me all the things a wife should know, so that when my husband returns he will be proud of me.'

'Oh, I do not think you need bother your head too much with such things,' Almería smirked. 'From the look in his eyes this morning, I think you already know how to please your husband well enough!'

In June the Turks tried to raid Crete. It was a calculated measure intended to compel the Venetians to break up their fleet, thereby ensuring that the Holy League would never be the powerful force they feared it might come to be. Since the wasted efforts of the previous year, the Venetians had worked frantically to build up their naval strength, building more and more galleys. Their commander of the fleet, Marcantonio Quirini, had skilfully penetrated the blockade of Famagusta, bringing help to the beleaguered citizens. Now he used his daring to execute a clever move to prevent a major landing on Crete. Even so, the Turks managed to launch several lightning attacks on the villages along the coast, capturing the peasants and enslaving them. Their purpose was to stop the Venetians from keeping the rendezvous at the Messina Strait. In Venice itself, the citizens were preparing for an attack at the very heart of their empire.

By now, however, the Doge had realised that the Turkish threat must be met by force. Since the only way to do this was to join the Spanish fleet at Messina, Marcantonio Quirini was ordered to take his galleys there, risking all that the measure entailed. It was a brave gesture that could win or lose an empire.

Sultan Selim II ordered his own commander to Lepanto, a naval base in a sheltered bay within the Gulf of Patras, where the fleet could be protected by twin fortresses on either side. It seemed as though the Sultan's forces were invulnerable. The commander of the fleet was apparently content to spend the winter of 1571 safely ensconced in his retreat.

On his journey to the appointed rendez-vous with the Venetians and the others who made up the League, Don John visited the city of Naples. The people welcomed him enthusiastically, seeing a saviour in this handsome young man, for there was no city on the Mediterranean that had not suffered from the Turks. Dressed in white and gold, and mounted on a fine, spirited horse, he drew the hearts of the Neapolitans along with their cheers as he rode into the city. It was possible that few of them noticed the soberly-dressed man riding a few paces behind him, though there were a few flutters in some female hearts as the handsome Spaniard passed by. There was something striking about the clean-cut features, black hair and bright blue eyes. It was noticed by two women standing together on a balcony decked with ribbons and flags.

'Is that not Captain Domingo?' the fair-haired girl asked as she saw him. 'The man who came to dine with Marco dei Giorlandi and his daughter in Rome.' She crossed herself piously. 'God rest her soul!'

'She should have stayed on Corfu – or gone home to Venice,' Katrine replied, pulling a face. 'Yes, I believe it is he. I wonder if he will be at the reception tonight.'

'Oh, I should think he's sure to be,' Isabel

replied, her eyes opening wide as she saw the look on her companion's face. 'You wouldn't dare, Katrine! What would your husband say?'

'He will not notice.' Katrine's mouth turned down sourly. 'He never notices anything I do... He is always too busy counting his money. That's what comes of marrying a merchant.'

Isabel looked at her, seeing the discontent in her face. Katrine's husband had given her fine clothes and jewels, but it was clear that she was dissatisfied in her marriage.

'You should have seized your chance with the Spaniard in Rome!'

'He never looked at me while she was there. Anyone could see that he was mad for her, though I don't know why. She was a cold cat.' Katrine's face was marred by spite. 'Anyway, she's not here now, and if I do not lie with him tonight, it will not be my fault!'

'Stop wearing yourself out with all this work,' Maddalena commanded. 'You have scarcely left the stillroom for a week. Tonight I am taking you to a masquerade ball at the Orsini Palace, so go and put on the gown and mask you will find on your bed.'

Venetia wiped her hands, frowning slightly. 'I'm not sure I want to go. I've heard that these affairs can be a little wild. I'm not sure that my husband would approve.'

'Nonsense!' Maddalena shook her head and laughed. 'He made me promise to introduce you into our society, and tonight will be as good a chance as any. Everyone will be there. Roldán will not expect you to hide away like a little mouse, my love. He is an intelligent man, and he enjoys company. If you want to hold his interest for more than a few months, there are more important things to learn than how to make a few preserves or remedies. Innocence is all very well in a bride, but you need more than that to be certain that your husband will be faithful to you.'

Venetia nodded, remembering how he had teased her just after they were married. He had told her that a clever woman could always twist a man round her finger, almost as if he were inviting her to try her feminine wiles on him. He had pointed out Paolo's devotion to his wife after so many years of marriage.

Would Roldán quickly tire of her if she did not learn these things? Maddalena seemed to think so, and she must be right. There was so much to learn while he was away, but she was determined that she would be everything he wanted in a wife when he returned.

Already, it seemed so long, though it had only been a few days. Every morning she took his letter from the little casket, reading each word over and over again. Pray God he would come back to her safely when the war was over!

'I shall go and get changed at once,' she said, laughing nervously. 'You will tell me what to say, won't you, Maddalena?'

Maddalena arched her fine brows. 'Usually it is best to say very little! A smile or a look is more effective. You are young and pretty – and married. You can flirt discreetly and no one will think the worse of you, but take care not to be lured into the gardens alone. Roldán will kill me if I allow you to be touched by scandal!' She laughed as she saw Venetia's surprise. 'Your husband's reputation with the sword would normally be enough to protect you from unscrupulous men, but he is not here.'

'Have no fear! I do not wish to be kissed in the gardens.'

At least, not by anyone but Roldán, Venetia thought as she hurried away. If only he were coming with her to this ball tonight!

It was the first time she had worn all the jewellery Roldán had given her. Dressed in the grey silk gown and black velvet mask that Maddalena had supplied, Venetia knew that she looked sophisticated and mysterious. Entering the Orsini ballroom on Paolo's arm, her heart jerked with fright as she looked around. There were so many people, strangers to her. Their jewels glittered and flashed in the light of many candles supported in huge iron chandeliers that hung from the arched ceilings. The floor was of polished marble, as were the columns and exquisite statues that adorned the long room.

'You are quite free to dance with any man who asks you,' Maddalena said. 'Do not take off your mask at any time, no matter who begs you to – and do not leave the ballroom. Otherwise, you may do as you please.'

'May I have the honour of the first dance, Venetia?' Paolo asked. 'Once you have been seen to dance, you will be besieged with partners.'

Maddalena having encouraged her, Venetia accepted his offer. It was a slow, stately dance, and Paolo was light on his feet. She enjoyed herself and was sorry when it ended, but, as he had forecast, she was immediately surrounded by young men wanting to partner her.

She chose the most insistent and hinted at future success to her disappointed suitors. There was a vast difference between dancing with a masked stranger and with her friend's husband. The man paid her extravagant compliments, his eyes sparkling behind the velvet mask. She noticed that he held her hand a little longer than necessary, and that his manner was distinctly ardent. Now she understood why Maddalena had been so insistent that she must not leave the ballroom with a stranger. It was not easy to keep him at a distance, but remembering her friend's advice, she managed to do so without either being cold or losing her temper.

'You are the loveliest woman here tonight,' he whispered, as their dance came to an end. 'Will you dance with me again later?'

'Perhaps...' She fluttered her fan flirtatiously. 'If you can tell me why I should favour you above any other man here tonight?'

'Because I have a prior claim. We have met before. I know you, madam, though you may not know me.'

She shook her head. 'I think you are trying to gain an unfair advantage, sir. I do not believe we have met. I have not been into general society much until this evening.'

'I know....' He smiled mysteriously, deliberately attempting to arouse her curiosity. 'There is much I know about you. Perhaps I shall tell you where we met – if you will promise me another dance?'

'You are a wicked flirt, sir,' she cried, enjoying herself. Maddalena had been right. This was amusing. It was the way she ought to have behaved when Roldán teased her instead of flying into a rage every time. 'Do not press me now. If I decide you deserve it,

I may dance with you again.' She gave him a little smile and turned away.

She was soon claimed by another eager gallant. Partner followed partner, each as charming as the first, although she suspected that their intentions were not always honourable. She had several invitations to view the gardens whispered in her ear, but refused them all. It was exciting to be courted by so many men. She had never been complimented so much in her life, and she found it enjoyable. If only Roldán had been here to see her triumph, they could have laughed about it afterwards when she lay in his arms. She would have liked to see a spark of jealousy in his eyes, so that she could tease him a little. Then, later, when she lay beside him, she would show him that he had no cause to be jealous.

It was towards the end of the evening that her first partner approached her again. She hesitated a moment, then gave him her hand.

'Now tell me, when and where did we meet, sir? I am curious to know how you can be so sure when I do not recall it at all.'

'Alas, I obviously made less impression on you than you did on me.' He sighed deeply. 'It was in a garden. I came in search of your husband – though he was not then your husband, I think?'

'No. It– It was just before we were married.'

Venetia looked at him curiously. Yes, there was a likeness, she decided. She had forgotten all about him. 'Did you find Roldán that day?'

'Unfortunately not. I had to leave Rome for a while, and when I returned, I heard that he had departed to join the fleet.'

'He will be disappointed to have missed you. You are English, are you not?'

'How did you guess?'

'I'm not sure. Were you a friend of Roldán before he left England?'

'Yes. A close friend at one time. We were almost like brothers. We studied together – fenced, swam and rode together.' He paused, staring at her oddly. 'He will return to Rome?'

'Oh yes. I am staying with friends until he does.'

'Then you are well cared for and protected. I am glad to hear it, for these are dangerous times with so many strangers in the city. Would your friends think it strange if I called on you occasionally?'

'Why should they?' Venetia gazed up at him. 'May I ask your name, sir?'

'Have I not told you? How remiss of me! I am James Lodden, and here in Rome on Queen Elizabeth's behalf. Although she is not a Catholic, she takes a keen interest in the Holy League and hopes to hear of its success.'

'Roldán told me that some Englishmen had joined the fleet. You were not one of them?'

'Alas no, my queen would not permit it.'

'I have heard much of your queen. There are so many stories abroad that it is hard to know what is true. She is much loved and admired by her subjects, I believe?'

'Indeed she is. They call her Gloriana.' Lodden's mouth twisted in a strange smile. 'Some call her the Protestant bastard, but we do not speak of these things in her presence.' He bowed low as the music ended. 'Thank you for allowing me to dance with you, madam. Please excuse me now. I shall call upon you soon, if I may?'

She nodded, and he walked away. Her eyes followed him as he mingled with the crowd and was lost to sight. If he knew Roldán well, there were many things he could tell her about him. He might even know the name of the woman he had loved... She was reasonably sure that Roldán no longer cared for her, but she could not help being curious about the woman in his past. Besides, the stranger was charming, and it could not hurt to let him call...

Roldán looked down into the eyes of the dark-haired girl, recognising the clear invitation. He had seen that look many times before in other women, and knew what it meant. Katrine was bored with her husband and wanted some excitement. Having seen the man she had married simply for his money, he could understand her dissatisfaction, but it made him angry. Were all women faithless whores? How could he be sure that his own wife had not already found someone to help her pass the time while he was at sea?

He scowled at Katrine, turning away from her to find a quiet corner on the balcony where he could be alone with his thoughts. Should he have told Venetia what was in his mind before he left? Yet even that would not have ensured her loyalty, if she did not truly love him.

Suddenly he was remembering another woman. A young, pretty girl with fair hair and misty blue eyes – eyes that always seemed to be filled with tears. How Marietta had wept when she told him about her husband's cruelty. She had shown him the bruises on her wrists where the earl had tied her with cords before venting his vile lust on her.

Knowing that the Earl of Lodeberry was depraved and a disgusting pervert, Roldán had believed all the stories she confided in him. He had felt pity for her, and when she turned to him for comfort, he had naturally offered her his services along with his heart – his tender, youthful heart. She was about his own age, sweet, innocent and in trouble. No young man in his position could have resisted what she offered. His father had accused him of seducing his patron's wife. In fact, Marietta had seduced him. He had wanted to comfort her and protect her from the attentions of the earl's son, who, she had told him, was continuously pestering her.

'What a fool I was,' Roldán said to himself. He stared at the dark blue of the night sky, a wry smile playing about his mouth as he saw himself as a raw, inexperienced youth.

The smile faded as he stroked the scar on his cheek. Carlton had seen them together. He had gone straight to his father, and the earl had taken a cruel revenge, taunting the boy as he watched his servants thrash him with a horsewhip. Seeing his fury, Roldán's only thought had been to protect Marietta.

'I forced her to lie with me,' he had cried as he staggered beneath the cruel lash. 'She is totally innocent!'

'She is a whore!' the earl grunted. 'I knew it when I took her for a bride, but she pleases me.'

Roldán had challenged him to a duel for insulting Marietta, but he had laughed, mocking him for his foolishness. The beating had been severe. He had been more dead than alive when a servant carried him to his father's house.

An odd glint entered Roldán's eyes when

he recalled that last conversation with his father. He had defended Marietta's honour so fiercely before he left for that fatal meeting with Carlton. He had caught the earl's second son as he was about to enter his mistress's house. Backed by three of his friends, he had challenged Carlton to a duel. The son had more courage than his father, and had looked at Roldán mockingly.

'You're a fool, but I'll fight you,' he had said.

It had been a desperate battle between them. Carlton was older and stronger and an experienced swordsman, but Roldán was driven by something deep inside: pride, and a need to regain his self-respect after the beating. At last he had plunged his sword deep into the other man's side. As the sword fell from Carlton's hand and he crumpled to his feet, he smiled strangely.

'You really are a fool, Roland,' he whispered, then he fell face down on the ground.

At that moment he heard a woman scream. It was a terrible, animal scream of pain that he would never be able to forget. She had come rushing out of the house clad only in a scanty nightgown. He had watched as she knelt beside Carlton, cradling his limp body to her breast. He had seen Carlton's blood seep into the white material, stunned and disbelieving as she sobbed out her grief.

'Marietta!' he whispered. 'I don't understand… I did it for you…'

She looked up at him then, the hatred blazing in her eyes. 'We used you,' she hissed. 'You were the scapegoat to hide our love from his father.'

'I did not know,' he said helplessly. He was shocked by the hatred and raw pain in her eyes. How could he have guessed that she was in love with a man she pretended to hate?

'You were a fool,' she spat bitterly. 'How could you imagine I wanted a boy in my bed? It was always him I loved. Now you've killed him – and I hate you!'

He had walked away with her taunts ringing in his ears. She had tricked him with her tears and false smiles. She was a faithless whore, just as the earl had said she was. For her sake he had endured a savage beating – and he had killed a man! A man he had liked and respected once. The bitterness of the humiliation she had heaped on him made him want to vomit. He had learned a harsh lesson. He would never trust another woman as long as he lived!

It was a vow that had stayed with him, making him the man he was today. Only his sense of humour had saved him from becoming totally bitter. He had taken women to his bed only to relieve a physical need – until he had met Venetia. His mouth curved as he remembered their last night together. How much he had enjoyed teaching her the pleasure of loving. He recalled the fire and the passion his caresses had aroused. She had responded so sweetly, with an innocence that delighted him: she at least was no experienced whore. He felt a deep longing for her, wanting her here beside him. At that moment he knew that his life was about to change. When the war was over, he would take her to Granada and spend his days in making her happy – and his nights. How he wanted her at this moment! The yearning moved in him, making him breathe deeply as he felt that he could almost smell her perfume. But no, she would never wear a scent that was so heavy and cloying.

'Captain Domingo? I thought I saw you come out here. I followed you as soon as I could get away.' Katrine drew a sharp breath as he turned towards her and she saw the blazing anger in his eyes.

'Go back to your husband, Katrine,' he said, his mouth curling with scorn. 'I don't want you.'

He pushed past her, leaving her to stare after him in dismay.

'May we not walk together in the gardens for a while?' James Lodden asked, taking advantage of Maddalena's preoccupation with a servant for the moment.

'No, I may not be alone with you,' Venetia

replied with a little smile to soften her words. 'I am sure you mean no harm, but my husband might come to hear of it – and he is a formidable swordsman!'

'Yes, I know.' James frowned, an odd look in his eyes. 'Yet he was my friend, and I believe he would acquit me of any dishonourable intention towards his wife. I shall not attempt to seduce you, madam. It is only that it is such a lovely day, and...'

'Very well.' The sun was tempting her outside, too. 'But we must stay within my friend's view in the courtyard.'

'It is enough.' He smiled, and offered her his arm. 'I am honoured by your trust in me. I believe you know I would do anything to serve you?'

Venetia nodded, giving him an uncertain smile. This was not the first time he had called since the ball at the Orsini Palace some weeks before. He was very attentive, always seeking her out if she made an appearance in society, and she found him a charming companion. He managed to give an impression of devotion without ever stepping over the line she had drawn. She rather liked him, especially as he had told her stories about Roldán when he was a youth – stories of tree-climbing escapades in the bishop's gardens, and midnight swims in the river when their tutor imagined they were safe in bed. It was all very innocent and amusing, but so far there had been no mention of a woman. Perhaps if they were alone for a while, she might find a way of asking the question that burned in her mind.

'Are you to attend the reception at the French ambassador's next week?'

'I am not sure.' Venetia gave him a beguiling look. 'Will you not tell me some more stories about Roldán?'

He laughed, and glanced down at her. 'Even if I wished to seduce you, I should fail. You are very much in love with your husband, are you not?'

'Yes.' She smiled shyly. 'That's why I want to learn everything about him.'

'Is there something in particular you wish to know?'

'Yes. I – I believe there was some trouble with a woman?'

'Ah yes. Marietta.' He frowned again, his eyes dark with some emotion. 'That was unfortunate, I'm afraid. She was married to – to a man who was far too old for her. She turned to Roldán for comfort, but her husband discovered the truth. He was rather a vindictive man. He had Roldán beaten. He very nearly died.'

Venetia gasped. So that was the secret in her husband's past! The colour drained from her cheeks as she remembered that he had named his ship the *Marietta*. He must have loved her very much. She felt the pain twist inside her. Could she ever really make him forget his first love? How could he forget a woman when he bore the marks of the beating he had endured for her sake? Venetia had seen him touch the scar on his cheek sometimes, and she realised that he must have been thinking of the woman he had loved and lost. It was a bitter thing to have to accept. She had never loved any man but him, and never would. Yet she must try to live and be happy with this shadow hanging over her. He was her husband, and she could not bear to lose him. So she must accept that his heart could never be all hers, however much it hurt.

Smiling to hide the pain, she looked up at James Lodden. 'Are you to attend the reception, sir?'

'Yes ... at least, I may go.'

'Ask Maddalena if she means to go. We could all attend together, if you wish.'

'I should like that very much,' he said, giving her a warm smile. 'Now, I think we must return before your friend suspects me of abducting you!'

'Do you think the Venetian fleet will come in, sir?' Roldán looked at his commander, sensing the doubts Don John had not voiced. 'We have been at Messina five days now, and there is still no sign of them.'

'They must come,' Don John said in a

voice low with passion. 'We need them, my friend. Many of our best men are with Alva fighting the rebellion in the Low Countries. I wish my brother the king was as committed to this fight.'

'Surely you cannot doubt that, sir?'

'If you had read my orders!' Don John frowned. 'The king is more concerned with saving galleys than beating the enemy, but I am determined on it, Roldán. This time, we shall see action. My opinion of the Turks as fighting men is not as high as it once was. I believe they can be beaten – and beaten at sea!'

There was a look of such dedication in his eyes that Roldán was fired with the same confidence, even though it had always seemed that the Turks were almost invincible at sea.

'I am sure you are right,' he said. 'With you to lead us, we shall not fail.'

'Nor should we if all my men were as loyal and as willing to fight as you.' Don John clasped his shoulder. 'We shall win, my friend – but we need the Venetians!'

'Forgive me if I seem to interfere, my dear,' Maddalena said, 'but I must ask this question.'

Venetia held the red rose to her nose, inhaling its sweet perfume. 'Was it not good of James to send me these flowers?' She looked at her friend. 'What is it you want to know?'

Maddalena looked uncomfortable. 'I am sure it is all... I know you would never do anything... You are not becoming too much attached to James Lodden?'

'Attached to James?' Venetia looked at her in surprise, and then started to giggle. 'Oh, Maddalena – how could you?'

'I do not think it is funny, Venetia! He calls here so often now that people... Well, some people are beginning to talk.'

The smile left Venetia's eyes. 'You cannot think... Maddalena, you must know I would never betray Roldán? He means everything to me. I allow James to call precisely because he is the one friend I can rely on not to try and seduce me.'

Maddalena sighed with relief. 'I knew it must be so, my dear. Will you forgive me for even asking you such a foolish question?'

'Of course!' Venetia embraced her. 'I shall tell James not to call quite so often – but you do not think I should give up his friendship altogether, do you?'

'No, why should you? It was just that Roldán is away and people talk, but let them.' Maddalena picked up one of the roses that the girl was skilfully arranging in a silver vase. 'They are very beautiful. Perhaps you should not encourage James too much for his own sake?'

'He has always known I love Roldán,' Venetia replied with a frown. 'But I shall not see so much of him in future.'

Word came on almost the last day of August that Marcantonio Quirini's galleys had reached Sicily. The Venetians were committed to the struggle. Suddenly there was a feeling running high among the League that this time something would happen. The Turkish fleet might outnumber them, but they had a leader who believed in success. There were still arguments to be settled and objections to be overcome, but the Venetians were keen to fight, and Don John agreed with them even though it went against his own orders. Roldán knew that his leader was risking his own future for the sake of the cause, and his admiration for him grew steadily. It was sure now that something would happen. Yet just how or what they should do was still undecided.

'The Venetians are pressing for an attack on Morea,' Don John said to Roldán when they were discussing the situation.

'Hoping for help from the Greeks?' Roldán suggested. It was possible that the rebellion there might help their cause.

'Others are encouraging an attack on the supply base at Negropont...' Don John mused, speaking his thoughts aloud.

'To draw the Turkish fleet out of Lepanto

into the Aegean sea? Yes, I would be inclined to that view,' Roldán said.

He knew that Gianandrea Doria was still playing for time, urging caution on his commander as he had on the previous expedition, but he was dealing with a different personality this time. Don John was undeterred.

As the first autumn storm struck in the second week of September, the young commander refused to be swayed by this warning sign. He stuck to his purpose, and at last an agreement was reached among the various leaders of the fleet. To Roldán's personal delight, the galleys were put to sea, their crews blessed by the papal nuncio, who remained holding his arms skyward until they could no longer see him. This was a holy cause. The time had come to fight for Christendom.

The ships sailed in precise formation. Don John had given orders that clearly defined the space that must be left between them so that the oars would not clash, yet leaving no room for an enemy to slip between. Roldán appreciated his leader's thinking. It was very much like a cavalry manoeuvre on land. Don John was, after all, primarily a soldier.

The normal Turkish formation was, Roldán knew, spread out in the shape of a crescent. It was of religious significance and copied a device they used on their flags. Don

John was of course aware of this, and he had taken it into account when drawing up his battle plans – plans that included a strict code of moral behaviour on board his ships. This venture had been blessed by the Pope himself. It was a holy war. Men were hanged for blasphemy. It was a harsh régime, but Roldán knew it helped to harden the determination of the men. Everyone was now aware of their total commitment to his fight. There was no longer talk among ordinary soldiers of turning back, though Roldán had heard one or two of the leaders express doubts. Yet Don John's dedication shone out like a beacon, and gradually his sense of purpose spread throughout the fleet.

For a week no one knew what was really happening. A veteran Knight of Malta who had fought the Turks before was sent out to try and find them. He discovered that their ships had raided the island of Zante in the Adriatic.

'Are they settled for the winter at Lepanto, as we thought,' Roldán asked, 'or are they moving towards Constantinople?'

It was a question even Don John's spies could not answer.

Towards the end of September, the Holy League's fleet reached Corfu. The island had already been attacked, as if the Turks hoped to frighten the Venetians by showing what they could do if they chose.

'Thank God Venetia was not here!' Roldán said as he saw the results of pillaging, wrecked churches and ruined homes. 'It is a mercy that I did not let her return to her friends.'

The thought of his wife at the mercy of vengeful Turks made him shudder. She had been fortunate that the Corsairs who had attacked her ship had been primarily inter-ested in profit. She would not have fared so well here. He struggled to put the thought of her from his mind. He could not allow himself to be distracted from the task in hand.

Roldán was in conference with his commander when a fregata brought in news that seemed almost too good to be true. The Turks had gone back to Lepanto, but more importantly, they were said to be short of rowers and to have the plague on board. If that were true, then their morale must be dangerously low. It seemed that fortune was on the side of the Holy League. Now the feeling that this was truly a crusade began to grow stronger.

It was decided at last: they would beard the lion in his den! The Turks had returned to Lepanto, and it was there that the battle would take place.

'Have I offended you?' James Lodden

asked, a hurt expression on his face. 'If so, please tell me what I have said so that I may beg your pardon.'

'You have not offended me.' Venetia frowned, playing with her fan. 'It is just that... Well, it was suggested to me that I was seeing too much of you.'

'Have I been too free in my manners? Have I stepped beyond what is seemly?'

'No, of course not.' Venetia sighed. 'Oh, this is all so silly! You are my friend – and Roldán's. I shall take no notice of what people say or think. Will you come with us to the masquerade ball next month?'

He took her hand, raising it to his lips to kiss it. 'I would not miss it for the world! You know I must leave you for a while. I have business in Naples – but I shall see you when I return. You will not allow this gossip to spoil our friendship?'

'No.' Venetia shook her head, and smiled at him. 'I am sure Roldán would be angry if I did. Come to me again when you return. Who knows, we may have some news by then.'

The fog had kept them in harbour for several days. October had seen the start of a patch of foul weather, which was a hazard and yet a blessing in disguise, since it helped to hide the fleet's approach from the Turks.

News of the fall of Famagusta had just

reached them and was even now spreading through the outraged Venetians' ranks. As at Nicosia, the Turks had promised terms and then slaughtered everyone. If there had been any doubt of the Venetians' will to fight, there was none now.

Roldán's face was grim as he heard the news. There was little hope that Venetia's father could have survived. It saddened him that she must know more grief, but it made him angry, too. These enemies of man and God must be destroyed!

Eight of the fastest Sicilian galleys were sent on ahead to discover the whereabouts of the enemy, while the bulk of the fleet moved slowly towards the Gulf of Patras. It was split into three separate parts. Marcantonio Quirini's command was on the flank that was expected to bear the brunt of the Turks' efforts to break their ranks. In the middle was Don John's own command, while the less trustworthy Gianandrea Doria's galleys were to his right.

Roldán's galleys were under Don John's personal command. He could see his leader on the poop, his imposing figure clad in a gilded breastplate. So much for the orders that said he must not place his own person in danger!

A solemn Mass was held throughout the fleet on 7 October 1571, and it was in every man's mind that the time for battle was close. The fleet had edged round the northern shores against a strong wind, the rowers having to pull hard to combat the heavy seas. On every catwalk the bosun was alert, ready to lash any man who did not do his work. Roldán's own ship was no exception, yet his bosun did not once need to use the whip. Not one man on board was chained to his oar. Each had been promised his freedom if he did his duty, and there was as much determination in their faces as in those of the fighting men.

The enemy's fleet had been sighted. There were nearly three hundred of them, most of which were war galleys. They spread out across the narrowing Gulf, menacing and chilling the hearts of Christian men. A green pennant could be seen fluttering from the flagpole of the Turkish commander's ship, and there was the odd sound of music as the Turkish soldiers celebrated the coming confrontation. In complete contrast was the silence on every Christian deck. It was almost as if the hand of God had stretched out to touch them.

Roldán felt the strange dedication in every man. He might have been in church rather than preparing for a battle. He crossed himself, whispering a private prayer. Every man on board followed his example. They were all armed and ready for the fight. All equally prepared to give their life for the cause, if need be, yet eager to defeat their enemy and live.

Don John passed through the ranks of his ships in a fregata, a cross in his hand. His message was clear: they were there to conquer or die. In death or victory they would win immortality.

'For God and Spain!' Roldán cried. 'Fight bravely, my lads, and you shall be rewarded on this earth as well as in heaven!'

His words brought cheers from all round. Immortality was a comforting promise, but a purse of gold was enough to bring a glint to every eye.

On the Turkish galleys, the slaves had been chained to their oars. If the ships went down, they had no chance of escape. The commander of the fleet had advanced by bringing up his own ship at the centre, letting the wings extend backwards and outwards, entirely blocking the entrance to the Gulf. His plan was to outflank and encircle the League's ships. The decks were crowded with the brightly-clothed and jewelled figures of the Sultan's janissaries, who brought their personal fortunes into battle with them, while archers crouched in every available space.

'God help us!' Roldán muttered to himself as he saw their numbers. They would need His help if they were to win the day. The

Turks were fierce fighters, and they had previously been invincible at sea.

Shots, loud noises and the crashing of cymbals came from the Turkish ships as the two fleets converged. These gestures of defiance were intended to frighten the Christians, but under their leaders' command the League's soldiers stayed firm. Not a shot had been fired from their guns as yet. They waited for a sign from Don John.

The sign came from a higher authority. The wind turned. It had been against them all morning. Now it was with them. God was with them!

'We have them now, lads!' Roldán cried, and the same thought was in all their minds.

The Turkish sails were hauled down and the slaves thrust into action. While they struggled to maintain their momentum, the League's fleet suddenly came to life. The sails filled with a God-sent wind, and every man's heart was lifted. It was surely a sign from heaven! At a signal from their commander, every ship raised a cross. Their Lord had died for them, now they were ready to offer their lives for His sake.

The two flagships were headed for confrontation. It was unusual for the commanders of a fleet to take an active part in battle, but this was no ordinary clash. Both men seemed determined on it. Don John had sent forward specially fitted galliasses, clumsy, heavy ships with a significant purpose. Their decks were crowded with arquebusiers, and the weapons were proving a deadly threat. The Turks wore only their silken robes, and the heavy shot ripped through their ranks. The result was that the precise formation of their advance was broken as galleys veered out of control.

Don John's own ship was steadily approaching that of his enemy. Clearly visible, he walked fearlessly between his men, encouraging them. As Roldán watched from his own ship, he saw his leader dance on the gun-platform and smiled to himself. The sober mood had given way to excitement. He felt the growing fervour among his own men, so he steadied them as a Turkish galley advanced.

'Hold your fire until you can be sure of your target,' he warned. Now he had no time to watch Don John's ship as his attention was given to the coming challenge, and he missed the moment of contact between the two flagships. 'Make ready the grappling-lines,' he commanded, his hand resting on the hilt of his sword.

A shudder ran through the galley as they were rammed. 'Follow me!' he cried. Not waiting to be boarded, Roldán led his men across to the enemy's deck. His soldiers were tough fighting men; they used their weapons to good effect, and soon the boards beneath their feet became soaked with blood.

Around them, the battle raged. A woman who had gone to war rather than leave her lover was one of the first to cross from the *Real* to the *Sultana*. She killed her first opponent with one savage thrust of her sword – revenge for the women the Turks had so often enslaved.

The fighting surged back and forth. Don John himself was wounded, but laughed it off. The Turkish commander died with a ball in his forehead. An armed slave cut off his head and hoisted his terrible trophy aloft. The battle on board *Sultana* was quickly ended as the Turks realised that their leader was dead. The green flag came down, and the Pope's banner replaced it. Trumpets rang out triumphantly as the Spaniards plundered the vast riches on board the conquered flagship.

Several Venetian galleys had been sunk, and some of the enemy's. The outcome was still uncertain, but the balance was suddenly tipped by an uprising amongst the Christian galley-slaves who had managed to break free of their chains. On the Venetian flank, the battle was almost won. Everywhere were feats of individual valour and collective bravery, and by late afternoon the battle was won. Looking at the wrecks littering the sea, which had turned red with blood, Roldán sheathed his sword. He had blood on his clothes, hands and face, but none of it was his own. By some miracle he had come through unscathed, apart from a few bruises. He was alive, and the war was over. It would be years before the Turks could recover sufficiently to menace the Christian world again!

He went down on the deck on one knee, crossing himself as he gave thanks for the safe delivery of his men and galleys and of his own life. Rising to his feet, he gave order for the wounded to be attended, and then he smiled. Now he could go back to Rome – and Venetia.

CHAPTER NINE

There were rumours flying around Rome. Some said that a great battle had been fought, others that the League's fleet had not encountered the enemy and were on their way home. Venetia did not care much one way or the other as long as it meant that Roldán was coming back to her.

She had been dressing for the Orsinis' ball when a messenger visited the house, and Maddalena came flying to her room. 'They say there was a terrible battle at Lepanto,' she cried, her eyes bright with enthusiasm. 'We were victorious! The Turks are defeated.'

'Then Roldán will soon be home!' Venetia said, her eyes blazing with excitement as her heart leaped within her. 'Oh, I do hope it is true this time.'

'The Neapolitans are dancing in the streets for joy,' Maddalena assured her. 'I believe it must be true.'

The two women embraced each other. If the threat of Turkish invasion was over, it was a great achievement for the League, and one that could hardly have been expected.

It could have been just another rumour, but

when they reached the Orsini Palace, everyone was full of the wonderful victory and no one could talk of anything else. Apparently a dispatch had reached Rome earlier in the day, and it was certain that the Turkish fleet had been roundly defeated. The mood was one of celebration. Everyone was happy. It was unexpected and miraculous, far more than anyone had dared to hope for. Wine flowed freely as the guests toasted the heroes who had fought so bravely.

Dancing with a string of excited young men, Venetia found that the wine and tales of valour had gone to their heads. She was hugged and her hand was squeezed by partners who had gone wild with delight; some of them tried to kiss her in the ballroom itself. The affair was rapidly getting out of hand, and she looked around for Maddalena, hoping that she would agree that it was time to leave, but there was no sign of her. The ballroom had been invaded by a party of revellers from the street, most of whom were quite obviously drunk. Accosted rudely by one of them, she shook off his hand and tried to force her way through the crowd.

'Let me help you out of this,' a voice spoke at her elbow.

'James! Oh, thank goodness!' Venetia cried as she recognised her rescuer, despite his silvery mask. 'I thought you were not coming here tonight.'

'I was late, having arrived from Naples only this afternoon. Let me take you away from this madness. I must speak with you urgently, Venetia.'

He sounded serious, and his mouth was set in a grim line. Not knowing what else to do, she allowed him to steer her through the crush, which was growing all the time. The citizens of Rome had invited themselves to what had been intended as a private function.

'I should find my friends,' Venetia said tentatively. 'They will be anxious.'

'We shall never find them in this,' James replied, removing his mask and thrusting a rather drunk young man out of their path. 'I have a carriage outside. I shall take you home at once, for it is not safe for you to be abroad on such a night. Anything might happen.'

Venetia hesitated, glancing at him uncertainly. Although she had known him for some months, she had never before been completely alone with him; Maddalena or Paolo had always been within calling distance. She looked around anxiously for her friends, but she could not pick them out from the crowd. What should she do? Was it not better to leave with a trusted friend than stay and risk being accosted by drunken strangers?

'Very well, I shall come with you,' she said at last.

'You know you can trust me, Venetia.' James smiled at her. 'I came here to find you. There is something I must tell you. It is very urgent.'

Her heart jerked as she saw the look on his face. What could be so important that he had come here especially to speak with her? Roldán! It must be something to do with her husband. James had come from Naples. He must have news for her.

'Has Roldán been wounded?' she asked, her knees beginning to tremble as she saw him frown. He was wondering how best to tell her what was obviously bad news.

His grip tightened on her arm as he steered her towards the street door. 'You must not be too upset yet, Venetia. Trust me, and all will be well.'

She swayed as the world spun round her. Roldán was wounded, she was sure of it. She could not bear it if she never saw him again, never held him in her arms. She stumbled, and James put his arm round her waist, supporting her as they left the palace. Tears blinded her eyes and there was a terrible pounding in her head. Outside, she clutched at him in panic.

'You must tell me,' she choked as the tightness swelled in her breast. 'How badly is he hurt?'

288

James looked at her with pity in his eyes, and she knew it was even worse than she had feared. 'I am sorry, Venetia. He is close to death. The nuns were caring for him, and he asked for you. I promised that I would bring you to convent.'

'Close to death?' She began to tremble, shaking her head as the pain swept through her. She would die if she lost him now. 'No! No, it cannot be true!'

'I shall take you to him.'

She scarcely heard what he said. There was a roaring in her ears and the world spun madly around her. His face was a meaningless blur as she reached out to grab his arm to save herself from falling.

'Help me...' she whispered as the darkness closed in on her.

He caught her as she stumbled, sweeping her up in his arms. A coach lumbered towards them from the shadows, and a servant helped him to lift her inside. Glancing over his shoulder, James gave a smile of satisfaction as he saw that no one seemed to have noticed the incident. He turned to the coachman, giving the order to move on.

'You know where to take us. Do not spare the horses. I want to be on my way to England by morning.'

Giving one more backward glance, he climbed inside, hardly bothering to look at the unconscious girl. She had served her purpose, and his eyes glittered with a cold triumph. His long-laid plans had worked even better than he had hoped. He had thought to persuade her to let him take her to her husband, but this would prove far less troublesome. If she woke before they were on his ship, he would drug her. It had been so simple to deceive Roldán's wife. He had known exactly how to play on her weakness. Now she was his prisoner, and the first stage of his revenge was complete. This would be far more satisfying than an assassination!

From the shadows, a black-cloaked figure watched the coach drive away. He had come too late...

'What can have happened to her?' Maddalena was distraught. 'Roldán will never forgive us if...' She broke off on a sob. 'I should not have taken her there this evening.'

'Nothing very terrible has happened,' Paolo said, trying to calm his wife. 'You could not have guessed what the outcome would be. Besides...' He frowned, hesitating. 'I think I saw her leaving with James Lodden. He had his arm about her waist. I called to her, but she either did not hear – or did not want to.'

Maddalena stared at him, her face registering the shock his words had given her. 'You don't think... You can't mean that she has run away with him?'

Paolo sighed deeply, troubled by his suspicions. 'She seemed very taken with him, and Roldán told me that she married him only because she had no choice.'

'You can't believe that!' Maddalena cried. 'She worships him. Only tonight she was so excited because the victory meant that he would be coming home.'

'Are you sure she hasn't been deceiving you? I've never been quite certain about her, though I know you like her.'

Maddalena's eyes flashed with anger. She had sensed Paolo's doubts before, but he had never put them into words. Much as she loved him, she could not bear to hear his criticism of a girl who was very dear to her.

'I don't know how you could be so cruel,' she cried accusingly. 'Venetia would never do anything as wicked as running away with a lover! She loves her husband, and she would do anything to please him. When I think how hard she has worked to make him proud of her, learning all the things she had no mother to teach her... Oh, Paolo, I can't bear you to think so ill of her. She is a dear, sweet girl and I'm very worried about her. She would never go off without telling us. I know something has happened to her. I know it!'

'Forgive me, my love.' He took her hand and squeezed it gently. 'You know her so much better than I, so I must bow to your judgment.'

'We must find her, Paolo.' She looked up at him, the tears glistening on her lashes.

'We will,' he said stoutly. 'If she has not run away, she must be somewhere in the city. Perhaps she got caught up with the crowds and lost her way. I shall organise a search-party at once.'

'Oh yes, please do,' Maddalena said earnestly. 'I have a terrible feeling that she is in danger! There was something about James Lodden...'

'You did try to warn her,' Paolo said with a frown.

'Yes, but she laughed because it seemed so ridiculous. He was always so correct.'

'If he is such a close friend, it is strange that Roldán has never mentioned his name,' Paolo's eyes narrowed in thought. 'I believe he has something to do with Venetia's disappearance. If she did not go with him willingly...'

Venetia's eyelids flickered, and she groaned as she felt the pain in her temples. For a while she lay in a kind of daze, unable to think clearly. Her limbs had a strange heaviness, and her mouth tasted awful. Had she been ill for a long time? She could not remember. She did not even care much at the moment.

Her eyes closed again and she drifted into sleep. She was sleeping when the man came in to look at her. He frowned, wondering if the drug he had given her had been too strong. It was two days now since he had brought her on board his ship. If she was suffering, it was her own fault: she had resisted too stubbornly when she came round from her dizzy spell. He had thought she would accept his word that they were on their way to Naples, but she had surprised him by insisting that he should return her to her friends' house.

'If you wish to see Roldán alive, you must come now,' he had argued.

'I cannot travel alone with you,' she replied stubbornly. 'Furnish me with the name of the convent, sir, and Paolo will take me there.'

Her resistance had surprised him, and he had forced her to swallow the contents of a special phial he had with him for the purpose of subduing her should it prove necessary. He did not wish her harm, but she was vital to his plan of luring Roldán to England, and she had brought it on herself. Revenge on his one-time friend had not been the original purpose for his stay in Rome, but it was something he had hungered for for a long time. If the girl was hurt, it could not be helped. He was about to leave the cabin when he heard her moan.

'Water...' she whispered weakly. 'Please can I have some water?'

He walked over to the bed, looking down at her. Her face was an odd colour and she was obviously ill. Damn it! He did not want her to die. If she died too soon, it would not be the complete revenge he had hoped for. He must keep her alive somehow until after his meeting with Roldán.

Pouring water into a pewter cup, he slipped his arm behind her shoulders, lifting her so that she could swallow. She gulped thirstily, her eyes glazed and unseeing as she stared at him. He felt a faint prick of conscience as he laid her back on the pillows. She was an innocent victim, just as Marietta had been, yet she had brought it on herself by marrying a murderer!

Roland Dominion had killed James's brother after first seducing his father's bride. At first he had scarcely believed it was true. As boys they had shared every secret, and surely Roland could not have acted so basely? Yet how could he refuse to believe Marietta's story? Roland and his friends had ambushed and killed Carlton. It hurt him the more because they had once been so close. The desire for revenge had simmered inside him over the years, flaring to a bitter intensity when he saw Roland in Rome. He had changed his name after leaving England as a fugitive, and now he was rich and a man of some importance.

At first he had sought revenge by arranging

an assassination, but both attempts had failed. It was a chance meeting in a garden that had shown him a much sweeter revenge. This way, Roland would suffer for longer. Glancing down at the girl's face once more, James Lodeberry's determination hardened. She would live because his revenge would not be complete without her. Somehow he would make her live!

'Gone? Where has she gone?' Roldán stared at his friends in disbelief. 'She cannot simply have disappeared?' His gaze narrowed as he saw the look on their faces. 'There is something you are not telling me.'

'We had all gone to the Orsini Palace,' Maddalena said, not quite able to meet the fierce, piercing look in his eyes. 'Everyone was celebrating the news of the victory. When I last saw her she was dancing, then – then the ballroom was invaded by a crowd of uninvited guests. Most of them seemed to be drunk.'

'You should have left at once.'

'That was Maddalena's first thought,' Paolo said, protecting his wife from Roldán's anger. 'We looked for her for hours. I finally persuaded my wife to come home, thinking that Venetia might have made her own way here.'

'How could she?' Roldán asked, his face tight with anger. He had trusted these

people to take care of his wife, and now...
As yet, he dared not even consider the facts.
'She knew no one but you.' The odd stare in
Paolo's eyes made him pause. 'What are you
hiding from me?'

'We thought she might have got caught up
in the crowds,' Paolo said, seeing that his
wife was too upset to go on. 'I have had my
servants searching for the past two weeks.'

'She has been missing for two *weeks?*'
Roldán felt a terrible numbness. A day or a
few hours was one thing, but two whole
weeks! 'You have found no sign of her?' He
stared at the other man's face. 'For heaven's
sake, man, tell me the truth! Is she dead?'

'I was able to discover only one thing,'
Paolo said slowly. 'I saw her leaving with
James Lodden – and there was an unreliable
report of her getting into a carriage outside
the palace. I say unreliable, because the
witness was drunk. He saw a woman being
helped into a coach and he thought she
might be ill, but he cannot remember
clearly.' Paolo saw the quick frown and
added hastily, 'Of course, we can't be sure
the woman was Venetia, but the colour of the
gown she was wearing matches the description. And her hair...'

Roldán was stiff with disbelief. 'Why did
he think she might be ill?'

'She appeared to faint...' Paolo hesitated,
feeling awkward. 'I am inclined to believe it,

because I think I saw her leave with Lodden.'

'Who is this James Lodden?' Roldán asked. His mind was a blank, refusing to believe this. 'Why should she leave with him? You're not suggesting...'

'Paolo thinks she has run off with him.' Maddalena could not bear to listen any more. 'She met James at a masquerade ball. He claimed to be a friend of yours from England, and because of that she allowed him to call. I – I think she quite liked him, but she would never have run off with him. She was so excited because the war was over...' Her words trailed away as she saw the fury in his face.

Anger had replaced the numbing fear. She had run off with a new lover! She had gone because the war was over and she knew that he was coming back to claim her. It was the only possible explanation. Why else would she leave with a man, without consulting either Maddalena or Paolo?

'I don't know a James Lodden.'

He was so angry that he could not think straight. The thought of being with Venetia again had sustained him on his journey from Naples after leaving the fleet. There had been some delay while the possibility of further attacks on the Turks was being considered; but as soon as it was decided that there were to be no further ventures this winter, he had put ashore at Naples and ridden overland, leaving his captains in charge of the galleys. Now he was being told that Venetia had run away. He wanted to kill the man who had stolen her from him – and he wanted to kill her!

He took a few paces about the room, still unable to accept the shattering news. Did Venetia hate him so much that she had run away rather than be his wife? She had seemed contented enough the night before he left, yet he had been tricked by a woman's smiles once before. He felt a sickness in his stomach.

'I'll find them,' he said, his face twisted with bitterness. 'And when I do...'

Venetia held the bedcovers to her chin as the door of her cabin opened. For the first time in days her head had ceased to throb so painfully, and she was fully aware of her situation. She had been abducted by James Lodden!

As yet she did not know why, but she meant to ask him today. She stared at him as he came in carrying a tray of food. At least she knew he did not intend to murder her; he had patiently nursed her throughout her illness. She was not sure just how long she had lain in a daze, but she had been slowly recovering for at least ten days.

'So you are awake,' he said. 'You look

better today, Venetia.'

'Who gave you permission to use my given name?' she asked, scowling. 'You are no friend of mine, sir.'

'I have just saved your life. Had I not cared for you, you must have died.'

'Because you almost poisoned me!' Venetia countered, her eyes dark with anger. 'Do you expect me to thank you for that?'

'No, and I am sorry I gave you too much of the drug. Had you not been so stubborn, it would not have been necessary.'

'Why was it necessary? Why have you done this wicked thing?' She glared at him, fury making her forget to be afraid. 'Roldán hasn't been wounded, has he? It was a lie to persuade me to go with you.'

'Please forgive me for the deception. You must understand that I mean you no harm personally, Venetia. Indeed, I find you attractive... It will not be difficult to make love to you. I shall enjoy it.'

'You will never touch me!' she cried. 'I don't know why you've abducted me, but it is not because you are in love with me, so do not pretend that.' She stared at him intently, suspicions racing through her mind. 'You are not a friend of Roldán, are you? You came looking for him on the day that he was attacked...' A gasp of horror escaped her. 'It was you! You were one of those who attacked him!'

'No, I was not one of them. They were in my pay, however. I wanted him killed, but now I have decided to get my revenge personally.'

'Revenge for what?'

'Your husband is a murderer. He killed my brother.'

'I don't believe you!' Venetia's lips curled scornfully. 'Roldán is too proud to stoop to such a deed. If he killed your brother, it was in a fair fight.'

'Your faith in him touches me, madam. I fear you are mistaken, however. He and his cronies waylaid my brother one night and murdered him. It was witnessed by my father's wife. Not content with raping Marietta, he killed my brother Carlton.'

'No ... I won't believe you,' Venetia whispered, feeling the torment swirl inside her. 'Why should he?' She could not bring herself to say the words. The man she loved was not capable of such terrible things. Yet what did she really know of him? His lovemaking could bring her tears of joy – but what did she know of the true man? They had spent so little time together, and he had told her nothing of his past. Yet she could not believe these terrible accusations. 'I won't listen to you. You are lying!'

'Perhaps I shall let Marietta convince you.' He stared down at her, his face hard. 'He was my closest friend, and yet he killed my brother. I learned to hate him, madam, and you may come to feel the same one day. It does not matter. When you are his widow, you will have time enough to reflect.'

'You– You are planning to kill him?' Venetia felt a chill of horror run through her. What made a man hate like this? To kill in anger was one thing, but to plot revenge so coldly was quite different. 'You think he will follow me?'

'I know he will follow you. It may take him a while to work it out, but he is no fool. When Maddalena tells him those stories you were so fond of hearing, he will understand. No one else knows about the things we did together.'

'So you really were his friend.' Venetia stared at him in bewilderment. 'How can you hate him so much?'

'He betrayed me.' James's eyes glinted oddly. 'We were as brothers. I can never forgive him for what he did to my family. He dishonoured Marietta, and I shall take my revenge with his wife. Then, when he knows what I've done, I shall kill him.'

'If Roldán thinks I have run away with you, he will not follow me,' Venetia said, looking at him defiantly. 'You may do as you will. I shall fight you, but I know that you are stronger than I. My victory will be in knowing that your plan must fail. My husband married me only out of a sense of duty. He will not bother to look for me.'

There was surprise and concern in his face. Surely she was lying! No man would be indifferent to such a woman. 'You think to put me off by confusing me, Venetia, but I'm not stupid. Roldán would be mad to let you go. He will follow you, and I shall kill him.'

She was silent. How could she convince him that he was wrong? Somehow she had to keep him at bay for as long as possible. Long enough for Roldán to rescue her. Would he come in time? Like James, she was sure that he would come after her if only to kill her. He had snatched her from Mahomet's harem. This Englishman would be no match for him.

'Perhaps he will kill you,' she said. 'If you touch me, he will not spare your life.'

'Your illness has protected you thus far,' James replied coldly. 'I am in no hurry. A ship's cabin is no place for seduction. There will be time enough when we reached England. I may wait until Roldán is safe in my dungeons. Perhaps I shall let him watch...'

'You are a fiend!'

'I see your strength is returning. I'm glad you are feeling better, Venetia! There would be no pleasure in seducing a woman who did not know what was happening to her.'

Venetia clenched her hands into tight fists, but she refused to be drawn. She must be careful. If he realised that she was almost well again, he might carry out his threats. For the moment, she must let him believe that she was still unwell.

As he left the cabin, she slipped down the bed, ignoring the tantalising smell of the food he had brought. If he thought she was not well enough to eat, he would leave her in peace. There was no chance of escape while she was on the ship, but it might be different when they reached England. Somehow she must escape and warn Roldán. She could not let him walk into a trap because of her!

'Tell me more about this James Lodden,' Roldán said to Maddalena as they finished eating supper. 'There is something odd about this. You say he claimed to know me well, yet I have never met him. At least…'

'He was always telling Venetia stories about you.' She looked at him across the table. 'He certainly deceived us all. He seemed to know so much about your life in England.'

Roldán frowned, a suspicion forming in his mind. 'There was someone … James was my closet friend…' His hand played with the stem of his wine goblet. 'I wonder if it could be… But why?' He looked up as a servant came into the room, speaking to Maddalena in a low voice.

She shook her head, then looked enquiringly at Roldán. 'There is someone to see

303

you. I told my servant to send him away, thinking that you would not want to see anyone, but he says the caller is most insistent. Perhaps he has news.'

'I shall see him.' Roldán got to his feet at once. 'Excuse me, Maddalena.'

Following the servant to a small reception room, Roldán saw the tall, black-cloaked figure waiting for him. He frowned, remembering the night the stranger had warned him against an attempt on his life. They had never met again, and he had almost forgotten the incident.

'You wanted to see me, sir?' Roldán's manner was impatient. He had no time for mysterious strangers. 'How may I help you?'

'I have come to help you, Roldán.' The stranger turned to look at him, pushing back his hood so that the light fell on his face. It was the lined face of a man who had lived and suffered, but the face of a stranger. 'I believe I may know where your wife is.'

'My wife!' Roldán took a stride towards him. 'Who are you, sir? We have met before, but I do not know you. You warned me once, and now you say you can tell me where Venetia is. Why should you concern yourself with my affairs?'

'I am known as Guido, but perhaps this will explain better than words.' The stranger flung back his cloak, revealing the distinctive silver cross he wore on his breast. 'We of the brotherhood do not forget our friends.'

The cross he wore was the symbol of the Knights of Malta, and suddenly Roldán understood. When the Knights had been besieged by the Turks in the castle of St Angelo in 1565, he had volunteered to fight with them. A small band of men of various nationalities had helped to defend the island when it seemed that all were doomed to die. Roldán had fought side by side with the Knights, sharing their hardships and helping to bury the dead. Outnumbered and under tremendous pressure, the Knights willingly sacrificed their lives to defend the gateway to Christendom. They had held on in the face of terrible odds until help came in the form of Don García's troops. The bond that had been formed between the survivors was one that could never be severed. Roldán had refused to accept anything for his services. One did not ask a brother for payment.

He smiled and held out his hand, finding it grasped strongly. 'You are welcome here, Guido. We have supped, but food shall be brought if you wish?'

'I have eaten. There is no time to waste, Roldán. Your wife has been abducted and is even now on her way to England.'

'To England!' Roldán's eyes were suddenly intent. 'You are certain of this?'

'I made it my business to be sure. Unfortunately, my work took me away from

Rome or I might have been able to warn her. The man who abducted her is your enemy. It was he who tried to have you murdered.'

'How do you know these things?' Roldán asked, but he was aware of the fraternity that spread throughout Christendom. The Knights and their people were concerned in many secret sects, their influence working in the background of politics, business and the church. They were a powerful force in a world that extended far beyond the confines of their little island. 'No, I do not need an answer to that. You say this man is my enemy... Do you know his name?'

'He called himself James Lodden, but his real name is Lodeberry. He is the son of the earl.'

'Yes, I know him.' A muscle flicked in Roldán's cheek. 'You are sure he has Venetia?'

'I saw him take her. I was too late to do anything, but I followed the coach. He took her on board his ship. She was unconscious. I believe he may have drugged her.'

'She was drugged?' Roldán's eyes glittered with fury. 'I'll kill him if he has harmed her! If he wanted revenge on me, he had no right to involve her.'

'Calm yourself, my friend. He wants you to lose your head. If you go back to England you may be in danger, and not just from

James Lodeberry. You killed the earl's eldest son, and his wife has accused you of murder.'

'She knows it was a fair fight.' Roldán frowned. Was it possible that Marietta hated him that much? Would she lie simply to wreak her spite on him? 'She was in love with Carlton. She used me to protect her secret affair from the earl. I believed I was relieving her of an unwanted menace.'

'I know your heart and I do not doubt you. Even so, I must warn you that you could face a trial for murder if you return to England.'

'Thank you for the warning, Guido.' Roldán smiled slightly. 'You know I have no choice, don't you?'

'Then I shall go with you. I have business there on behalf of the brotherhood, and it may be that I can help you.'

Frustration clawed at Roldán's guts. The merchant ship seemed slow and clumsy when time was so important, but he had sent his galleys to winter in Sicily and had had little choice. In any case, Guido was right when he said that a Venetian merchantman would attract less attention. It would be asking for trouble to sail into an English port in a Spanish war galley. England and Spain were not at war, but relations between them were not as friendly as they might have been.

Once, King Philip II had hoped to marry Elizabeth of England and convert her to the true faith, but she had kept him dangling on her string too long. If Spain's king thought of England now, it was with anger; the Protestant queen encouraged privateers to attack Spanish galleons loaded with silver and gold from the New World, while pretending to be outraged at their actions. Elizabeth was a thorn in Spain's side, but she managed to keep her allies guessing so that neither the French, Dutch or Spanish really knew what was in her mind. As a soldier, Roldán admired her courage, though he could not accept her religion.

Seeing the ship's captain coming towards him, Roldán walked to meet him. 'Well, Gómez, how much longer before we reach England?'

'With a fair wind – three days.' Gómez sensed his impatience and frowned. 'We've made good time, sir.'

'Yes, I know. Forgive me, I am out of my mind with worry. Two weeks were lost before I even knew she was missing.'

'You found her before, sir. The odds were against you then, it should be easier this time. England is a civilised country, not a slave port.'

'Yet I have a terrible fear, Gómez. At least Mahomet was single-minded about what he wanted: it was simply a question of money.

James wants revenge. Who knows what he might do?'

'You know I am ready to help in any way I can.'

'I may need your help, Gómez. I must be certain of a ship when the time comes.'

'It will be waiting, never fear. If it was not for your generosity, I would not have a ship.'

'That was payment for past favours. I am in your debt once more, my friend.'

Roldán moved away, ignoring the captain's denials. He had always paid his debts, as James Lodeberry would discover when they met. His face was grim as he looked out over the sea, watching the trail of white foam behind them. He was going back to England, back to a country he had not seen for eleven years.

He had blocked the past from his mind deliberately, giving his whole endeavour to the new life he had made for himself, forcing the bitterness out of his soul. Eleven years... How much had happened in those years!

His uncle had welcomed him like a son, prepared to give him a home and a life of ease; but he had preferred to carve out his own future. A successful voyage to the New World had set his feet on the ladder of fortune, then the two years as a galley-slave when only his strength of purpose had kept him going, and the months on Malta.

Skirmishes at sea with the Corsairs, and now the victory at Lepanto. It had been a good life. A soldier's life. If it was his fate to die in England, then so be it. All that mattered was Venetia.

If his enemy had harmed her… He felt a deep, twisting agony inside. For a while he had believed that she had left him to run away with a lover and he had wanted to kill her. Now he knew that she was in danger because of him – because a man who had once been his friend believed Marietta's lies.

If Venetia was dead, he would kill the bitch who had betrayed him. He would hang for it, but if the woman he loved was dead, he would not want to live…

It was dark and cold inside the coach. Venetia hugged her cloak tightly to her, staring resentfully at the man sitting opposite. Her arm was still smarting from the way he had bundled her inside when they left the ship. She had tried to pull away, but he had merely tightened his grip, forcing her to get into the coach.

'Where are you taking me?'

'Somewhere safe, where your husband will not think of looking for you.'

'You will achieve nothing by this!'

'But I already have.' He smiled complacently. 'You would be well advised to put all thought of escape from your mind, madam. I have been patient with you so far – but I can be less than kind if I choose.'

'You are a rogue, sir.' She glared at him. 'I wish I had never met you. You deceived us all into thinking you respectable.'

'But I am very respectable.' James laughed nastily. 'I have been on a mission for our beloved queen.'

There was something odd about his words, as though he meant exactly the opposite. It was very strange that he should have spent so much time in Rome if he was working on Queen Elizabeth's behalf. Perhaps that was another lie, Venetia thought. Perhaps he was really a traitor to his own queen… She felt close to despair. No one would believe her even if she told them of her suspicions. She was a foreigner in a strange land, and a prisoner. She would have no chance to talk to anyone.

The journey seemed to go on and on for hours. There was little to be seen out of the window but trees and fields and hedges. It was winter, and the trees had no leaves. Everything looked bare and brown, adding to her sense of misery. She felt so cold! Closing her eyes, she tried to sleep for a while. Some time later, she was woken by a sudden jolt. The coach had come to a halt, and there were voices outside. Servants were attending to the horses. Poking her head through the open window, she saw that they were drawn up outside a grey stone building. It seemed to be some kind of a fortified manor house with towers and walls and tall iron gates, rather ancient and forbidding. She shivered as James got out and helped her down.

'Well, how do you like your new home?' he asked, sneering.

'It– It looks like a prison.'

His soft laughter sent shivers down her spine. 'How accurately you describe it, madam! Benedict Towers was just that when it belonged to my ancestor. He used it to imprison traitors while they awaited trial. No one incarcerated here ever left again – except to go to his death. A fitting place for my little tryst with your husband, don't you think?'

'Y– You are mad,' Venetia whispered.

'No, I am quite sane,' he said, taking her arm as he forced her to walk towards the grim buildings. 'Now, I should like you to meet someone.'

'Who?' Venetia stared at him in surprise. 'Surely no one would choose to live here?'

There was a strange expression on his face. 'Perhaps when you have met her you will understand,' he said, his eyes glittering in the moonlight. 'I know she will want to see Roldán's wife.'

There was something very chilling about his manner. She could not imagine who this mysterious person might be, or why she should want... She!... Of course, it had to be Marietta. But why should the Earl of Lodeberry's wife choose to live in a place like this?

Her feeling of foreboding grew as they passed beneath a heavy stone arch into the entrance hall. She had thought it was cold outside, but in here the chill seemed to bite into her flesh. Everywhere had an air of neglect, as if no one ever came here. Glancing about her, she saw rusting suits of armour and moth-eaten tapestries, testaments to a time gone by. What furniture there was had a dull, damp look and there were cobwebs over the fireplace.

'No one could possibly live here,' she said. 'I demand to be taken to a comfortable house.'

'You will be comfortable enough in your own quarters, madam. This part of the house is never used. I do not come here often, and Marietta never leaves her room, except now and then at night.'

'Is she a prisoner, too?' Venetia looked at him sharply.

'She chooses to live in solitude,' James replied harshly. 'Ask me no questions. You will soon see for yourself.'

He gripped her arm again, his fingers bruising as he steered her up the wide stone staircase. Their feet echoed eerily in the emptiness. Despite the candles burning in sconces at intervals along the walls, it was a house full of shadows – and something else. There was an air of oppression hanging over it, as though the ghosts of long-dead traitors lingered on within its walls. Venetia shivered as she pictured the wretched prisoners chained in dank, airless dungeons, knowing that they would leave this terrible place only to meet their deaths. Would she ever leave here alive?

'So you feel it, too,' he said. 'I have sometimes thought I can smell the stench of decay in parts of the house. I hate it! If I had my way, I would tear it down stone by stone.'

'Why don't you?'

'Marietta likes it here. She will never leave.'

Now there was a sick, crawling sensation in her stomach. Why did Marietta want to live here? It was dark and depressing. Surely any woman would prefer a country cottage – and what of her husband? Why did he allow his wife to remain here?

'Does– Does the earl not object to her living here?'

'He does not know. Nor would he care if he did. As far as my father is concerned, she is dead.'

The mystery was growing, but Venetia realised that it was useless to go on asking questions that received only veiled answers. She glanced at James, sensing a kind of nervousness in him as they turned into a long, dark corridor. Here there was scarcely any light, and she could only just make out the door at the end. It must be where he was taking her. She swallowed hard, feeling her nerves tighten as he stepped forward and knocked on the door. There was silence for a moment, then, as he raised his hand once more, a woman's voice bade them enter. It was a young voice, light and almost musical in tone.

He lifted the latch, pushing Venetia before him into the dimly-lit room. It was even colder in here, the only light coming from one small candle. Her first thought was that it was so bare, not like a woman's chamber at all. There were no pictures on the walls, no books or sewing frames, no tapestries, no flowers or mirrors. Just a table, a stool – and a bed.

As Venetia's eyes turned towards the bed, she saw a figure lying hunched up beneath a coverlet. She glanced at James, but he made no move to rouse the woman, and as they waited, she stirred, rising slowly to walk towards them. She was bent like an old crone, her movements almost painfully slow. This could not be Marietta! What was going on here?

The woman stopped short of them. Her

pale blonde hair caught the light of the candle, still as beautiful as it had been when she married the Earl of Lodeberry. She looked into the shocked eyes of the girl standing in front of her, a harsh laugh breaking from her lips.

'That's right, look at me, girl! Have you ever seen such a loathsome sight?' Her laughter rang out loudly, sending chills down Venetia's spine. 'I've been cursed – by the Devil or God. My face was once as beautiful as yours, then I was struck down by grief, and now I am so ugly that no one can bear to look at me.'

One side of her face was twisted, the eye almost closed beneath a sagging lid. Her mouth hung slackly, and a dribble of saliva ran down her chin. By contrast, the other side of her face was smooth and unmarked. As she hobbled forward, Venetia saw that one hand was bent, the fingers like skinny claws.

'Marietta,' James spoke at last. 'I have brought you Roland Dominion's bride.'

'What?' The right eye gleamed with some fierce emotion. 'Who is she? His wife? His! That murderer...'

'I found her in Rome and brought her here to you. What shall we do with her now, Marietta?'

CHAPTER TEN

England. The country he had left in anger eleven years before. It was strange to stand on English soil again. The language seemed heavy on his tongue, though he spoke it easily enough, but there was no sense of homecoming. He had been cast out, deserted by family and friends alike for a crime he had not committed. He could be taken and hanged on the word of a lying whore. His eyes moved around the inn yard, the frown leaving his face as he saw the Knight coming towards him.

'I must go to London,' Guido said. 'Where shall you begin your search?'

'I do not think he will have taken her there. I doubt that it would satisfy his lust for revenge to see me hanged. There must be more to his plan. I believe I should perhaps call on the earl and his wife.'

'Will that not be dangerous?'

Roldán shrugged. 'He will not be expecting it. By the time he thinks to call his servants, I shall be on my way. Besides, I have something to say that may give him cause to think first. Marietta has deceived too many people for too long.'

'I shall make what enquiries I can on your behalf, Roldán, and if there is a chance of reaching the queen's ear, I shall intercede for you. If she pardoned you for any past crimes, you would be able to continue your search in safety.'

Roldán gripped his shoulder. 'You may waste your breath, sir, but I thank you for it. Elizabeth has no love for Catholics. Why should she listen to your pleas?'

'Perhaps there are reasons enough,' Guido said, smiling slightly. 'Elizabeth is no fool, and I have something to tell her that she may consider worthy of reward. Meanwhile, we must part. God bless you, Roldán.'

'And you, sir.'

Roldán watched as the Knight rode away, then he turned to mount his own horse. He must find James, and quickly. The obvious place to start was at the earl's large country estate, where they had spent so much of their boyhood together.

It was a grey, misty morning. Roldán halted his horse at the top of the rise, gazing down at the sprawling mansion in the valley. It was just as he had remembered it, the buff stone walls faded by time and the changing seasons. Here, he had learned the meaning of humiliation as a young boy. Sent to serve in the earl's house by his father, he had quickly discovered that he was as nothing to the noble lord. His innocence had fled as he began to know the nature of his master. The earl was steeping in vice, as evil as he was repulsive to the youth's eyes.

Marietta had looked like an angel when she came to the house as a young bride. He had believed her totally innocent, disbelieving the earl when he swore that he had taken her from a brothel, where she had catered to the whims of men since she was little more than eight years old. Was it in that den of vice that she had learned to deceive so well? After that fatal day, when he had seen her weeping over her lover's dead body, Roldán had learned to pity her. It was not her fault that she had been corrupted from an early age. Now, he was not sure whether he hated her or merely felt contempt for her lies.

If Venetia was dead, he would kill Marietta, but for now he was concerned only with discovering the whereabouts of his wife, and he urged his horse forward at a steady walk. The earl would scarcely be awake. He would still be in his chambers – to which there was a secret entrance. Roldán and James had chanced on it together. They had thought it a huge joke to spy on the earl, until they witnessed the loathsome acts he perpetrated on a young pageboy. James had vomited, his face as white as death. Roldán had felt pity for his friend. What must it be like to have such a father – to know that his blood ran through your veins? Roldán's own father might be a gambler, but he was at least a godly man. The youths had never used the passage again, but today it would serve a purpose.

Entrance to the house itself was easy for someone who knew every part of it so well. Finding the door to the secret way, Roldán brushed away sticky cobwebs, feeling his way through the gloom. It seemed the passage had not been used in years. Perhaps old age had cured the earl of his vices, or perhaps he flaunted them more openly now that his sons were all grown to manhood. Except for Carlton...

As the wooden panel slid open, Roldán stepped into the earl's closet, from where he could hear the sound of snoring. Making his way into the adjoining bedchamber, he smiled with satisfaction. As he had expected, the curtains were still tightly drawn about the bed. He pulled one back, gazing down at the unsightly spectacle of the earl in repose. Without his wig, his head was bald and speckled with brown spots. The years of evil living had left their mark on his pitted skin.

Roldán felt a sickness in his stomach as he leaned forward to shake the old man's shoulder. There was an unclean stench about him that made the younger man draw back in disgust. He stood ready to silence him if he tried to raise the alarm, but the earl merely grunted, opening his eyes to stare at him short-sightedly.

'Damn you, Robert! What's to do?' he muttered. 'You know I need me sleep these days.'

'It isn't Robert, sir.'

'Who is it, then?' The earl stared at him. 'Come closer; you know I can't see.'

'Has age finally caught up with you, or is it the reward of a mis-spent life?'

The earl eased himself up in bed, peering at the face he could not see properly. 'Who are you? You're not one of my servants. There's not a man among the lot of them!'

'No, but there is no need for alarm, sir. I have not come here to kill you. I want information about your son James.'

'What has that fool been up to now? Don't blame me for his meddling, sir. I've no control over him. Hang him if you must, but let me sleep in peace.'

'Where can I find him?'

'How should I know? He never comes here, not since Marietta…'The earl squinted at him. 'I've heard your voice before, but I'm damned if I can remember when…Was it at Court? Have you come from Walsingham? I tell you, I know nothing of me son's affairs.'

'Nor I, sir, except where they concern my wife. James has abducted her and I want her back.'

'Has he, by God! I never thought he had it in him. Always seemed to me as if he lived like a monk.' The earl scratched his head. 'Well, now, if you tell me who you are, I might tell you where to find him.'

'You had me beaten for seducing Marietta. You told me that she was a whore, but I refused to believe you. I was a romantic young fool!'

'Young Roland?' A chuckle broke from the earl. 'Come back, have you? Never thought I'd see you again. Marietta did for you, didn't she? The bitch! I knew she was cheating me with Carlton, but I went along with her. You were always too arrogant! A good beating was what you needed.'

'You knew about Carlton?'

'Of course. That's why I let you live. I hoped you would save me the trouble of getting rid of him. We always hated each other's guts. He was the only one of my sons who dared to stand up to me.' The earl laughed again. 'Pity you didn't make a thorough job of it! I had to finish him myself after they carried him home.'

'Carlton wasn't dead?' Roldán stared at him in horror. 'You– You killed him yourself?'

'He deserved it. Thing was, Marietta saw me, so I had to beat her.' The earl's face twisted with spite. 'I thought I'd killed her, but she managed to get away. James helped her, of course; he was in love with her, too. You weren't the only fool, Roland. He thinks I don't know where he took her, but I'm sharper than he.'

'James was in love with her? He never mentioned it to me...' Suddenly it all began to make sense. Now he understood why his boyhood friend had listened to Marietta's lies. 'Where shall I find him, sir?'

The earl hesitated, then smiled maliciously. 'Well, I suppose I owe you something for the beating...'

Sitting in front of the small fire, Venetia hugged the blanket round her shoulders. It was so cold in this place. She was not sure how many days she had been kept a prisoner, since each day was much the same as the one before. Marietta came with food, stopping for a few minutes to stare at her while she ate, almost as though it fascinated her to see another woman. She seldom said very much, though she had asked a few questions about Venetia's family. She had seemed surprised that the Venetian girl could understand some English if it was spoken slowly and clearly.

At the beginning, Venetia had been nervous of her, but Marietta did not appear to wish her harm. That first night, the girl had expected to die. It had all seemed so grim and awful. When James asked what he should do with her, Venetia had thought it was the end. But the excitement had soon faded from Marietta's eyes, and she had merely shrugged and turned away.

'Do as you please,' she had said. 'You brought her here.'

'I thought it might amuse you. She could be company for you, Marietta.'

'I don't want company. Take her away.'

James had obeyed without arguing, leading Venetia through more passages until they reached another wing of the house. Here, it was apparent that some effort had been made to keep the rooms clean.

'My own rooms are here. I do not think you will be too uncomfortable.'

The chamber he showed her into was clean and adequately furnished. Looking round, she saw that there were most of the items a woman might need for her comfort.

'I intended this for Marietta, but she prefers the other wing.' He frowned, seeming almost awkward, as if now that he had her here, he did not quite know what to do. 'Will you be comfortable?'

'Yes…' Venetia bit her lip. 'But will you not let me go? I can understand why Marietta is so bitter, but what good will it do to keep me as your prisoner?'

'I cannot let you go free. Perhaps I made a mistake in bringing you to this place, but it is too late now. Roldán will come for you –

and when he does, I shall kill him!'

He had left her alone then, locking the door behind him. Venetia had run straight to the window, looking for a way of escape, but her room was high above the ground. There was no way out. She had not wept. She was determined that nothing would break her spirit. Roldán would find her.

She looked up as the door opened and Marietta came in with a tray of food. As usual, she locked the door before setting the tray down on the table. Then she stood by the door, watching as Venetia got up.

'Will you not eat with me, Marietta?'

'I have eaten.'

'Then stay and talk to me. It is so lonely with no one to speak to.' Venetia gazed at her. 'Do you not think so?'

'I am used to it. Who would want to talk to me?'

'You mean because of your face?' Venetia looked at her steadily. 'It is not your fault. How did it happen?'

'Do you really want to know?' Marietta's voice was sharp with scorn. 'I suppose you pity me?'

'I don't despise you. I think it is a cruel thing that a woman as lovely as you were should be so afflicted. Surely sympathy is not so wrong?'

'I don't want your pity. It was Roland – your husband. He did this to me. I was struck by the grief he caused me. He raped me, and then he killed the man I loved.'

'No!' Venetia drew a sharp breath. 'I don't believe you.'

Marietta laughed harshly, seeming amused that she refused to believe her story. 'Well, that says something for you. At least, you've a mind of your own, and that's more than most. Men have always believed everything I say – except one. My husband. I hated him.' A strange expression passed across her face. 'Maybe I'll tell you the truth one day.'

'Won't you tell me now?'

'Eat your food before it goes cold.' Marietta turned away. 'James should not have brought you here. It was all so long ago – and there's been enough suffering.'

'Please, won't you tell him to let me go? If anything happens to Roldán, I shall die.'

Marietta stopped, her back towards her. 'You love him very much, don't you?'

'He is everything to me.'

Venetia stared as the door was closed and locked behind her. She felt a tingle of excitement at the base of her spine. Surely she had managed to reach Marietta's inner being? She might yet turn out to be a friend. Perhaps with a little persuasion, she might tell James to let her go. He would do it for Marietta.

Two days had passed since Marietta's last

visit. A servant had been sent with the food instead. Why was Marietta avoiding her, Venetia wondered. Had James forbidden her to come, or was it for another reason? Had she begun to get through to her?

Hearing the key turn in the lock, Venetia looked up hopefully. Perhaps it was Marietta. Perhaps she could persuade her to talk to James. The hope died as she saw that it was James himself. He came inside, locking the door and removing the key.

Venetia got to her feet, her knees trembling. There was something odd about his manner. A strange expression showed in his eyes as he looked at her. 'What is it?' she asked. 'Something has happened.'

'Roldán is in England. He paid my father a visit. I was warned, or he would have found me at my lodgings.' His eyes glittered with excitement. 'He will come here next, Venetia, and then I shall have him... But first I intend to have you!'

Roldán was here in England! Oh, how she longed to see him again, but if he came here he would be in danger. For a moment she was so shocked that she did not realise what he meant; then, as she saw the look on his face, she understood.

'No!' she cried. 'This is madness. What good can it do you to force yourself on me? You will gain no pleasure from it.'

'I want him to know what it feels like. He

raped Marietta.' James moved closer to her. 'I loved her. I still love her, though she shrinks from me. He did that to her, Venetia.'

'No, that isn't true.' She backed away from him, shaking her head. 'I don't know what really happened, but it wasn't Roldán's fault. Ask her… Ask her for the truth.'

'Always you defend him! How he must adore you – and how much it will hurt him to know that I have had you!' He reached out for her, his fingers grasping the silk of her bodice. She gasped as he tore it away, crossing her arms to cover her breasts. 'I shall delight in telling him how you pleaded for mercy. Go on, Venetia, beg me to spare you!'

'No…' she whispered defiantly. 'I'll die before I beg for mercy from you.'

'Then I shall just have to…'

'Leave her alone, James! I forbid you to touch her. I won't be the cause of another woman's grief. I was the victim of men, so I duped them. She is innocent. Leave her be.'

James spun round, his eyes widened as he saw Marietta in the open doorway. She had a bunch of keys in one hand, and a long, wicked-looking knife in the other.

'Marietta,' he breathed. 'What are you saying? This is for you. It's your revenge for what he did to you.'

'Fool! I don't want this kind of revenge,

James.' She fixed her right eye on his face. 'Kill him if you can. You must, or he will kill you – but leave her alone.'

'I don't understand you, Marietta. It was for you… All this was for you.' He stared at her in bewilderment. 'You know I love you!'

'You are a weakling, James! Your father beat all the guts out of you long ago. Only Carlton was man enough to stand up to him.' Her voice was full of scorn. 'Roland was the scapegoat to cover my affair with Carlton. He wounded your brother in a duel, but it was your father who killed the man I loved. Yes, I loved Carlton. I went to his sickbed, and I saw my husband holding the pillow over his face. I tried to stop him, but he laughed and told me I was too late … and then he beat me. He hit me again and again. It was the beating that caused the seizure that left me like this, not my grief. I lied to you, James, because I was bitter, and because I knew you would believe me. I needed you because there was no one left to help me.'

'No…' His face was deathly pale as he stared at her in disbelief. 'Please, Marietta, tell me it isn't true?' he begged as he walked towards her, forgetting Venetia in his horror. 'You couldn't have lied to me all these years.'

Neither of them was looking at her. Slowly Venetia edged towards the open door, hardly believing it when no one tried to stop her. They seemed to be caught in a world of their own. She slipped out of the door while they were still staring at one another, fleeing down the passage in a sudden panic, knowing that she must get away from this terrible house.

Reaching the top of the stairs, Venetia paused as she heard a scream. It was so terrifying that it sent chills running through her. The world seemed to whirl, and she clutched at the banister to steady herself. She must not faint. She must not! She had to escape from this place, and the horror in the room that she had just left, or she would die. Taking a deep breath, she ran down the stairs.

There was only the door between her and freedom. Lifting the latch, she opened it and went out, running blindly into the night. From the darkness a large shadow loomed towards her. It was one of the servants. She screamed despairingly, and then a pair of strong arms closed about her.

'Venetia, my darling,' a voice said. 'Thank God I've found you.'

'Roldán!' She looked up into his face, relief washing over her. 'I knew you would come, but you are almost too late. If it had not been for Marietta...' She shuddered violently. 'I think ... I think James has killed her...'

'My God!' Roldán glanced beyond her to the stairs. 'Guido, take care of my wife.'

'Roldán– No!' she cried, but he was already past her, taking the stairs two at a time. 'Come back; he'll kill you!'

'Let him go, lady.' A stranger moved towards her out of the darkness. 'He will do what must be done.'

'But– But James intends to kill him. I must stop him. I must!'

Guido caught her arm, holding her gently but firmly. 'You can do nothing to help him. It is his destiny. Have no fear, my child. He is a brave soldier, and God is with him.'

Venetia looked at him in wonder. 'Who are you, sir? And why do you say that God is with him?'

'A carriage is outside, and there is someone waiting for you.' Guido smiled at her. 'I believe you will be glad to see Almería again?'

'Almería is here?' Venetia caught a sob in her throat.

'Your husband thought that you would need her. Now, let me take you to her. It will be best if you let her look after you. Do not bother yourself with details. Roldán will explain everything later.'

'But…' The protest died on her lips as she gazed into his face. This was a good man. There was a kind of serenity about him that calmed her. 'You are sure that Roldán will not be killed?'

'He is not alone, my child.' Guido turned her round, and she saw that the courtyard was full of armed men, some of whom proceeded to walk past her into the house. 'Come now, let me take you to your woman. You are safe now. It is all over.'

Roldán stopped as he saw the man blocking his path. There was a wild look in James's face as their eyes met and held.

'James,' he said softly. 'You know why I have come?'

'To kill me. I would do the same in your place.'

'I shall kill you if I have to, but I have come to arrest you. You have been accused of treason.'

'Treason!' The colour drained from James's face. 'You know what that means? I shall be tortured until I tell them the names of my friends. I beg you, give me a swift death – in the name of all that was between us once.'

'Venetia is safe. You may stand your trial. I do not desire your death for revenge. I am not a vindictive man.'

'She is alive – but I have known her.' James's eyes glittered. 'Oh, how sweetly she moaned beneath me...'

'Liar!' Roldán cried. 'If you took her, it was by force!'

'The first time, she struggled a little, but I

soon taught her to beg for my caresses. It has been several weeks, and she thought she would never see you again. She told me that you married her only from a sense of duty.' James laughed as he saw his dart strike home. 'She has a certain mark on her shoulder.'

James must be lying to arouse his anger, but there *was* a tiny mole on Venetia's shoulder. 'Describe it to me,' Roldán muttered grimly, 'and then you die.'

'It is shaped almost like a star.' James felt a thrill of pleasure as he saw the fury in the other's face. 'Such fire, such sweet passion. I envy you, my friend...'

Anger raged in Roldán. He knew that it was probably all lies, but even so, the pain seared him. Venetia was a passionate woman, and it was possible that she had responded to another man's embrace. Yet the picture James's words aroused in his mind made him want to deny it in the only way possible. Drawing his sword, he advanced on his enemy.

James retreated, the way he had come, a look of desperation in his eyes. 'You will allow me the honour of a fair fight?' he asked. 'My sword is in my chamber.'

'Of course. This is merely a precaution in case you try to escape.'

'I shall not run away. I have waited for this day a long, long time. It was I who tried to have you killed in Rome ... or had you

333

guessed that?'

'You blame me for Carlton's death,' Roldán said. 'But you know that my sword did not directly cause his death, don't you? You know that he was alive when he was carried into your father's house.'

James's eyes glittered strangely as he continued to retreat slowly. 'You raped Marietta! You assassinated my brother!' He sounded almost hysterical. 'Now you know what it feels like to be betrayed.'

Before Roldán had a chance to reply, James thrust open a door and darted inside. Roldán followed swiftly, knowing that in a house like this there must be many secret ways to elude an enemy; he was determined that James should not evade justice. Inside, he saw that they had entered a large, empty chamber – empty save for the accumulation of long-forgotten armour that must have lain rusting for years. While he was still assessing the situation, James seized a long-handled pike from a pile near the door, and stabbed at him.

'So this is your idea of a fair fight!' Roldán muttered, dodging out of the way.

'It's more chance than you gave Carlton!' James stabbed again, viciously.

'Do you really believe that?' Roldán stared at the strained face of the man who had once been his friend. What had happened to change him into this desperate fugitive?

For answer, James lunged at him. Seeing a similar weapon on the wall, Roldán abandoned his sword and snatched the heavy pike. The clash of metal reverberated loudly in the high-ceilinged room as the two men thrust at one another. The poles crossed as the antagonists pitted their strength in a test of stamina, each trying to make the other lose ground. They were breathing hard, well matched in build and determination, but James had led a life of indulgence at Court, while Roldán's body had been honed to the perfect fighting machine. Hours of practice had built muscles of iron in his back, thighs and shoulders. He forced his opponent steadily backwards, his superior strength gradually prevailing. Suddenly he gave a great push, sending James staggering back, then, with a swift, upward motion he brought the pole of his pike under James's weapon, tearing it from his grasp. The head of his pike descended to prick at a point just below James's Adam's apple.

'Now choose yourself a sword, and we shall continue.'

James stared in disbelief as Roldán threw away the pike and picked up his sword. 'You could have killed me...'

'We'll fight like gentlemen,' Roldán said. 'I'm no murderer.' He stood back while James selected a sword. 'On guard, sir. This time there will be no quarter given.'

They saluted each other with their weapons, the blades clashing with a new fierceness. By allowing James a second chance, Roldán knew that he had given away much of his advantage. Fencing was a skill often indulged in at Court; it needed less strength than martial combat, and James had always been a fine swordsman. As youths they had practised together daily.

They were evenly matched in skill, that much was obvious at once. At first neither could gain superiority as they thrust and parried, each forced to retreat in turn. Both were breathing heavily as the fight progressed around the large chamber; both stumbled and recovered; both scored glancing hits, and it was only after a prolonged period of fierce fighting that Roldán's fitness began to tell. This was not a fencing match, but a contest to determine life or death. Roldán was used to such contests, having come face to face with death many times, but the strain was beginning to show in James. Beads of sweat appeared on his brow as he was forced to retreat once more. Now he was gasping for breath, his thrusts becoming wilder and wilder. He made a last, desperate lunge at Roldán. Their blades met and slid away, Roldán's sword plunging beneath his arm and burying itself in his side. He gave a cry of disbelief, sinking to his knees as his own sword clattered to the ground.

Roldán stood back, watching the changing expressions on his face: surprise, then fear and finally a smile of mockery. James's eyes met and held those of the man he had planned to kill.

'She was mine,' he whispered. 'You've won – but you will never be able to forget...' A crimson froth bubbled from his lips and he fell face down to the ground.

'You've killed him, then!' Guido's voice brought Roldán's gaze to the doorway. 'The queen will not be pleased. There was much he could have told us about the plot against her life.'

'I would never have taken him alive, if I could,' Roldán looked at him. 'He was once my best friend. As boys we shared everything. A swift death is better than slow torture.'

'You are too soft-hearted, my friend. You had best keep such sentiments to yourself,' Guido said with a frown. 'Elizabeth has agreed to hear your story, but you could still hang if she had a mind to it. Pray that her ministers do not tell her that you must be implicated in the plot.'

'I am grateful for all you have done.' Roldán sheathed his sword. 'Venetia? She is with her woman?'

'They have been taken to the house you know of. I sent a guard with them, and they are safe enough. Now I should like you to identify a woman, if you can.'

'She is dead, then? Venetia said she thought that he had killed Marietta.'

'It is not a pretty sight,' Guido replied grimly. 'You had best prepare yourself for a shock.'

Venetia was wearing a soft robe of green velvet. She had bathed, and Almería had washed her hair. It was so good to feel really clean again – and warm. A huge fire was burning in the grate of the room she had been shown to by a smiling servant, and Almería had brought her a tray of delicious food.

'Who does this house belong to?' she asked, as her nurse set down the tray.

'I do not know, my lady, except that the servants appear to know the master. No doubt he knows what he is doing.'

'Yes, he thinks of everything. He brought you with him, and my clothes.' Venetia sighed, touching the ruby pendant at her throat. 'I wonder if I should delay supper until he comes?'

'He will not expect it. It may be hours before he is free to join you, or even days.'

'What do you mean?'

'James Lodeberry had been plotting to assassinate the Queen of England. It is believed that it was to be part of a plot to set a Catholic on the throne.'

'So I was right!' Venetia exclaimed, shocked. 'I suspected that he might be a traitor to his own queen because of things he had said, but I did not imagine that he meant anything as wicked as this! But what has this to do with my husband?'

'He was with the guards sent to arrest Lodeberry. He may have to return to London to make his report to the queen herself.'

'Yes, that is possible,' Venetia acknowledged with a sigh. Was there to be more delay before she saw her beloved husband?

She sighed again, obediently sipping the wine that Almería handed her. She ate a morsel of cold chicken and a snippet of cheese after the woman left, but pushed away the pies and sweetmeats. It was frustrating to know that Roldán was delayed by business. She longed to be in his arms, to feel his lips on hers. If only he could be here with her now. There was so much she wanted to say to him.

Her hair was dry now, and the fire had made her sleepy. She was tempted to go to bed, but some inner instinct kept her still sitting on her stool, staring into the flames. It was so good to be free, to know that there was... She stiffened as she heard the sound of footsteps outside her door, and got to her feet as the latch was lifted.

'Roldán,' she whispered, her heart beginning to race.

He stood in the doorway looking at her. She wanted to run to his arms, but shyness or some intuition held her back. Her knees trembled as he advanced into the room. How much she loved him!

'You should be in bed,' he said, and there was a harsh note in his voice that disturbed her. 'I thought you would be asleep.'

'I waited – in case you came to me.' Why were his eyes so cold? Was he angry with her?

'I wanted only to be certain that you were comfortable, Venetia. I shall not disturb you further.'

'Will you not stay with me tonight?' Her heart was thumping as she gazed at him almost pleadingly.

'Tomorrow we must begin our journey to London. You should get some rest.'

Roldán stared at her, feeling the old desire move in him. He wanted her badly. The invitation in her eyes set his pulses racing, but there was a knot of pain twisting in his guts as he recalled James's dying words: 'She was mine... You will never be able to forget...'

Would he ever be sure of her again? Guido said that she had been abducted, but Paolo believed that she went willingly. She had certainly encouraged James to call on her. How could he be sure that she was not as faithless as Marietta? She was his wife, and he would have to conquer his doubts, but not tonight.

'Go to bed, Venetia,' he said, then turned and left her staring after him in dismay.

Tears slid slowly down her cheeks as she gazed at the closed door. She had longed for this moment so much, and now... What had changed him? He was so cold – as if he no longer wanted her. What had she done? Why had he turned from her? Surely he could not blame her for what had happened?

She had longed to be in his arms; now she felt empty. If Roldán did not want her, what was the use of living?

The Palace of Whitehall was thronged with richly-dressed men and women. Venetia stood by a window, gazing down at the gardens. She was temporarily alone. Roldán was somewhere about, having left her in the care of Lady Symonds, a rather stern-faced lady of the Court.

'I must seek an audience with Her Majesty,' he had said. 'Lady Symonds will show you where to go.'

Venetia had merely nodded. She was almost afraid to speak to him now lest she give herself away. His reserve during their journey had clearly shown that he no longer felt anything for her. Whatever he had once felt for her had gone. It was breaking her heart. She was confused and hurt, bewildered by the change in him. Always, before, she had felt that he was attracted to her physically, but now she might not exist for him.

Lady Symonds had brought her to this long gallery where everyone seemed to be walking and talking together, then she had been left to her own devices. In fairness, the Englishwoman had tried to make conversation, but Venetia answered in a detached manner. How could she laugh and listen to gossip when the pain inside her made her want to die? Only her pride had kept a fixed smile on her lips. Roldán must never guess how much he was hurting her...

As Roldán got to his feet, he felt the Queen's eyes on him. She had extended her hand to be kissed, and he sensed that she was not really angry with him, though her greeting had been sharp.

'Well, sir, I am waiting for an answer.'

'Lodeberry fought desperately, ma'am. He was determined not to be taken alive. He preferred death to being put to the question.'

'Indeed?' The toe of Elizabeth's satin shoe tapped the ground. She was dressed in a gown of rich satin embroidered with jewels and gold thread, her red hair curled and perfumed beneath a coronet of pearls. She looked every inch a queen. 'Well, sir, you have rid me of a traitor, but robbed me of valuable information. I am not sure whether I should reward you or send you to the Tower. My ministers are of the latter opinion. What say you?'

'I am a Catholic, ma'am, and I have chosen to make my way in Spain – my mother's home – since there was little for me here.' He met her eyes boldly. 'Yet I have always admired Your Majesty, and I would never raise my sword against you. You are the rightful ruler of England, and I hereby give you my solemn promise that I shall never conspire to deprive you of that right.'

'Pretty words, sir. Can I believe them, I wonder?'

'If Your Majesty is pleased to spare me, I shall leave England within a few days.'

'A few days?'

'I would like to see my father before I leave.'

'Ah, yes.' Elizabeth looked at him thoughtfully. She had always prided herself on her instincts about men. Somehow she did not believe that this one was a traitor. 'You are a brave soldier, so I have been told. You fought with the Knights of Malta – and at Lepanto. I believe Christendom owes you a debt. I am a Christian prince, though circumstances have changed the precise form of my beliefs. Yet I do not wish to quarrel with the

Catholics in my realm. I would have all my subjects live in peace. Do you believe this?'

'Yes, ma'am. I pray that God will help you to achieve the peace you desire.'

'Amen to that.' A smile flickered in her eyes. 'I like you, Roland Dominion. You have our permission to visit your father – and to stay or to leave our land, as you wish. There is always room for a brave man in my service.'

'You are generous, ma'am.' Roldán kissed her hand again. 'But my home and fortune lie in Granada. Now, if you will excuse me, I must find my wife.'

Venetia was hardly aware of the laughter around her. She felt numb with misery as she stared out of the window. What was she doing here? All she wanted was to be alone. She turned sharply, thinking to find a quiet corner where she could wait for Roldán, and bumped into a man. His clothes were extremely fashionable, richly embroidered with pearls, and he was wearing a large emerald earring in one ear. She was too distressed to notice that he was also very handsome.

'Forgive me, madam,' he said, his eyes brightening as he saw how lovely she was in her pale grey gown. She was less richly dressed than some of those present, but she was the most beautiful woman he had seen at Court in many a day. 'I am a clumsy, fool!'

'No, no, it was my fault,' Venetia murmured. She tried to pass him, but he moved slightly to block her path. 'Excuse me, sir, I must go.'

'Why so much haste?' he asked, a flicker of amusement about his sensuous mouth. 'I am Harry Greenwood. May I have the honour of knowing your name? You are new to the Court, I think?'

'I am merely waiting for my husband,' Venetia said. 'I see him coming, and I must go to him. If you will please stand aside?' There was the glint of anger in her eyes as she looked up.

Harry Greenwood obeyed, watching with a wry smile as she walked past him to meet a rather grim-faced man. Obviously she was not used to Court ways. A pity, but she would learn in time! He shrugged his shoulders and moved off in search of easier prey.

'Whom were you talking to?' Roldán asked, his mouth hard. He felt the anger stirring in him. Could he not leave her alone for a few minutes without her flaunting herself for some man? 'You were supposed to be with Lady Symonds.'

'Sh– She left me alone,' Venetia replied defensively. Why was he so angry? What had she done? He could not be jealous just because that man had spoken to her, could he?

Gazing up into the furious blue eyes, Venetia felt a little jolt to her heart. He was jealous! Very jealous. He thought that she had encouraged the stranger's attentions. The ice began to melt inside her, sending a rushing surge of joy. If Roldán was jealous, it meant that he was not indifferent to her. Something was wrong between them, but it did not matter; he still wanted her. Somehow she would break through the barrier he had erected to keep her at a distance. She was no longer the child who had feared to face the truth. She was a woman, and she would use a woman's ways to reach him.

She smiled at him, laying her hand on his arm. 'That impetuous gentleman was Harry Greenwood, or so he said.' Her eyelashes fluttered delicately. 'He wanted to know my name, but I would not tell him. You were not jealous, I hope?' She gave a gurgle of laughter. 'I believe he was trying to flirt with me a little. Should I have indulged him, do you think?'

'Did you wish to?' Roldán glanced down at her. She was so beautiful, and he wanted her. He had denied himself for four nights, but he could not hold out much longer. Especially when she looked at him like this. Damn it! She was flirting with him.

'I would rather flirt with you.'

'Would you, Venetia?' A slight smile entered his eyes. How charming she was in this mood. 'It cannot be as much fun to flirt with your husband as a stranger.'

'When you were away, Maddalena taught me to flirt discreetly with strangers. She said that I must learn how to hold your interest, my lord.' Venetia's eyes danced with mischief as she saw a little pulse begin to beat in his temple. 'I wanted to learn all the things that a wife needs to know – but preserving fruit is not as much fun as flirting! The only trouble was that I wished you were there so that I could make you jealous.'

'Oh?' His brow arched, and a gleam started in his eyes. 'Why was that, madam?'

'So that I could tease you as you have so often teased me, sir.' She smiled at him, her love shining from her eyes, unafraid and free. 'I used to imagine you flying into a rage so that I could see the fire in your eyes. You would shout and threaten me, and then...'

'And then?' he asked softly, the hot desire stirring in his loins.

'And then I would show you how much I love you,' she whispered. 'I would kiss away all your doubts, my lord. I know you have doubted me, and I cannot blame you. Marietta destroyed your faith in women. Because of that, I can never have your whole heart, but I shall be content with what you give me. I love you, Roldán. Only you. I loved you from the first, though I fought against it. I shall love you until I die – even

347

if you reject me.'

His arms ached to hold her. James had lied! He was a fool to have believed ill of her for an instant. She was not Marietta. He had always known that she was different, but his pride had stood in the way. He was a blind, stupid fool to have listened to the rantings of a sick mind. This was neither the time nor the place to tell her all that was in his heart. So he took her hand and kissed it.

'Forgive me,' he said humbly. 'I have been unjust. I shall explain everything later – when we are alone.'

CHAPTER ELEVEN

'You can leave me now, Almería,' Venetia said as her husband came into the room. 'I shall not need you again tonight.'

She was wearing a light garment that clung to her body, emphasising the firm breasts, tiny waist and slender hips. Her hair hung about her shoulders in a cloud of titian silk. Roldán could smell her perfume as he moved towards her, the same scent that had haunted him for months, and it inflamed his senses.

'You are so beautiful,' he breathed, reaching out to touch her hair. A shudder ran through him as he felt a deep hunger for her. She was his now. His wife. And she loved him. 'Am I dreaming, Venetia, or did you really say that you love me?'

'I love you more than life itself! When James abducted me, my only thought was for you. I wanted you to come for me, but I was so afraid that he would kill you.'

'He hated me so much.'

'It was because of Marietta. He loved her, even after...' Venetia choked, unable to go on. 'She suffered so terribly for what she did. Shut away in that terrible place because

349

she could not bear anyone to see her.'

'Hers was a cruel fate,' Roldán agreed. 'When I saw her face, I knew that she had suffered far more than I; and I knew I did not hate her for what she did. I began to pity her long ago. Then, when I realised that her lies might rob me of the woman I loved above all else, I wanted to kill her. As for James…' He shrugged his shoulders. 'Who knows what made him the way he was. It was not only Marietta.'

'Marietta saved me from him,' Venetia said, tears stinging her eyes. 'I do not think that she could bear to see another woman suffer as she had. When she came into the room, he was trying to force himself on me and she told him that it was all lies, but he would not believe her. Then, when he did, he killed her. He could not bear to face the truth.'

'So she repented at the last. God rest her soul.' Roldán touched his wife's cheek, stroking the soft skin. 'James lied to me. He taunted me with cruel gibes that he knew would wound me. I did not believe him until he described the mole on your shoulderblade.'

'Do I have one?' Venetia frowned, as he nodded. 'Then he must have seen it while I was ill. The drug he gave me was too strong, and I almost died. If he had not nursed me through it, I probably would have done. So, you see, he was not all bad.'

'Then I am glad that I gave him a swift death. It was what he asked, but I could not have let him be tortured.'

'No, I know that.' Venetia's eyes were sad. 'He was your friend, once. Why must life be so cruel sometimes?'

'Do not waste your pity, my love. You have been restored to me, and that is all I care for.' He gazed down into her eyes. 'I shall take you to meet my father. I want him to see that I have done something worthwhile with my life, and then I intend to take you home to my estate in Granada. I believe that the Turkish threat is ended, for the time being, at least, and I am tired of fighting. I want to spend my life with you – and our children.'

'Oh, Roldán,' she whispered chokily. 'Can it be that you truly love me? Please say it. Say that your heart is all mine.'

'Can you doubt it?' he asked with a lift of his brow. 'Did you not know it when I held you in my arms? I thought you knew, but still withheld your love from me as a punishment. That was why I lost my head that night... Venetia, my darling, words in themselves mean so little. It is easy to say you love me, and lie. Surely my love was there in everything I did?'

'Yes, I know it now, but say it to please me?' She looked up at him appealingly. 'I know I am foolish, but words mean so much to a woman.'

'Then listen well, my love, for I may not say it often. I am a man, and men prefer to show their love in other ways.' He reached out and touched her hair, letting the strands run through his fingers. 'I loved you first when I saw the sun set fire to your hair. You were so beautiful that I thought you a goddess, but you seemed to hate me from the start, and then your father told me that you were promised to another. I knew I could never have you, yet I refused to accept it. When I tricked you into kissing me that first time, I hoped you would fall in love with me. I told myself that I wanted only your body, but in my heart I knew that I loved you as I had loved no other woman. If I could not say it, it was because I was afraid that you would use my love to destroy me.'

'As Marietta did?'

'Yes.' He smiled wryly. 'I was young then, and full of ideals. I thought to comfort her and save her from a cruel husband. She used me to hide her love affair with Carlton. When I discovered the truth, it was too late.'

'And so you began a new life in Spain as a mercenary?'

'Among other things…'

'Yes, Guido told me that you helped to defend Malta.' Venetia lifted her hand to his face, and he turned it up to kiss the palm. 'I want to know everything about you, Roldán. There must be no secrets between us ever again.'

'We have a lifetime to learn about each other.' He drew her into his arms, bending his head to kiss her gently. 'I want to make love to you, Venetia. You cannot know how long these months apart have seemed...'

'As long for me as for you, my lord.'

'Truly?' he asked, his pulses quickening, as she nodded. 'And you know that I love you with all my heart?'

'With your heart, your mind and your body,' she said. 'Maddalena told me that I must appeal to *all* your senses if I would hold your interest for more than a few months.'

'Indeed? It seems that Maddalena has been overly busy! She taught you to flirt... What else has she taught you?'

'Why don't you let me show you?' Venetia's eyes gleamed with mischief. 'You once told me that a clever woman could make her man a slave. Tonight, if you wish, I shall show you how to be a slave of love.' She took his hand, smiling at him shyly but with a confidence he had not seen in her before. 'You must first promise to do everything I ask.'

'You intrigue me! I have a suspicion that I should not give way to you, madam – but just for this once...' There was a flame leaping in his eyes as he let her lead him towards the bed. 'What are my mistress's commands?'

'Show a proper respect when you address me,' Venetia said with mock severity. 'Tonight you are my slave. First, you will stand meekly while I undress you; then you will lie down on the bed, and...'

'This sounds promising,' Roldán murmured wickedly. 'Did Maddalena tell you all this?'

'Well...' Venetia blushed and avoided his eyes. 'She hinted at some things, and I thought of the rest for myself.'

'Ah...' He grinned suddenly. 'It gets even better. I had no idea what was going on in that head of yours. Your slave bows to your commands, my lady.'

'You are not to touch me,' Venetia said. 'You must leave everything to me.' His own words... How magnificent she was!

His eyes glinted with amusement, but he merely bowed his head in assent, playing his part and allowing her to have her way. Was this the innocent child he had first taken to his bed, he wondered. That girl had given him much pleasure, but this was a woman standing before him: a passionate woman with a sense of humour. How much she had learned. He rather liked this new side of her nature.

It took all Roldán's will-power to hold back as she began to untie the strings of his shirt. The touch of her hands on his skin sent his pulses leaping. He was racked with a hot desire, tempted to bear her swiftly to the bed beneath him, but he restrained himself, letting her have her way.

'Lie down now,' she whispered. 'I want to look at your body ... I want to make love to you.'

'As my mistress commands,' he breathed. 'But I'm not sure how long I can play this game of yours, Venetia.'

'You must,' she said. 'You promised.'

Her hands began to stroke his smooth flesh, slowly, tantalisingly. Then her lips followed where her hands had been, setting him on fire. He reached out, but she shook her head. 'Not yet,' she whispered. 'Not until I tell you.'

A groan broke from him as her lips moved surely to the sensitive areas of his body. It was a totally new experience for him. Women had always been merely warm, pliant bodies beneath his; never had a woman taken the dominant part with him in the intimacy of love. The sensations she aroused in him were exquisite, sending him on a dizzy spiral of desire. Then she did something unbelievable; her legs straddled him. When he realised what she intended, his breath exploded in a gasp.

'Now you may touch me,' she whispered. 'Put your hands about my waist. Lift me...'

He needed no further urging. The waiting

had been sweet torture, but the fusing of their two bodies was beyond all expectation. He had never known such pleasure. His face twisted with a kind of agony as they swiftly reached the climax of love together, and Venetia arched her body, crying out wildly.

Afterwards they lay side by side, his arm draped across her damp back. She opened her eyes and turned her head to look at him, smiling lazily.

'Well, my lord, are you pleased with me?'

'You are a saucy wench, and I doubt not that I should beat you for your impertinence! If a man is not to be the master in his own bed...' A soft chuckle broke from him. 'I shall have my revenge, sweet tormentor. You shall pay for this, I promise you.'

'I know well that you always exact full payment, my lord.' She gazed up at him innocently, but he saw beneath the mask.

'Ah, I have taught you too well, Venetia. Had you known it, you always had the power to make me your slave.' He smiled ruefully. 'I may yet have cause to curse Maddalena and her meddling.'

'No, my lord, I want no powers over you – except the one I exerted tonight. In a marriage, must there always be a master? Could we not be as equals, sharing our happiness, our love – and our sorrows?'

'We are matched in love, my darling. Why not in all things?' He smiled and bent to kiss her lips. As he did so, a flame began to leap in his eyes. 'And yet, I have a mind to see if I can torture you, my green-eyed houri. Oh, how right Ali was!'

'Did you really pay Mahomet five thousand ducats for me?'

'Yes. I would have paid him fifty times as much, had he but known it.' Roldán shook his head. 'Do not think to distract me, wench! I shall not be satisfied until you beg for mercy.'

Venetia gurgled with laughter as he rolled her over on to her back. Soon her mirth gave way to stronger emotion, and she moaned as the fever mounted in her blood. 'Oh, please,' she murmured. 'Please ... now...'

'Not yet,' he replied wickedly. 'You are not suitably repentant.'

'You are cruel, my lord.'

'Do you humbly beg my pardon?'

'No... Yes!' She clung to him. 'Do not leave me now, I beg.'

'Could I leave you?' he whispered. 'I am but a man, Venetia. Will you promise always to be like this?'

'Only if you never change.'

He laughed, catching her to him in delight as he ended the conflict in the way they both desired so ardently.

'I am glad to see you, Roland. I had thought to die without setting my eyes on you again.

Now, at least, I have the chance to beg your pardon.'

Roldán looked at the frail figure lying in the bed, and felt the pain twist in him. 'You should not beg my pardon, Father,' he said. 'You were right. I was a foolish child to be taken in by Marietta's lies.'

'You were young, and she was old in deceit and lies.' The baron sighed, reaching for his son's hand. 'I sent you away, and regretted it from the moment it was done. I have not done right by you, my son. I thought only of your brother's inheritance, and, as you see, he does not even trouble to visit me now that I am dying.'

'Would you like me to bring him here?'

'No, it does not matter. Will you stay with me? It can only be a few days now.'

'Father...' Roldán's voice was harsh with pain. 'Of course I shall stay.'

'Do not grieve, my son. I have lived my life, and I am ready for death. God in his mercy has brought you here.' His hand gripped Roldán's. 'Are you happy?'

'As happy as any man has a right to be, and far more than I deserve. I have brought my wife. Would you like to see her?'

'Yes. Bring her to me. I am glad that you have married. Your brother has no wife, as yet.'

Roldán walked to the door, beckoning to Venetia. 'He wants to see you, my love.' He took her hand, leading her towards the bed. 'Father, this is Venetia.'

Venetia looked down at the man's face, seeing traces of the pride and strength that had once been his – the qualities he had passed on to his son. She felt the tears prick behind her eyes, and she bent to kiss his cheek.

'I am glad to see you, sir.'

'You are the kind of woman I had hoped Roland would marry,' the baron said. 'You remind me of his mother. She had black hair, but she was beautiful like you – and she had such a temper! Yet there was goodness in her heart.'

'I, too, have a temper,' Venetia confessed, 'though I am learning to control it.'

The baron smiled. 'Will you not sit beside me for a while? Roland, you may go. I would be alone with your wife for a time.'

Roldán smiled, a flicker of amusement in his face. He was growing used to the way Venetia charmed every man she met, young or old. They had spent a few days at Court before coming here, and he had had to keep a tight rein on his emotions until he began to see that her love was all his own. He could hardly blame other men for falling in love with her! He left the room, glancing back to see that the two people he loved were holding hands.

For the next ten days Venetia divided her

time between her husband and his father. In the mornings she walked or rode about the estate with Roldán, meeting the tenants and getting to know them. In the afternoons she sat with the baron, reading to him from the Bible or simply holding his hand and listening to him talk.

She was holding his hand when he died, and her tears of grief were genuine. She had come to know and love Roldán's father, and she was glad that she had been able to give him some comfort at the end of his life, something she had not been able to do for her own father.

They stayed in England until the baron was laid to rest; then they sailed for Spain and the new life awaiting them there.

Venetia stretched, and held a hand to her back. She was carrying her first child, and the last few months had not been easy, though she was beginning to feel much better now. She had hidden her discomfort from Roldán as often as she could, for she knew that he worried about her. He had surrounded her with every comfort, and she was in danger of becoming spoilt.

Hearing the ring of his booted feet on the tiled floor, she looked up expectantly. It was unusual for him to return at this hour of the day. He normally spent the whole morning inspecting his estate, returning to her to spend the afternoon in the shade of the patio. He smiled at her as he came in, and she felt the old magic in her blood.

'How are you, my love?'

'I am well enough. My back aches, but that is to be expected.' She looked at him enquiringly. 'You have not come home just to ask me that, so is something wrong?'

'There would be something wrong if I did not care about your health,' he replied, grinning at her. 'But you are right. I do have something to tell you.'

'I knew it was so.' She laughed up at him. 'You have that look on your face... Tell me, then!'

Roldán leaned against the table, gazing down at her with an odd expression in his eyes. 'You are certain you feel better?'

'I am quite certain.' Her nose wrinkled, and she shook her head at him. 'If you do not tell me at once, I shall scream, and tell the servants that you beat me!'

He chuckled, knowing the threat was merely that. 'I have decided on a new business venture.'

'Oh?' She stared at him, wondering at the excitement in his eyes.

'I have bought some merchant ships. I have a taste for trading...'

She felt a pang of dismay. Did that mean he would be more often from home? Was it possible that he had begun to tire of their life here? She knew it must seem very quiet to him after the years of being constantly on the move.

'Will you be going away soon?' she asked, trying not to let him see that she was upset.

'I shall not leave you, Venetia. If I make any trips, it will be when you are able to come with me.' His look chided her for having no faith, understanding what she would not say. 'I have a partner in the venture. He will travel abroad while I stay here.'

'A partner?' She looked at him in surprise, unable to read what was in his mind. 'You don't mean Captain Gómez, do you?'

'No. This is a man of great experience. A man I know I can trust.' He smiled at her. 'I would like you to meet him, but only if you feel well enough.'

'Of course I do,' she said stoutly.

'You must not be too upset, my love.' He bent to kiss her cheek. 'It will be a shock for you, but you must think of our child.'

Her heart began to pound as he walked to the door. What was all this? He could not mean… A spasm of fear mixed with excitement caused her legs to shake. She stared at the doorway, her mouth going dry as a man came in. He stood looking at her, obviously as shocked as she was.

'Venetia…'

'Father?' she choked, rising unsteadily to her feet. 'Father, is it truly you?'

His hair was white, and he looked much thinner than she had remembered, but as he came towards her, she saw that it really was he. He was alive!

'I thought you were dead,' she whispered as he moved swiftly to catch her in his arms. 'Oh, Father, I can't believe it's true!'

'I believed you were dead until a few weeks ago,' he said, as their tears mingled. 'My darling little girl! How I have suffered, believing that I should never see you again. I blamed myself for deserting you.'

'Father...' Venetia sobbed, clinging to him. 'Father...'

Several minutes passed before either could speak again. Then Venetia accepted a kerchief from her husband and dried her eyes, smiling as she saw Roldán's quizzing look.

'What happened?' she asked. 'Gómez was sure you were trapped on Cyprus.'

'And so I was. I was a fool, Venetia. I should not have tried to save everything. Now it is all lost.'

'That is not important. It is you ... your life, that matters.' She smiled and hugged him. 'Tell me how you escaped.'

'It was after the fall of Famagusta. We had come to terms with the Turks for the surrender, then... I was herded with the other prisoners who were to die, but I saw a face I knew among our captors: a man I had traded

363

with in the past. I knew him for an honest man, and he still owed me a considerable sum...' Marco dei Giorlandi paused, looking grim. 'Now I am in his debt. He saved my life, Venetia, hiding me away until – until it was all over. Then, when the news of Lepanto reached us, he helped me to leave the island.'

She knew that he had been careful to make light of his suffering so as not to distress her, but she could only be grateful that he had escaped and was here with her now.

'It is a miracle,' she said. 'I still can't believe it.' She glanced at her husband and then at him. 'How did you know where to find me?'

'I chanced to meet Captain Gómez, who told me the whole story, and so I made my way here as quickly as I could.'

'And now you are to be Roldán's partner,' she said. 'It is wonderful! I think I must be dreaming.'

'It was the best thing I ever did, asking Roldán to take care of you. Without him, you would have disappeared without trace.' He glanced at her husband. 'I have no words to thank you, sir.'

'I need none. As you see, I have my reward. Your daughter is my wife, and I need nothing more.'

'I see that you have made her happy, sir. For that alone I am forever in your debt.'

'Oh, please!' Venetia cried impatiently. 'I want to hear more about this business proposition. Is it safe to venture far these days? I do not want to lose my father now that I have found him again.'

'As you see, your daughter has become something of a tyrant, sir,' Roldán said with a sad but false air. 'I doubt not that I have been too lenient with her of late because of her delicate condition.'

Venetia saw the gleam in her husband's eyes, and shook her head at him. 'Do not believe a word he says! Roldán always, but always, gets his own way.'

'Except for one or two or more occasions I might mention – but I shall spare your blushes, my love.'

'Devil!' she muttered, seeing the unrepentant look in his eyes. He would never change, nor did she wish him to. He was the man she loved, and that love would last her lifetime. 'Tell me the truth, you wretch!'

'The Turks have re-equipped, as we expected,' Roldán said, frowning. 'However, war is expensive. The Venetians have paid two thousand five hundred gold sequins of tribute for this year.'

'That is outrageous!' Venetia cried.

'Perhaps,' her father said mildly. 'Yet to continue the war would cost us far more. We shall trade under the Venetian flag, and your husband's galleys will protect us. There is nothing to concern you, Venetia.'

She looked at the two men uncertainly. By making their own treaty with the Turks, the Venetians had effectively destroyed the League. Would it lead to trouble between Spain and Venice? The two countries were uneasy allies at the best of times. Yet even as the doubts clouded into her mind, she knew that Roldán would overcome any problems this raised, as he had overcome everything else that threatened them. Her love flowed out towards him.

She smiled at her father and then at her husband. 'I might as well save my breath,' she said in a resigned tone. 'I have no chance against the two of you.'

'No chance at all,' Roldán said with a wicked grin as he slipped his arm round her waist, 'I think...'

The publishers hope that this book has given you enjoyable reading. Large Print Books are especially designed to be as easy to see and hold as possible. If you wish a complete list of our books please ask at your local library or write directly to:

Magna Large Print Books
Magna House, Long Preston,
Skipton, North Yorkshire.
BD23 4ND